DARK JUSTICE:
MORGAN

DARK JUSTICE SERIES, BOOK 1

DARK JUSTICE: MORGAN

DARK JUSTICE SERIES, BOOK 1

JENNA RYAN

This book is a work of fiction. Names, characters, places, and incidents are the product of the author's imagination or are used fictitiously. Any resemblance to actual events, locales, or persons, living or dead, is coincidental.

Copyright © 2017 by Jenna Ryan. All rights reserved, including the right to reproduce, distribute, or transmit in any form or by any means. For information regarding subsidiary rights, please contact the Publisher.

Entangled Publishing, LLC
2614 South Timberline Road
Suite 109
Fort Collins, CO 80525
Visit our website at www.entangledpublishing.com.

Amara is an imprint of Entangled Publishing, LLC.

Edited by Tera Cuskaden
Cover design by Kelly Martin
Cover art from Deposit Photos and Bigstock

Manufactured in the United States of America

First Edition October 2017

AMARA
an imprint of Entangled Publishing LLC

To Stan Stark, for being such a great neighbor.

And to everyone at Beacon Community Services for being such wonderful friends!

Prologue

"I don't believe you, Alexa. I won't believe you." Georgia Fixx crossed her arms in a defensive gesture. "You never liked Owen, so now you want to turn him into a villain. God sakes, we've hardly been married any time at all, and you're telling me to divorce him. He's my husband—and he's not a monster."

Alexa Chase drummed her fingers on the steering wheel of her Honda Accord. Her idea had been to get her sister out of the city, somewhere she could be certain they were alone. But in retrospect, a late-night drive might not have been the best choice. "I didn't say Owen was a monster. I said he was a criminal. He works for a man named James Mockerie, who imports drugs and exports weapons. I found the proof, Georgia."

"By sneaking and snooping and playing on his son's affections."

Alexa twitched away a pang of guilt and regret. She *had* used Owen's son; however, the cause had been justified. Did she feel like slime for having done it? Absolutely. But God help her, look what she'd discovered.

"The FBI had no business approaching you." Georgia glowered at her. "And you had no business helping them. Spying for them. Stealing for them."

"I took books and codes, passwords and disks. Evidence of Owen's involvement in Mockerie's organization, which, by the way, is vast. I handed that information over to the FBI." Alexa negotiated the next curve at a higher-than-normal speed. She tended to drive fast in the desert outside Las Vegas in any case, so given the circumstances, she simply took her mood out on the road.

"There's an animal!" Georgia shouted, bracing.

Alexa swerved to avoid a jackrabbit.

"You drive like a maniac." Her sister's reproach ended on a pout that was pure Georgia. "How do you know Owen wasn't forced to work for Mockingbird?"

"Mockerie. The truth of his involvement was in the evidence I discovered. Your husband is a willing participant, always has been." Alexa softened her tone. "He also had three wives before you."

"So he made wrong choices. Who cares? We all do it. Fourth time lucky, then."

"They're dead, Georgia."

"What?" Genuine shock flitted across her sister's features, followed swiftly by denial. "No. You're lying. Or mistaken. Or...something." She grabbed the sides of her hair, tugged hard. "Why are you doing this to me?"

"Because I want you to be safe. To live. Not to wind up like his three other wives."

"You work for him. Shouldn't that...? I mean, how can you...? Oh, hell, I don't know what I'm saying. I *do* know Owen would never try to kill me. You're insane for thinking that. You're also driving way too fast."

"I know." Sighing, Alexa touched the brake. When nothing happened, she pressed down harder. "Shit!"

"I agree." Georgia sulked. She refolded her arms in defiance. "You're a mean sister to do this to me."

Alexa looked ahead, then behind, then at the winding desert road. "The brakes are gone," she said. "Dammit, they're totally gone." Had they been gone before? Maybe. They'd felt a bit spongy after she and Georgia had left the city.

Georgia scowled. "How can the brakes be gone? You just had the car tuned up."

Alexa downshifted. The engine screamed, but the car only slowed a little.

They were on a long slope, she realized. Her heart hammered against her ribs, and the air she breathed felt like fire in her lungs. She tried the emergency brake. Nothing happened.

She wouldn't panic, she promised herself. It wasn't in her nature to overreact in any case. But how the hell could she slow the car when they were flying downhill?

"This isn't funny, Alexa." Grabbing the edges of her seat, Georgia planted her spiky heels on the floor mat. "You're going to get us both killed."

"I'm actually trying really hard not to do that." The tires squealed as Alexa took another corner. She couldn't execute a shift or a one-eighty turn without the brakes. All she had right then were the automatic gears and a fleeting hope that the road would level off before she careened out of control.

"Slow down!" Georgia shouted. Her voice was high and tight, her tears audible. "You're doing this on purpose to prove a point. Except I still don't believe you about Owen, so please stop playing stupid games." She hitched a shuddering breath. "You *are* playing games, right?"

"No." Swearing, Alexa set her teeth and geared down

again.

The back end of the car swung out. Georgia shrieked, and the road blurred, then suddenly, miraculously, leveled off.

Alexa geared down one last time and brought the car to a sliding halt. As her senses continued to scramble, she noticed that the front end was less than six inches from the edge of an unbarricaded canyon.

Still clutching the steering wheel, she let her head fall back against the headrest. "Holy crap."

Her thoughts settled, slowly. Prying her fingers loose, she forced herself to breathe normally. To breathe at all.

She exhaled. Her phone. She needed to find it. Had to call someone. Her contact at the FBI. She had his numbers programmed, work and personal.

"I can't move, Alexa." Her sister seemed unable to make her lips form the words. "Everything's frozen."

"We're all right," Alexa told her. "Not dead, anyway." It took her a moment to locate the phone inside her Kate Spade bag. While she searched, she heard Georgia gasp.

"Car, car. Car!" She pointed. "We're still moving!"

Feeling the movement, Alexa whipped around in her seat. "Get out," she said. Then she felt a bump behind them and she grabbed Georgia's wrist. "Wait. It's okay. We were moving backward, not forward. The rear bumper is pressed against the rock wall. We're good." *For the moment*, she added silently.

It amazed her that her hands didn't shake as she speed-dialed her FBI contact's number.

"Jamieson," a man's voice answered. "Is this Alexa Chase?"

"What? Yes. I'm—my sister and I are…" She combed her fingers through her hair, regrouped. "I need to talk to Agent Marshall."

"Marshall's dead, Ms. Chase. He was shot and killed this afternoon in his Arlington condo. Are you intact?"

"No, yes." *Get past the shock*, she ordered herself. "The brakes on my car failed. I'm—I don't know where I am exactly. North of Las Vegas. My sister's with me."

"Get out of the car," Jamieson said tightly. "Get out of sight. Don't let yourselves be seen. I'm sending help. Look for an amber light. Intermittent signal. Two flashes, one flash, then three. Repeated. Do you understand?"

Alexa glanced at Georgia, stricken and silent beside her. "Yes." Gripping the phone harder, she asked, "Is Fixx behind this? Did he kill Marshall?"

"Him or James Mockerie. At the moment, I'm going with Fixx. Get off the road."

Reaching over, Alexa shoved her sister's door open. "We need to move, Georgia. Now!"

"I don't want to go." Georgia's lower lip wobbled. "I want Owen. Except..." She turned imploring eyes to her sister. "Do something, Alexa. Please."

"Don't let anyone see you," Jamieson repeated. "We'll get you out of there ASAP, but you need to understand. You and your sister are marked women. And marked in the world of Fixx and Mockerie means you're targets. From this moment on, Ms. Chase, you and Georgia Fixx are officially dead."

...

There was nothing Owen Fixx disliked more than being woken from a sound sleep. Six hours minimum, no interruptions—that was his credo. Lately, he'd been running at about 30 percent.

"What?" he demanded after the third ring of his cell phone.

"We damaged the brake line on Alexa Chase's car."

The man on the other end sounded tense. Never a good sign in Owen's opinion. "From the tone of your voice, I'll speculate that your attempt at sabotage failed. She's still alive."

"She's a better driver than we figured. Or crazier. We lost her. Car was empty by the time we found it. Plenty of rock formations in the area. They could have hidden anywhere in the dark."

Putting the phone on speaker, Owen donned his burgundy silk robe. "You're not making me happy here."

"She was with her sister, Mr. Fixx."

Owen gave the remark a moment's thought. He hadn't yet grown tired of Georgia when Alexa Chase had done her nasties and turned traitor on him. He'd estimated another six months to a year of play from his fourth wife's feisty nature before he would have been forced to eliminate her. However, business came first and his business was lorded over by an extremely vicious man.

James Mockerie didn't take failure well—not for long at any rate. Screw-ups usually resulted in slow death. Torture was his candy, and Owen had been witness to the languorous consumption of it numerous times in the past.

"Get Alexa Chase," he told his man. "If her sister's with her when she dies, we'll consider her collateral damage."

"Are you...?"

"Get Alexa Chase." Owen enunciated each word. "Set up a team. Devise a solid plan. Fuck up again, and heads will roll."

"I know. We'll get her, sir."

The man sounded both frightened and determined. Which was how Owen liked his people to be. Cause them to cringe too much, and they became ineffective. On the other hand, battles needed to be fought and won before they escalated into full-blown wars. War meant Mockerie, and his interference was something Owen preferred to avoid.

"I'll do what needs to be done on my end," Owen said. "Make sure you call me with better news next time." He disconnected before the man could reply.

Open-ended threats worked for him. Owen's people knew he'd kill anyone who screwed him in a blink. Which was a merciful ending, all things considered.

Owen Fixx was a man who considered matters very thoroughly before he acted. At least on a professional level.

Picking up his phone, he punched in a number. Whatever the cost emotionally and/or financially, he intended to avoid any unnecessary forays into hell. Not that the idea of meeting the devil frightened him. In his opinion, Lucifer was merely a weak shadow cast by a much more virulent being. A man known in the West Coast drug and weapons world as James Mockerie.

Chapter One

"More whiskey." A man with a belly the size of a watermelon leaned his tattooed forearms on the bar. "Make it a triple."

Amber Kelly leaned her own arms on the bar across from him and met his bleary gaze. "Are you driving, Harry?"

"Truck's got a busted rear axle. I'm hoofing it. Jack Black, Amber. Keep it coming, and I'll give y'all a frigging big tip at closing time."

He would, too. Then she'd hand it back to his wife because Liz and Harry Carver had five teenage boys and Harry preferred hard liquor to hard work. Motioning him over to the pool table, Amber poured a glass of watered-down whiskey and wished like hell two a.m. would arrive.

She'd spent the past month of her life in this backwater Tennessee town. Four endless weeks living with a new name and managing a mediocre bar in a sequestered region of the Smoky Mountains. The scenery was spectacular, the townspeople off and on friendly…

And God alive, her sister Rachel was the most infuriating pain in the butt on the planet. Where the hell was she on the busiest night they'd had in ten days?

"Getting low on beer here," a man called out. He winked at Amber across the crowded room. "Friday poker should never be played straight."

So claimed the cardsharp banker who owned the best house in Black Creek and held the mortgages on 45 percent of the rest.

With a placid smile, she began refilling pitchers. She didn't bat an eyelash when the door slammed open and a scrawny man with a floppy gray mustache shouted, "Where's my boy?"

"Not here." She kept her eyes on the flowing beer. "Not tonight."

The man was across the floor in a flash. Paulie Murkle reminded her of a revved-up cartoon rabbit, from his twitchy pink nose to his long, thin feet. He blinked his eyes rapidly as he demanded, "You tell me true, Amber. Is he off drinking and diddling that waitress of yours?"

"Could be. She's not here, either." Amber placed a mug of draft on the bar. "I'll put this one on your tab, Paulie. I can't change how Jess or Rachel act, and neither can you."

Paulie snatched up the mug, slopped foam. "Girl's a drunkard and not fit to work here."

Setting five pitchers on a tray, Amber slid them to her lone server. "She's not a girl. And I say she is fit to work here. You're starting to piss me off with your attitude, so let it be and go play poker with the bank."

"I don't play cards with assholes. Hows come you hired someone without experience to work the tables? You shoulda found another like Wendy." He waggled his brows at the fifty-something server who made a point of ignoring him.

Amber fought a wave of irritation. "Rachel's a good person, Paulie. Just maybe not cut out for small-town life."

"Then let her hightail it to Memphis and leave my Jess be."

"Your Jess turned twenty-six last week."

"My Ethan turned twenty-nine last month. What's your point?"

"They're old enough to make their own choices."

"The hell they are." Beer dripped from Paulie's mustache onto the bar. "They stay on the farm with me till I say not."

Please, God. Whisk me to Kansas or California or Little Rock, Arkansas. Anywhere that isn't here at this moment.

With a patient smile, she said, "I'll try Rachel's cell again. She's bound to pick up at some point. Meanwhile, go on over and shoot pool with your fishing buddies."

She speed-dialed her sister as she spoke, and turned away to let her mind slide back twelve short months, to a time when life had been much simpler—or so it had seemed.

Georgia—Rachel now—had sashayed in to see her one night, newly married to Owen Fixx. As hotel manager, Amber had been working an emergency relief shift, dealing blackjack in Fixx's casino. She'd been surprised by the elopement, but happy for her sister. Until six days later when the FBI had come knocking on the door of her Las Vegas condo...

Her world had taken a definite turn for the worse after that visit. While an oblivious Rachel had settled into married life, fear and suspicion had become Amber's constant companions. She'd transitioned from hotel manager to internal spy in less time than it took to pull the arm of a slot machine.

The discoveries she'd made about her new brother-in-law had stunned her. She'd amassed a file full of damning evidence—thanks in part to the dangerous game she'd chosen to play with his besotted and equally guilty son.

She wasn't proud of her actions in that regard, but she'd weighed the odds and taken the risk. Fixx was a monster, and that monster had been living and sleeping with her sister.

A B-movie of bad memories played in Amber's

head. She'd done what the FBI had asked. She'd gathered information and turned it over to her government contact. End of spy story, finally. Fixx would be arrested, Rachel would get a quick divorce, and Amber would find a new job. No one need ever know what she'd done.

Wrong. Someone in the FBI had known. The evidence she'd unearthed had mysteriously vanished, and it had taken every aspect of the life she'd been living with it.

Amber and her sister had been handed over to the US Marshals office and placed in the Witness Protection Program. They'd been given new identities and relocated to Tennessee, where old-style music played day and night, people believed in spooks, and Amber was slowly but surely going out of her mind.

Her gaze flicked through the crowded room to the jukebox in the corner. One of her customers was a diehard Tanya Tucker fan. The playlist really, really, really needed to be updated.

"Answer," she ordered as her sister's cell phone continued to ring. Instead, Rachel's voicemail kicked in. Rocking her head from side to side, Amber waited it out. "Yes, I know, you're unavailable, blah, blah, blah..." When the message ended, she said simply, "Call me. Now."

Setting her phone down, she glanced at Paulie, who was jabbing a pool cue into the stomach of a man twice his size. A few minutes later, she heard a ring and saw her sister's name on the screen.

"It's about time, Rachel." She turned away. "Where the hell are you? Paulie's on the verge of skewering his neighbor."

"Sounds like my kind of guy," a man's voice drawled back. "Listen, sugar. I got your sister all snug and cozy here with me. Sorry she can't talk right now, but I can and I want you to listen. We're coming for you. In fact, sugar pie, a couple of us are already there."

Chapter Two

Gage Morgan loved the King. Not weirdly loved him, but his early music had an edge no other musician could match.

He sat in his open-top '59 Caddy outside the gates of Graceland, slouched down in the driver's seat, savoring his second bottle of Michelob. "Blue Moon of Kentucky" played quietly, traffic was light, and he had a sweet buzz going on—one he hoped to make a whole lot sweeter after this meeting he'd been talked into showing up for ended.

McCabe, the man who'd talked him into it might be a US Marshal, but he wasn't his boss in the true sense of the word. As a US Marshal himself, Gage didn't mind hearing him out. What could it hurt? He wouldn't give a rat's ass no matter what McCabe said. You cared, life got messy, and he'd been there, done that too damn many times already.

Gage heard the footsteps McCabe didn't bother to disguise and smiled as he took another pull on his beer. "Your boots need new soles, my friend. Left one more than the right."

"Your senses are still good, Gage. Means you can only be

on your second or third beer, and that makes me uncommonly lucky at quarter to midnight on a Saturday."

"You're luckier than you think. This is only my first beer."

"You could use a shave and a haircut." McCabe vaulted over the door, accepted the bottle Gage handed him. "Yeah, I know, same goes for me." He drank deeply. "It's been a long day."

"I'm not available."

"Tell me something I haven't heard before."

"Just trying to save time. I'm in a funk."

"Who isn't? Bad weather's blown in."

"Does this particular weather involve a woman?"

McCabe chuckled. "Two of them, actually."

"Smart?"

"One's smart, the other's resentful. You take this assignment, you'll figure out which is which soon enough."

"Major funk here, McCabe." Reaching for another beer, Gage twisted off the cap, but he swirled rather than drank. "What's the story?"

"They're in the Witness Protection Program—have been for the past month. One of them's missing, presumed taken. The other's gone to ground, no idea where. She's not trained, not really, but she has a surprising amount of common sense. It might keep her alive long enough for you to find her."

"Making her the smart one."

"There you go. You've got it figured out already. As a bonus, she's a looker. Tall, black hair, gold eyes. No idea what her ancestry is, but you won't be disappointed."

"Can't be disappointed by what you never see." Gage kept swirling his beer. "How she looks doesn't matter to me. What's the bottom line?"

"She was asked to gather information for the FBI about one Owen Fixx."

Shit. Gage let a humorless smile cross his lips. "Owen

Fixx? The weapons and drug dealer who works for a sadist known as James Mockerie? That Owen Fixx?"

McCabe slanted him a shrewd look. "Intrigued?"

"No. And I'm sure as hell not suicidal."

"You were once."

"Yeah, well, I have more to live for these days. I'm thinking about getting a dog."

"Dogs are a commitment, Gage. You go wherever, whenever, and suicide missions were your style long before you left the LAPD."

Which he'd done for reasons that'd had him shying away from relationships ever since. "Talk to me about Mockerie." Gage let his gaze roam past the gates of Graceland, heard "That's All Right " in the background, and forced himself to stay in the moment. "What's he up to these days?"

"Same as always. Anarchy. Word is, he's found a lucrative overseas market for his weapons. Anywhere wars break out, his people are there, guns, bombs, and drugs at the ready."

"You create hell around you, those who have to live in it need to escape any way they can. What happened to the information your looker dug up?"

"It disappeared."

Figured. Gage laid his head on the headrest. "How is it Mockerie's minions got a line on her? Did the resentful woman talk?"

"She ran. Maybe she talked. Details are sketchy. All we know is that she's missing." His lips curved. "And here's the kicker: she's the clever one's sister."

Great, just fucking great. "So we're talking blood and affection and the potential for panic at some point because, hello, not a trained agent. Jesus, McCabe, this isn't just suicide, it's sloppy suicide. What's clever sister's name?"

McCabe polished off his beer. "Her real name was Alexa Chase. You want the current one, you'll have to come in and get it, along with the rest of the details. This is a one-man job as far as I'm concerned. I don't want send in a team of people. I just want to send in the best."

Gage seriously wished he'd been born with Elvis's mojo, but no such luck. On the other hand, Elvis had been dead and buried for forty years. There was no dog in the offing for the King. No looker with black hair, gold eyes, and curious ancestry, either. He turned his head on the rest. "I'll mull it over, get back to you."

Ditching his bottle, McCabe vaulted from the Caddy. "Time's a factor. Don't mull for more than an hour. You've got contacts in the area, Gage—more than a few, if memory serves. That makes you the right man for the job in my mind. You know where to find me."

Unfortunately.

Using his knee to bump the retrofitted CD player to another disk, Gage switched to gospel. And took a painful journey back through hell.

...

James Allan Mockerie had two stunning women on retainer. They'd been his mistresses back before he'd murdered his wife, but these days, they were simply a pair of exquisite call girls who came to him as required.

He missed his wife in a strange and unhealthy way. Unhealthy to his vast business empire, certainly. From the moment he'd met her, she'd dazzled him. And as he'd discovered, to be dazzled was to be distracted.

His anger started mounting, and he couldn't seem to control it. So he blocked the memory and shuffled his thoughts accordingly.

There were problems that required his attention. The one that weighed heaviest on his mind involved his associate,

Owen Fixx.

Secreted in Fixx's plush Las Vegas hotel office, Mockerie watched the action in the casino below through a wall of elegant smoked glass. The gaming floor was packed, as usual, with everything from cowboys in distressed denim to Texas millionaires in diamond-studded belts. The money they dropped helped fuel his empire. That and booming overseas sales.

He recognized his associate's sharp double rap on the door.

"Come," he said when the knock repeated. Propping a booted foot on the desk, he swiveled Fixx's office chair just enough to let his approaching associate know he was considering something weighty. Then he stopped the motion and showed his teeth. "You look unhappy tonight. More problems on the wife and sister-in-law front?"

Lines of strain showed around Fixx's annoyingly handsome eyes. "The problems are being handled. The information that was stolen is back in my hands, and our FBI insider is going about his business. I put a fifty thousand dollar reward out on the pair of them. I got word two nights ago that my ex has been located. She was living in a small town in Tennessee."

Mockerie kept his teeth fully visible and his own eyes shielded behind a pair of round sunglasses. His hair was long and flyaway under a hat that had belonged to his father. His white T-shirt, leather vest, and jeans had all seen better days. He wore a ring, the only piece of jewelry he owned, on what remained of his left middle finger.

He toyed with that ring while Fixx took a subservient seat across from him.

"Your casino's doing well." Mockerie studied his missing half finger. "Ka-ching, ka-ching." His gaze rose. His teeth vanished. "Where is she now?"

"My tracker caught up with her in Mississippi."

"Is your tracker reliable?"

He watched Fixx deliberately blank his features. "I sent the best I've got. He's taking his directions from our inside man. I don't think it'll be long before he'll have her sister, as well."

"You hope. The information Alexa Chase stole might be back in our hands, but that doesn't mean the threat's been eliminated. She could have all kinds of shit tucked away in that cunning brain of hers."

"If she did, she'd have given it to the authorities when they brought her in."

"Assuming she trusts the authorities. I wouldn't tell all to anyone in the government. You're smart, you withhold, just in case the so-called good guys decide your usefulness has ended and the wolves can have you. Get them, Fixx. Both of them. I want to see their squirming, terrified bodies stretched out on long tables." Mockerie's smile returned. "If I don't see theirs, you can count on the fact that I'll be seeing yours."

・・・

Months of spying, of subterfuge and over-the-shoulder glances, had taught Amber that panic was her worst enemy. It was right there, always, waiting to wrap its bony fingers around her throat. But instead of letting it intimidate her, she'd learned to use it. To take advantage of her heightened senses and focus on what mattered. What would keep her alive.

She didn't have time to think, not really. Even as Rachel's kidnapper spoke to her, she looked up and saw two large men staring at her from the back of the room. They grinned and started to move forward through the crowded tables.

Amber's first instinct: survive. She grabbed what came to

hand—two full bottles of whiskey. Breaking them both, she sent the contents flying. Then she lit a match.

Chaos erupted instantly. She threw three more bottles of whiskey into the mix. Flames shot upward in huge spikes and spread.

She could no longer see the men, but she knew they were there, hopefully trapped in the pandemonium. She ducked out through the exit next to the bar, stopping only long enough to swing the emergency backpack she'd had ready and waiting for a month up over her shoulder.

There was a tunnel. The former owner of the bar had told her about it when she'd arrived. Something to do with Prohibition and smuggling booze down from the hills. Whatever its original use, Amber was grateful for its presence that night.

When she emerged in a back alley, she climbed out, tried to settle her nerves, and took a look around. She didn't hesitate. She stole the first truck she saw that had keys in it.

Thoughts she couldn't control spiraled through her head. Rachel had been taken by someone connected to Owen Fixx. That was a given. Obviously, Fixx wanted both of them. Maybe they'd snatched Rachel partly as a backup in case they missed her. Whatever the plan, Amber had no intention of going along with it.

She headed northwest. The Dakotas meant nothing to her or her family. No safe harbors to be had in those states. But there were mountains where she could lose herself while she considered her limited options.

She drove through the night, slept some, and when she felt it was safe, used a payphone to call the message center for her WPP emergency contact. She relayed the available facts in code and slept a little more.

When she woke, she bought sandwiches and Coke from a crappy highway rest stop and told herself to keep going. What was the cliché? A moving target was harder to hit?

She only stopped long enough to take a fast shower at a campsite where a group of Boy Scouts were toasting marshmallows and scaring one another with ghost stories. If scary was what they wanted, Amber could have given it to them in spades.

She drove in circles at times. It was mostly a deliberate act, though, once or twice, when fear snuck in and clouded her mind, she wound up on a dead-end road in a dead-end town that came straight out of Edgar Allan Poe.

By late Saturday night, she decided to risk another call to her contact. Because the truck was low on gas, she found a station off the highway and pulled up to a row of poorly lit pumps. She paid with cash taken from the bar and really, really hoped she'd get lucky in the all-night café next door.

She did. A cell phone left unattended on a table presented itself while she headed for a back booth. Instead of sitting, she bought a local newspaper and returned to the truck. Ten minutes later, on a side road that read like a cow path, she had her contact, Tom Vigor, on the phone.

"Got it, Snowbird." Tom sounded like a half-drunk hillbilly, but Amber knew he could outthink the US Marshals' top people and play a game of chess at the same time. The old man grunted, then said, "Someone stole your mama's jewel box, and you don't know where to look for it. We'll hope the rings inside are brass and not real gold. I'm looking at my call display. Who's Myra Pinkerton?"

"No idea." Amber let her gaze roam through the shadowy night. "I grabbed her phone from a café."

"Then we can talk."

"If you say so. I don't know where the guy who threatened me was calling from. I think Rachel might have been running off with a local farmer named Jess Murkle. Knowing her, Miami or New Orleans would have been the destination."

"What's Jess Murkle like?"

Amber studied an odd-shaped shadow. "He hangs his head when he talks to his father, but on his own, he's cocky and snide. Develops a swagger that gets bigger the more he drinks. And he drinks quite a lot."

"So does Rachel, as I understand."

"No question she loves her whiskey and tequila. It's our mother's legacy. Our father's was cocaine."

"And yet you remain clean and sober."

"I'm a throwback to my Puritan ancestors." She wished she'd bought an energy bar when she'd stopped for gas. "Can you do anything for me? For either of us?"

"Been working on it since I got your message. Given Fixx's connection to James Mockerie, I'm being extra cautious. We know there's at least one person on the take somewhere in the ranks of the FBI. We also know or can figure that Mockerie'll want you taken out as badly as Fixx does."

Closing her eyes, Amber allowed ripples of guilt to wash through her. "Fixx's people might have missed me, Tom, but they have my sister. I'm afraid they'll hurt her, or worse."

"They won't harm a hair on her head until they get their hands on you."

"Bullshit." She opened and narrowed her eyes. "They could do all kinds of horrible things to her after what happened in Black Creek, and I'm not there. For whatever reason, they haven't used her phone to contact me again since I left town, but I'm sure they will eventually."

"Now, Snowbird…"

"Don't patronize me," she warned him. "I'll agree they probably won't kill Rachel right off, but one thing I know about Fixx is that he's a coldblooded, spiteful bastard with as much mercy in him as a scorpion. Rachel's my sister, and I gathered more than enough evidence to destroy him. He'll see her as expendable. Maybe you're right and nothing will happen until they have me, but they'll sure as hell try and use her to draw me out. Using can mean a lot of things, from the threat of pain to actual torture. I can't let that happen."

"Now, you listen to me, missy." Tom firmed up his tone. He still sounded like a hillbilly, but a determined one. "I've been in this game for a long, long time. I'm telling you, Fixx—and Mockerie, for that matter—will want the both of you brought in alive and unharmed. Mockerie in particular likes to inflict the first cuts. It gives him pleasure to see that initial spurt of pain. Once it's over, he'll leave the rest to Fixx. He won't want to see either of you again until you're dead. Our sources suggest he'll spend up to six hours staring at a corpse."

Amber frowned at her phone. "Who the hell are your unfortunate sources?"

"Stories for another time. I keep the identities of any and all operatives to myself."

"So, you're what? A super spy ,and being a US Marshal is your cover?"

She noticed he didn't answer her directly. He simply reverted to his backwoods banter, yucked out a laugh, and said again, "Help's a'comin', Snowbird. You hold on to that thought. Now, if you're sure Myra Pinkerton's phone isn't bugged, let's you and me get our facts straight concerning the contents of that jewelry box we mentioned earlier."

Amber's head began to throb. "Right, my mama's jewels. I know the drill."

"Good girl. You go back for that box then and keep telling yourself, Rachel will be fine. Dig deep, Snowbird."

"Yeah, to the belly of hell," she muttered.

"You need to start smoking."

"I hate cigarettes."

"Try a little weed. Or do you call it pot?"

"A rose by any other name. I'll dig, but I won't smoke. I

don't like weeds, plant or human." She took a bracing breath. "I'll be in touch, old man. I hope."

Lowering the phone, Amber ended the call. Then she tossed Myra Pinkerton's cell into the woods, started the truck, and headed back to the Smoky Mountains.

Chapter Three

Gage wanted to kick his own butt to Los Angeles and back—and keep right on doing it until his brain rebooted. He should've known by then that not giving a rat's ass meant not taking one of McCabe's assignments. "Fuck me," he said softly over Elvis's "Tiger Man." Fuck, too, the situation—and the woman who'd been part of it for screwing him up inside.

But he kept on driving until he reached a town called Diggerton, Tennessee, where broad banners proclaimed the start of a local pumpkin carving festival.

Okay, not an uncool thing, but not his reason for going there, either. Fifteen years ago, a group of investors calling themselves the WEED Group—Willis, Earp, Elliot, and Deacon—had opted to build an amusement park two miles outside of town. No surprise, they'd run short of money. Then the economy had taken a hit and, well, sometimes it was wiser to cut and run than to go on pissing money down a rat hole.

And on the subject of rats… Gage gave his ass a final mental kick before turning his full attention to the minefield of potholes that only loosely resembled a road.

He swore because it made him feel better, and pictured McCabe's face as he did so. What had McCabe said? Something about black hair and gold eyes. Gage knew only a handful of his counterparts would take on a job like this, as intriguing as it sounded.

James Mockerie was a killer, a man without a soul. Word had it he'd murdered his wife a while back. Gage couldn't remember the details of the story, or even his wife's name. *Something Welsh,* he thought. Rowella, Rowena. Whatever the case, he could imagine Mockerie doing the deed himself. The man was reputed to be much more hands-on than Owen Fixx, though God knew Fixx had a hell of a nasty nature.

Reaching down, Gage cut to the running lights and slowed his Ram 4x4 to a crawl. The rig could handle potholes just fine, but the mini landslides ahead presented more of a challenge.

Cut and run, he reflected as he worked his way over the rubble. The amusement park investors had done it. If he were smart, he would, too, before any of this became something that mattered.

The gates appeared in front of him, crooked and rusting, barely clinging to their concrete foundations. With the moon up and the stars out in full force, he could see the silhouette of a giant Ferris wheel alongside the skeletal remains of wooden roller coaster tracks. The WEED Group must have lost a bundle.

Arming himself, he hopped out. He knew where to go. He only hoped she knew, as well, because he'd never been overly fond of amusement parks. The funhouse clowns had scared him shitless as a kid, and his asshole cousin had sealed the deal by locking him inside the reptile tent after hours.

There were no tents here, reptile or otherwise—only derelict buildings, splintered booths, and dead carnival rides. What a waste.

He headed for what appeared to be the carousel. Two horses remained. One of them was missing its head; the other had tipped forward onto its nose.

Throughout the park, an eerie wind rustled the autumn leaves. Rodents scrabbled in the wreckage, and a couple of owls hooted high in the trees. But no human sounds reached him. Maybe she'd gotten her signals crossed when she'd talked to old Tom. Or maybe she believed he was her enemy, too.

Keeping his weapon out of sight, Gage called her new name. "Amber? I have your mother's jewelry box. The rings inside are brass."

Still no movement. No response.

He raised his hands, palms out. "My name's Gage Morgan. I'm here to help you."

Finally, he detected a whisper of sound—a quiet brush of fabric across metal. Turning toward it, he watched her emerge from full darkness to shadowed moonlight. She had a gun, a big one, pointed straight at him. What he could see of her expression didn't look remotely friendly.

"Tell me who sent you," she said. "And don't lower your hands until I'm satisfied."

He let his gaze slide over her body, then slowly back to her face. "I work for a man named McCabe. Tom Vigor contacted him when he got the message about your sister." Since her mistrustful expression showed no sign of changing, he advanced, slowly and with his eyes locked on hers. "It's dark, Amber. Whoever I am, you can count on the fact that I'm trained. If I move and you shoot, you'll be shooting at air."

She didn't alter her stance or look away. "How well do you know Tom?"

"We met a few times, back when I was part of the LAPD."

She lowered her gun a fraction. "You worked for the

LAPD? Tom's a very talkative man. He told me a lot about his family. Do you know his son, Tommy Jr.?"

Gage nodded, continued his steady advance. "Thomas Vigor Jr., homicide detective. Loves playing the ponies. Like father, like son. Two kids. Wife's name is Clare. I've been to four barbeques at their place. Their oldest graduated three years ago."

"Two years ago," she corrected.

He shrugged. "I've been out of the loop for five."

"And now you're a US Marshal and work for a man named McCabe."

"From time to time. When the mood strikes," he added with a shrug. She adjusted her grip on the gun. "Tell me about McCabe."

"His enemies call him the Reaper. The rest of us wait for him to call us. It's complicated," he said before she could press the point. "Look, we can toss this ball of suspicion around all night and hope Fixx's people don't show up, or you can decide to trust me and we'll go from there. If it helps, I didn't jump at the chance to take this job."

The gun dropped another notch. Her mistrust level didn't budge. "Then why did you?"

"Rent's due, car needs work. Put the gun away, Amber, and we'll find someplace safe to talk."

Her gaze slid sideways as an owl swooped down, probably to grab a mouse. "I thought I'd gotten it wrong—the location Tom was trying to tell me about in code." Her eyes met his, and yes, they were amazing. "I'm not an agent or anything close to one. I managed a hotel in Las Vegas before this nightmare started. I can read faces and body language, pick up on subtle vocal changes. I considered psychiatry as a career, but I didn't have the patience to go through the years of training."

He grinned. "We're two of a kind in that regard."

"I despise men like Owen Fixx, more in some ways than I do the James Mockeries of the world, because the Fixxes settle for adopting other people's nasty habits instead of delving into their own psyches to see what they can dig out."

Okay, that almost made sense, even if he wasn't sure why she was telling him any of it. "You're scared," he said when she stopped talking.

Her eyes closed briefly. "Yes. My world—the one I created for myself—is a lot more glamorous than this one. To say nothing of a lot less dangerous."

Gage half smiled. "Welcome to the realm of dark justice. McCabe believes in the people he sends to deal with impossible situations. Not many others do. Not anymore. Am I shaking your faith?"

"You would be if I'd had any to begin with. As it is…" As the sentence trailed off, the gun dropped all the way. "I can shoot, but I'm not a marksman. I'm guessing you are. If you wanted me dead or captured, that's what I'd be. You're more attractive than I tend to like, but that's a personal prejudice and not relevant to this situation. I'm not happy to be back so close to Black Creek when I was a fair distance away from it before. Either you, Tom, or McCabe, whoever he is, better have some kind of plan or Fixx's men are going to be all over us. I'm terrified of him, and he's terrified of James Mockerie. With reason, I get that, but still, dead's dead and I'd rather not wind up in a grave just yet. Not me and not Rachel."

"Whose real name is?"

"Georgia. She likes Rachel better. We both like our new names better."

Interesting. But Gage had too many other concerns right then to go into it. He nodded at the derelict arcade. "A couple of those booths are semi-intact. We can use them for shelter while we talk."

"Meaning we're not done?"

"If you're asking can I take you to a safe location, the answer's no."

"Because that would be too straightforward, and God forbid any part of this should make sense." She waved him off before he could respond. "Doesn't matter. I don't want to go in. I want to find Rachel. Tom thinks she's alive, and I have to believe he's right. In a way, I dragged her into this nightmare. I'm going to make sure she gets out of it alive."

"That could be a tall order." He kept his eyes on the shifting shadows as they walked. "Why Snowbird?"

"Our family lived in Wyoming. My parents took us south every winter when we were very young."

"Did Tom give your sister a code name?"

She laughed a little. "He called her Grouse."

Gage grinned. "Enough said. Do you trust Tom?"

"More than I trust you; however…options." She squared her shoulders beneath her black, all-weather hoodie. "I don't appear to be overburdened with them at the moment. There's a turncoat agent in the FBI, maybe more than one and in places other than the FBI. Nothing I've been told or that I'm thinking inspires any real confidence in authority figures." She slid him a sideways look. "Jury's still out on the LAPD and the US Marshals."

"It shouldn't be." Gage shoved his hands in the pockets of his leather jacket. "Two of my former LAPD coworkers, guys I believed in, were on the take. Big time, big take."

"Did they take from Fixx?"

"More likely Mockerie. A lot of his drugs and weapons are shipped out of Los Angeles. An exodus like that requires a substantial number of people to look the other way. It's a problem, but not the immediate one. Not yours. Although Fixx will likely have access to Mockerie's list of inside sources."

She studied him as they drew closer to the mostly upright

booth. "How is it you entered the picture?"

"I was in the vicinity. Tom called McCabe. McCabe contacted me." Gage made a visual sweep of the tree line. "How tough is your sister?"

"She hates pain. She'll talk if she's threatened with more than a small amount of it. Do you know her story?"

"McCabe filled me in when I agreed to help him. Was your father in the military?"

"What? Yes. For a while before he got married." She frowned. "Why?"

"What about your mother?"

Her answering smile was false and tight. "Don't ask. Her parents, my grandparents, were wonderful." She tipped her head at a considering angle. "I sense you want to know my ancestry."

"You're an astonishingly beautiful woman, Amber. And cops are curious by nature."

"So was I once. My mother was born in Iran. Her father was French, her mother came from India. My father's much more of a cultural jumble, mostly on his mother's side. Irish, Egyptian, Romanian, Aboriginal Australian, the list goes on… One of the shadows just moved."

"Yep. Noticed." Gage had her on the ground before she could jerk away, though he doubted she would have. "Left wall of this booth is solid." He rolled to his feet, weapon drawn. "Use your gun if you have to. Hesitate, home in a crate."

"Great positive reinforcement," he heard her mutter in his wake, but his mind and eyes were already focused forward, to the spot between the trees and fence where he'd glimpsed the movement.

Seconds later, a gun went off in the vicinity of a sad-looking octopus ride. Dangling cars creaked like coffin lids in the gusty October wind. Gage heard another shot and grinned. Show time.

The chase was the best part. Got the adrenaline pumping and sharpened his instincts.

He hoped Amber would have the good sense to stay put. He figured the odds on that were about sixty-forty.

Overhead, a large tree branch creaked. He let a pair of shots go and waited through the unnatural silence that followed.

"You know I'm here and on you," he said softly. "You keep running, I'll keep shooting. Chances are I'll be luckier than you."

Squeezing through a gap in the fence, he listened. The sound of someone thrashing in the underbrush drew him farther to the right. He sent another shot into the neighboring trees, then stuffed his gun and headed for the sound.

The target, a male, broke free as Gage approached. Firing backward, the man began to zig-zag. Gage caught him a split second before he slammed face-first into the trunk of a bent oak.

Fists and feet flew. If he'd been in the mood to play dirty, Gage would have broken one of the guy's arms. As it was, he didn't want to leave Amber alone for any length of time. He flipped the prisoner onto his stomach, set a knee in the small of his back, and pressed until all resistance stopped.

"Smart man." He added more pressure. "Now, let's see who you are."

Redrawing his weapon, he turned the man over and regarded the shadowy features that glared up at him.

The guy was big, scarred, and sullen, his intentions unknown. Until Gage looked into his eyes.

Chapter Four

A leaf crunched behind her. Amber didn't think. She simply surged out of her crouch, spun, and kicked. The approaching person let out a startled shriek and landed on the ground.

"Oh, shit, crap." When she swiped the hair from her eyes, Amber realized what she'd done. "I'm so sorry." She went to her knees beside a gasping female.

The young woman had a frail build, and she whimpered as she struggled to catch her breath. "I can't see." She panted and whimpered louder. "I can't see!"

Amber winced. "I'm sorry, I really am. I thought you were a—" She hesitated, substituted, "—someone else."

"Buddy?" The whimper became a wail. "Are you here? I think we're getting ripped off. Why can't I see?"

"Because it's dark, and your eyes are closed," Amber told her. She caught the woman's flailing hand, shoved up the sleeve of her jacket, and glanced at her arm. "I'm guessing you and Buddy were meeting someone." She sat back on her heels. "A guy with a gun, maybe? Or does Buddy carry a gun, and he's the one who was shooting up the park?"

The woman didn't answer. She was too busy trying to pry her eyelids apart.

"Okay, well, I'm still sorry I kicked you. When you're ready to stand, I'll help you."

Amber heard footsteps behind her, one set walking, the other stumbling. She swung her head around.

"What's going on?" Gage asked. "Who's she?"

"If the guy you're with is Buddy, they're together, waiting for someone who's probably long gone should he happen to have witnessed any of what just went down here."

Gage gave the man in front of him a shove that sent him to his knees. "Looks like we screwed up a drug deal. My heart's not broken. The girl can't be more than seventeen, and her friend's so twitchy he'd be more likely to shoot his supplier than pay him. Which also wouldn't break my heart. And yes, I do have one somewhere. It murmured enough to worry the New Age hippies in the commune where my old lady dumped me."

Amber frowned. "Your mother dumped you in a commune?"

"Don't look so appalled, Snowbird. I've always been grateful for the favor." He made a head motion. "Is she hurt?"

"Not much." Standing, Amber dusted off. She had no idea why, but this semi-normal conversation calmed her nerves to some degree. "Why were you grateful to be dumped in a commune?"

"Because the alternative was a hell of a lot worse. A couple of the guys who were there way back when taught me a lot of useful stuff. Biker Joe—he died five years ago—got me up on my first motorcycle when I was seven. It didn't suck."

Amber had no idea why she wanted to laugh. Maybe she was on the verge of hysteria.

"Rather than explore that fascinating subject," she said, "I'll ask instead, what are we going to do with these two?"

The girl was still using her fingers to work her eyes open. The man, twenty-three at most, with his hair hanging in greasy rat tails, glowered at Gage like a snarly adolescent.

Gage shrugged, drew Amber aside and out of earshot. "I've got his gun, and I'm not in the mood for a trip to the local cop shop." He scanned the trees behind them. "We'll tie him up and leave her to set him free. State she's in, that could take the better part of two hours."

Contrition set in as Amber regarded the girl. She pitched her voice to the same low level as Gage's. "I kicked her. In the sternum. I might have fractured one of her ribs."

"Yeah? Huh. Lucky shot or some kind of training?"

"Mixed martial arts. It's a fitness thing, but I like knowing I can defend myself."

"How's Rachel in that regard?"

"She's into yoga."

"Your skill's more useful. I need a couple pieces of rope." Gage handed her his gun. "I've got supplies in my truck. Move closer, and go for a knee cap if he tries to get up. I don't imagine he will. He's in his own world right now, singing some song I don't recognize and playing air guitar on his back."

"Why your gun?" she asked, examining it.

"Makes less of a bang than yours."

Small favors, Amber supposed. Her life had come down to a series of those. Whatever could be done to attract the least amount of attention.

"I'm not used to this running-in-the-shadows stuff," she confided when Gage returned. Because her hands threatened to shake, she forced her mind to step sideways into her safe zone. "Numbers have always been my strength." The man on the ground continued to sing, but now he was playing air drums. The girl had her hands over her ears now and was whimpering even louder than before. "I could keep track of three blackjack games at once in Las Vegas. Spotting cheaters was a piece of cake."

Gage gave the rope around the young man's ankles a tug. Once again, he drew her away from the pair. "So, a hotel manager and a cardsharp rolled into one. Your boss got himself a bargain with you."

Amber's temper sparked. It helped her shaking hands but did nothing to improve her mood. She controlled her annoyance long enough not to plant her foot in Gage's sternum.

Straightening, he took his gun back. "Very good, Snowbird. I saw the shutter come down on your expression. You know how to manage your emotions."

"Some of them," she admitted. "My sister's missing, I've been living in hell for the better part of a year, ever since the FBI asked for my help, and for all I know, you're one of Fixx's clever traps. He's full of those, as I discovered. You say you work for a man my WPP emergency contact trusts, and you had all the right answers to the questions I asked, but how do I know I can trust you all the way?"

Smiling, he stuffed the gun in his waistband, strolled closer to regard the prostrate pair. "You don't. But you either come with me or stay with your new friends. Odds are part of your business. You decide." He nudged the young man's ankle, received a mumbled response. "It's either them and a pumpkin carving contest in Diggerton, or me and a dash for the Canadian border."

She brought her eyes up. "That's not what I…"

"Doesn't matter what you want," he interrupted. "You've got two options, right here, right now. Three if you want to go solo. Not the best choice in my opinion."

Their gazes remained locked until Amber's brain stopped scrambling through the wild possibilities and settled down to the more logical probabilities.

"Why Canada?" she asked.

His smile widened. "I like maple syrup and changing leaves. We'll go by way of Vermont. Fixx won't expect that."

She glanced away, then back. "Is it too soon for me to say I hate you?"

"It's never too soon for that." He motioned her away from the glowering man and his still-whimpering companion. "But I wouldn't expend too much of my hatred at this early date. 'Cause, honey…" Wrapping a hand around her ponytail, he gave it a warning tug. "You ain't seen nothing yet."

. . .

"I want to talk to Owen." Rachel fussed with the rope that bound her wrists. "You can't keep me in this skanky motel room forever. The owner's not stupid enough to believe anybody would stay here for more than a couple of nights."

The man by the door grinned broadly and kept chewing his gum.

"I'll scream," she warned him. "I'm good at it."

"You scream, you die," her captor drawled. "Up to you where you go with that."

Rachel opened her mouth, fully intending to follow through, but she snapped it shut when the man produced a gun. She lifted her chin instead. "You wouldn't dare."

He shrugged and kept on chewing his gum. "We're waiting for my boss, sugar plum. Your sister's too smart for her own good. Two of my men got burned real bad. Unlike everyone else who scrammed out of there, they walked into the fire to find her. Sorry to say, they never did, so now the search is on."

Rachel stomped her tied feet. "I want to talk to Owen," she demanded. "Nothing that happened in Las Vegas was my fault. I didn't want a divorce. I don't even know how I wound up getting one. Owen will understand, he'll listen."

The man began to whistle around his gum "I ain't saying he will, I ain't saying he won't. All I'm saying is I got orders and we're waiting for my boss to get here before we do anything."

"Fine." Rachel wanted to punch that wad of gum right down the bastard's throat. "I'm screaming."

However, once again, the sound died in her throat.

Ahead of her, the motel room door opened, and a man walked in. Danger rippled the air around him. But that was only part of what stopped the scream. The real shock was the unexpected sight of someone she knew. Someone who hadn't been a threat in her past life.

Someone whose current facial expression terrified the living hell out of her.

...

"So, no Vermont, no Canada, no maple syrup," Amber remarked.

She wondered if the lake-sized potholes on these back roads might swallow Gage's truck and solve her problem that way. Except that Rachel was still out there and in danger. Alive, she hoped, but probably half expecting her ex-husband to help her.

Gage had retrieved her backpack and ditched her stolen truck before they'd left the amusement park. She had to assume he'd known what he was doing. Still...

"This is the worst nightmare ever," she said through gritted teeth. "And the longest. I can see where the concept of Limbo might come into things."

"You're quick on the uptake, Snowbird. It could save your life."

She glanced at Gage in the driver's seat beside her. Dark hair—too long. Green eyes—too mesmerizing. Lean build, sexy stubble, amazing profile... He was so not what she'd anticipated in terms of help. Couldn't McCabe have sent someone who looked like Sydney Greenstreet?

He glanced at her, and for a moment, she thought he'd read her mind. She wouldn't blush, she promised herself. She'd passed that stage in her life years ago—and what in God's name was she doing anyway? So the man was hot as hell. It was hardly the time for her to be noticing that.

Banking her frustration, which wasn't a hard thing to do in the face of her still-mounting terror, she asked, "I understand the double-talk and the distance back at the amusement park, but do you really think Fixx's trackers are close enough behind us that they might intercept and interrogate a couple of junkies?"

"I think his people could be anywhere from here to the Mississippi delta. But given the fact that McCabe said your sister ran off with a Black Creek farmer and no mention of him was made when the guy holding Rachel threatened you, it's a good bet that farmer's not likely to be plowing the lower forty come next spring. So to answer your question, I think his trackers could be anywhere."

Guilt shattered the outer layer of Amber's fear. "In other words, odds are Jess is dead."

"Yep."

"I hate that this sounds completely self-serving, but do you also think he talked before he died? Told whoever where he lived?"

"That, or whoever caught up with him traced him to Black Creek. Either way, once a location was established, his usefulness would have been at an end. And you're allowed to care about your own life, Amber. The FBI approached you, not the other way around."

"They didn't approach Jess Murkle, though, did they? He had no part in any of this."

"Don't count on that. He was a drinker. So is your sister. Liquor loosens tongues. You have no idea what she might have said to him, or what he might have done if what she said sounded profitable. And you can lose the disgusted look. People get jaded in my world. As a wannabe shrink, you should understand that."

Unfortunately, she did, or she was starting to. "Okay, fine," she allowed. "Circling back to the pair in the amusement park, will it always be necessary for us to talk in code around strangers?"

Gage checked the rearview mirror. "What any stranger hears that isn't true can't hurt us. False trails. We create as many as we can between where we were and our actual destination."

"Which is?"

"Hidden Valley."

A headache loomed, possibly a migraine, but pain merely heightened Amber's mistrust, to say nothing of her confusion. "We're going where salad dressing's made?"

Gage grinned. "Is that Hidden Valley still around?"

"Who knows?" She blew out a breath. "Talk to me, Gage. Tell me something that's true, something that makes sense. What's in Hidden Valley? And don't say 'us, when we get there.'"

"I'm not big on clever quips, though it sounds like someone in your life is or was." Gage worked his way around a large, potentially deep puddle. "Hidden Valley's a retreat. I know the people who run it."

Amber's suspicion doubled. "Are we talking commune?"

"Yes and no. For us, it's a quiet and sequestered sanctuary. One road in, same road out. There's Pepsi on the seat behind us and a bottle of Advil in the glove box. If Fixx's people did follow you to Diggerton, the junkies in the park will point them toward Canada."

"What if they're following us right now?"

"Bridges, Amber. We'll cross them when we get to them."

He hit the high beams, but that only made the surrounding landscape seem more macabre.

"Sleepy Hollow," she murmured as the eerie atmosphere seeped into her bones. "I'd say Frankenstein, but the Smoky Mountains don't have enough European flavor for that."

"Have you been to Europe?" he asked.

"What? Yes." She dragged her gaze away from the skeletal trees, set it on his face. Which only confused her more considering her earlier mixed feelings about him. "I worked in the casino at Monte Carlo for two years. It was a fascinating experience, but not a great fit." She slanted him a shrewd look. "Why would you ask that question when I'm ninety-nine percent sure you already knew the answer?"

"I prefer to hear certain facts firsthand. Plus, I'm trying to distract you. I sense your mind's on overload. I was told Rachel worked in a boutique in Fixx's Las Vegas hotel. Apparently, she caught the main man's eye."

Although an analysis of Rachel's life wasn't Amber's topic of choice, he'd been right about the overload factor. She breathed in and slowly out. "Okay, fine. Rachel's beautiful and flamboyant. She loves glitter and all the nightlife she can get. Black Creek smothered her. I had a feeling she'd bail."

"She likes men."

"They're drawn to her."

"Like flies to sugar?"

Amber smiled. "More like honey in this case."

"What about you?"

"Men aren't as drawn to me. I put up barriers, deliberate ones. It goes back to college. Some professors have different agendas than their students. Authority carries a certain amount of power, or so some men think."

"In other words, you avoid the Owen Fixxes of the world."

"In as much as I can." She thought about Owen's son and pressed on her throbbing temple. "On the rare occasions I can't, I suck it up and go to a quiet place in my mind."

"So, astonishingly beautiful with a touch of Zen." He regarded the side mirror.

Amber's eyes narrowed instantly. "Something?" she asked.

"I saw a light. It's gone now. What was your first impression of the great and powerful Owen Fixx?"

Now there was a question, she reflected. A complex one that took her on a winding journey back to a more innocent time. Or so she'd believed back then. "I met his son Gareth before I met him," she revealed.

"Met his son where? In Monte Carlo?"

"No, on a flight from Chicago to Las Vegas. We were seat mates. We played blackjack. I won every game. Numbers and odds," she added with a smile. "Gareth's not as perfect or as polished as his father. We had a drink when we landed in Las Vegas, and he asked me if I'd heard of the Moroccan Hotel. He said his father owned it and he was looking for a manager."

"So, to answer my original question…"

"I thought Fixx was a prick. But he paid well, and I knew I wouldn't have much contact with him. Rachel came to Nevada a few months later and got a job in the same hotel. When she and Owen started seeing each other, I did what I could to revise my opinion."

"Did you succeed?"

"Not really."

"Making you and Rachel different on a number of levels."

"On every level." Amber glanced at her own side mirror. "I love her. She's family. She drives me crazy, but I don't want anything to happen to her. Fixx was an aberration. He's a snake who can act. He fools a lot of people."

"He didn't fool you."

"He wasn't trying to, not in the same way as Rachel. I saw a light, Gage, maybe a mile behind us. Should we be worried?"

He maneuvered the truck around another long puddle "There's no way to speed on this road. We'll be all right for a while." He arched a dark brow at her. "Were you ever involved with Gareth Fixx?"

"You really like loaded questions, don't you?" Releasing her ponytail, Amber shook out her long hair. "The short answer is not right away. He was interested, but I had doubts. I worked for his father; Rachel was dating his father. The situation was awkward, or it could have been if…" She folded her arms. It was a telling gesture, but how could she not feel uncomfortable after using someone as shamelessly as she'd used Gareth? "Move on, okay?"

"If you want. Word is Fixx has two sons."

"Word's wrong. Gareth's his only son. If you're putting Luka in the number two position, he's Fixx's nephew. Fixx took him in when his sister died. Luka was ten, Gareth was eight. There's always been a strong rivalry between them. Fixx also has a brother, Tony, who comes and goes and makes everyone he meets think of Indiana Jones."

"Is Tony part of his brother's business?"

Amber gave in and reached for the Advil. "I never found anything to connect him to Owen's criminal activities. On the other hand, there's nothing to connect Luka or Gareth, either, but I know they're involved."

"Between the son and the nephew, who's the better actor?"

"Gareth, definitely." She twisted the top off a Pepsi. "He's a part-time musician. It's very seductive when a man can sing and play the guitar. But truth be told, Gareth's up to his ears in Daddy's bad business. Luka's his polar opposite.

He doesn't bother with pretense. He's plain old in-your-face bad. It might sound weird, but I like that about him. You get what you see, end of story."

Gage's gaze flicked to the rearview mirror. "What did Rachel think of her newly acquired relatives?"

"She liked and trusted both Gareth and Luka. And Tony was her big brother from the moment she met him. I told you, Rachel and I are different on every level. Our perception of Fixx and his family was just another case of that."

"Talk about some of your other differences," he suggested.

"Yeah, right, where to start with that long list." And how far back should she take it? "It probably won't surprise you to hear that I was cynical and suspicious as a child. When I was five, my best friend talked me into swapping my really cool Raggedy Ann doll for an old hand-knitted piglet that smelled like mothballs. I cried all night, then I stopped crying and promised myself I'd never be an easy mark again. Rachel preferred to live in a Barbie doll world. She got married in a blingy princess ball gown and wore a tiara."

"Which you never would have worn."

Amber felt her inner feline rising and offered him a slow smile. "Do I look like a princess to you?"

"No, you're a siren. Beautiful, dangerous, and scary as hell to any man with functioning genitalia."

Her smile faded. "That light behind us is creeping closer."

"Road's improving."

"Not that I've noticed." Amber turned in her seat and almost bit her tongue off when the front tires struck a rock. "Can we lose him?"

"Oh, we can do a lot better than that." Reaching back, he grabbed her pack and dropped it in her lap. "We're on a high point of land. Narrow road, no guardrails. There's a canyon on our left. I'm going to slow down at the next bend. When I tell you to jump, tuck and roll. When you stop, head for the trees. Take this." He handed her what looked like a small cell phone. "It's a comm link. It has a one-mile radius. Keep it switched on, and I'll find you."

Never in her life could Amber recall having so many instructions fired at her in under fifteen seconds. "Are you sure—" she began.

But he cut her off with a firm, "This is as slow as it gets, Snowbird. Go. Now."

It must have been his tone. Either that, or she'd gone as crazy as he obviously was. Amber grabbed the link and her pack, shoved the door open, and jumped.

Her martial arts classes had taught her how to fall without injuring herself. However, when she factored in the momentum of a moving vehicle, everything she'd learned about a safe landing flew from her head. She hit hard, tumbled, and wound up on her stomach with her face buried in a patch of wet leaves.

"Ouch," she mumbled.

She struggled to slow her spinning mind as she rolled over. A series of crashes reached her from the road ahead. The sound penetrated her mental haze. It also got her moving.

Head for the trees, Gage had said. Which trees? There were an awful lot of them on this side of the road.

Working herself into a crouch, Amber switched on the link and waited for the light to blink green. When it did, she zipped it inside her pocket, hoisted her pack, and struck out for the woods.

She heard a final crunch of metal on rock and knew exactly what Gage had done. He'd shot his truck over the edge of the cliff into a fathomless canyon where no one in their right mind would dare venture at night. If there happened to be a lake at the bottom, so much the better.

How long would the diversion last, Amber wondered as

she ran. Two or three hours? Until morning?

A horrible thought suddenly occurred to her. Halting, she spun to look back. Gage's truck had gone into the canyon. But what if it hadn't been empty when it left the road?

Chapter Five

Gage waited in the bushes, well concealed from oncoming headlights. He rubbed his sore right knee as he shifted position. He was out of practice. Jumping from a moving vehicle required timing and finesse. He'd almost slammed his head into a boulder before he'd stopped rolling. He only hoped he'd done a better job of directing Amber or all of this would be for nothing.

The truck shadowing them approached with caution. It came complete with a double set of high beam headlights and a row of powerful fog lamps on the roof. Gage spotted two people inside as it crept past.

Could be Fixx's men, but not necessarily. Poachers were rampant in these mountains. If that's what these two were, they wouldn't be reporting any accident they might have happened to notice to the local sheriff.

The driver braked. The taillights glowed red. A window slid down. Gage heard voices, but he couldn't tell what was being said. All he knew was that one of the men inside had a distinct Southern drawl.

A few seconds later, the window slid back up and the truck moved on. Slowly at first, and then with a burst of speed as it neared the next bend.

Gage continued to wait, but the sound of the engine simply faded into the night. Interesting. He grimaced as he stood and hoisted his backpack onto his shoulder. Disaster averted or not?

He took two steps and gave his knee an experimental flex. It hurt like hell, but nothing was broken. He'd be good to go for a few miles.

Raising the comm link to his mouth, he started across the road. "You there, Snowbird? Say yes, and make my night."

"I'm somewhere," she replied. "But please don't ask me to describe my surroundings. I landed on my flashlight and broke the case."

"Never buy plastic." He regarded the screen. "I've got your position. You're due east of me. It shouldn't take long to— Shit!"

"What? Shit what? Gage?"

He ducked behind a large stump. "Truck's coming back."

"Does that mean they are Fixx's men?"

"It's a good bet." Gage stayed low. "Don't move," he said. "Leave your link on. I'll find you."

Could still be poachers, but he doubted it. More likely, Amber had been spotted and followed to the amusement park. Unless someone had tapped into Tom Vigor's phone line. Someone who knew Tom's list of codes...

There were suspects within the US Marshals office ,a half dozen or more. McCabe knew about them, and so did Gage. Knew their names at any rate, as well as where they worked and why they were suspected. Unfortunately, there was no evidence to support those suspicions.

In Gage's opinion, it wasn't a turncoat US Marshal in the returning truck. Fixx would have sent his own people to deal with this problem. And those people would be armed to the teeth.

Fuck life and his own susceptibility. He could have been home, listening to the King and getting quietly drunk. Or playing poker with a couple of cops on the Memphis force. Barring those things, Mary Ellen was usually up for a round of dinner and sex... And why in God's name should the thought of sex with Mary Ellen pale now that he'd met Amber Kelly?

Gage swore long and hard when he stepped in a rut and twisted his bad knee. Screw it. McCabe deserved to burn in hell for inflicting this assignment on him.

He raised his comm link. "I'm coming up behind you, Amber. Don't freak."

"I never freak." She materialized next to him and nodded at the base of a sprawling beech tree. "I left my link over there. I've learned to be paranoid."

He spotted the outline of her backpack. With an ironic smile, he let the memory of Mary Ellen fade even further into the background. "Paranoid's good. Odds are eighty-twenty those are Fixx's bloodhounds back there. Does he have any favorites on his payroll?"

"Not that I know of. I saw a man with a missing finger once. Or part of a missing finger."

Grinning, Gage grabbed her pack. "Hell, honey, you saw Mockerie."

"I did not." She stared in astonishment. "Long hair, worn-out hat, faded jeans, old cowboy boots, still shy of forty... That's James Mockerie?"

"Yep. The hat hides his face." Gage pulled a flashlight from his pocket and switched it on. "He has a scar that runs from his left eye to the corner of his mouth, and a crushed left cheekbone that didn't heal properly."

"I think I saw part of the scar." After tying her hair back into a sleek ponytail, Amber swung the pack onto her shoulder and pocketed her comm link. "I missed the crushed cheekbone. I only got a quick glimpse." She used her index fingers to point in opposite directions. "Which way?"

"South, and picking up the pace wouldn't hurt."

"You're limping," she noted.

"Rock and roll, Snowbird. It's been a while since I've jumped from a moving vehicle. Last time I did, I came away without a scratch. My partner wasn't so lucky." And why the fuck had he gone there? "It was a long time ago," he said with a shrug. Too bad a long time ago would always be yesterday for him. "It's tricky terrain. Stay ahead of me and keep your eyes on the ground. I'll watch for predators."

She turned to study him. "You're a man of mystery, Gage Morgan. I'm not sure I like it, but I can live with it—for a while."

"Yeah?" He trapped her chin with his hand before she could evade him, ran his thumb lightly along the curve of her jaw. Something inside him shifted when he looked into her eyes. Unwilling to examine what it might be, he let his hand drop. "Okay, let's just back that last part up a bit. You're not thinking of trying to ditch me, are you?"

Her answering gaze was direct and unflinching, and, dammit, it almost had his thoughts slipping sideways again to a woman named Lydia and a time he desperately wanted to forget. Not that that time and this were related in any way. Amber was waking feelings he'd assumed were dead. One touch and he wanted more. A moment away from the madness, a good long taste of her incredible mouth, a night of wild, uncontrolled— Whoa. *Back off,* he ordered himself. Where the hell had all that come from? And what was she saying to him now?

She sighed, glanced away. "Any potential ditching will depend on what you expect me to do. I want my sister back safe and unharmed before Fixx gets ahold of her."

Gage swung the flashlight beam around. "You don't think Fixx would understand why she went into hiding?"

Amber's eyes glittered, but her expression didn't alter. "I think he'd understand just fine about the hiding part. It's the divorce that will have sent him over the edge. I'm not sure who made it happen or how they pulled it off, but I dug into his affairs, Gage. His business and his personal affairs. Owen Fixx had three wives before he married Rachel. All three of those wives wanted to divorce him. And all three of them died before they could."

Gage knew precisely where this was going, but he wanted to hear her say it.

Amber looked westward. "Owen Fixx is a coldblooded killer. He's a man who deals in illegal weapons and drugs. He's also completely insane."

. . .

They walked in silence for some time after that. Amber had no idea where they were going, but she assumed Gage had a plan in mind.

She wondered if her story about Fixx had sounded melodramatic. Or maybe Gage simply had no reply for it. In any case, she welcomed the break. It gave her time to collect her thoughts and gear down from an intensity level that wasn't her normal state.

He'd touched her, and for a moment, the danger around her dissolved. It had been a very, very long time since any man had moved her. *Why now?*

"I used to be calm no matter what happened." Deliberately moving away from him, she turned a small circle as she walked. The woods had thickened considerably, and the ground underfoot felt increasingly treacherous. "Never got ruffled, never worried about things I couldn't control."

"You dealt." Gage checked out the path with his flashlight, then switched it off and threw the woods back into murky black shadow.

"For the most part, I liked managing Fixx's hotel. The facilities were amazing, the staff was great, the guests were mostly happy. Fixx was an asshole, but I worked around that. Uh…" She pointed at a movement between the trees. "Please say not a bear."

He used the flashlight again. "Deer. I think."

She summoned a serene smile. "Are you always this reassuring?"

"I'm making a special effort in your case."

Amber couldn't help it. She laughed. "Okay, so, are we still going to Hidden Valley, or has the destination changed?"

"Destination's the same, but we'll need a vehicle."

"Meaning we what? Hijack one? Because I doubt you planted a second truck, and mine's…" She waved a hand behind them. "Not accessible."

"There's a town about a mile west of here. It's called Halo. It's just off a north-south highway."

"Which is good because?"

"Plenty of tourist traffic. We won't stand out."

"We will if the people after us—well, me—happen to be in the vicinity."

"Would you recognize them if they were?"

"Probably not. Fixx has a deep pool of muscle and fire power. He pays well," she explained. "Bad guys with skills like that."

"Good guys with skills don't mind it, either."

"Long as they stay good and don't switch sides." Because to doubt Gage's character was to invite the terror she'd been living with since Rachel had disappeared back again. She glanced up as an owl hooted high in a tall pine to her left. "Do you know someone in Halo?"

"In a way," was all he said.

Amber left it alone. Her body was bruised and scraped, her head hurt, and her thoughts were far too tangled to straighten them out. Better to keep her eyes open, let him take the lead, and see where she wound up.

Half a mile farther on, the woods thinned and small houses began to appear. Mostly they were shacks and trailers that had settled at odd angles in the mud. Any vehicles she spotted were up on blocks or too old and rusty to be drivable.

Gage grinned in profile. "Never judge a book, Snowbird."

"I wasn't," she said, then frowned at what looked like an old boxcar with windows cut in the side. "Okay, maybe I was. A little. But a truck with working doors would be a definite advantage."

"We only need to make it to Hidden Valley."

"Which is how far from here?"

"Less than a hundred miles."

"Practically walking distance."

"You've obviously never lived in L.A."

"I've visited. Didn't consider going from place to place on foot." Her frown deepened. "Seriously, Gage. We're not going to steal one of these deathtraps on wheels, are we?"

"Wouldn't be my first choice."

A cluster of lights came into view, possibly with a street between them. Amber heard music above the sounds of frogs and crickets. Sucking up her uncertainty, she hitched her pack higher. "Is the idea for us to stroll through town like casual tourists?"

"Not exactly. Do you have a cap with a visor?"

"Yes, but that won't disguise – "

"It will if you stick to the shadows. And there'll be plenty of those in the local bar. Servers'll be young and pretty. You won't get a second look."

"Excuse me?"

Gage chuckled. "Nothing personal, but low tops and push up bras tend to draw a man's eye."

"Right. In we go."

The music, a twangy mix of country and blues, grew louder. Smoke drifted out of a barely lit building that stood apart from the others on the street. Everything appeared old, saggy, and tired, even in the dark. Trucks were parked helter-skelter near a sidewalk that was little more than a strip of raised wooden slats.

They passed a pair of teenagers, busy making out in the alley next to the bar. The girl, she reflected, could have been Rachel seven or eight years ago. Or Amber right now…

Jesus, where had that come from? She wasn't going to do this. Gorgeous or not, Gage Morgan was off-limits. She needed to focus on staying alive and finding her sister.

Blocking the provocative mental image, she poked Gage's back. "Why are we going inside? Trucks are out here."

"Curiosity." Gage looked up and down the street. "Knew it," he said, then took Amber's arm before she could ask. "Stay behind me and stick to the shadows."

She was tempted to offer a salute, but it was hardly the time. Instead, she tugged the cap she'd dug from her pack lower and followed him through the door.

Straight into Merle Haggard's backwoods garage. At least that's how it felt on the surface. Good old boys sat around a motley collection of tables while a Merle wannabe across the room did his best to imitate the original. The bartender, a tall, bone rack of a man, could have been a close cousin to Paulie Murkle. In front of him, sashaying between tables and bystanders, a pair of young women who'd squeezed themselves into skintight jeans and shirts made for twelve-year-old boys kept the beer and whiskey flowing.

It made the place she'd had in Black Creek look like a Nashville palace.

Gage stayed close to the outer walls. His gaze, Amber noted, never stopped moving. Until it landed on a pair of men at a table near the back of the room.

"Yeah, you just keep right on sizing up the staff," he said softly.

Amber squinted at the men. "Do you recognize them?"

"I know the type. Question is, do either of them look familiar to you?"

"No. Well…" She took a second, longer look as one of the pair lit a cigarette. "Maybe. The guy on the left. The twisty ring, and the buzzcut. I'm not sure."

"What about the other guy?"

"No."

"Good enough. Our work here's done."

"Simple as that? I thought we'd be… Ah, hello." She stared up, way up from the wall of male chest that had materialized in front of her.

"Dance." The man to whom the chest belonged grabbed her arm.

Gage kept his smile easy. "Lady's with me, pal. Let her go or say good-bye to a few vital parts."

The man's heavily whiskered grin was wide and drunkenly anticipatory. "Hell, I've swatted June bugs bigger'n you."

"Yeah? Any of those June bugs carry a Glock?"

Confusion had the grin fading. "You got a clock?"

"He means a gun." Amber willed her heart rate down. Big and dumb were no match for a cop with a weapon. She hoped.

Irritation took over, and the man jerked on her arm. "Asshole pulls a gun on me, I don't swat. I squash. Dance," he growled again.

Amber heard a *click* from below.

"You got balls, big guy." Gage kept his voice level and his eyes on the tables ahead. "You want to keep them, you let the lady go, walk over to the bar, and order another drink."

Amber held her breath while the man wrestled with his drunken pride. Finally, he snorted. "Hell, ain't no bitch worth losing Tom, Dick, and Harry. Rather have whiskey anyway."

He shoved Amber for show before turning toward the bar.

"Shit," Gage said under his breath.

A split second later, Amber understood why. The man whipped around so fast she almost missed the motion. Her backpack went flying as Gage knocked her aside, avoided the worst of a straight-armed blow, and shouted something she couldn't hear above the sudden scrape of a dozen chairs. Someone whistled, someone else hooted, and one of the servers let out a shrill scream.

On her butt with her head spinning, Amber struggled to make sense of the sudden eruption of motion in front of her.

Gun, she thought hazily. There was one in her pack—assuming she could find it.

She located Gage's pack near the wall. He'd have a spare inside, right? Cops were always armed to the teeth.

She opened the flap and rummaged inside. A shot rang out, followed by another series of screams. When a pair of hands yanked her to her feet, she grabbed a long, heavy object, pulled it out, and swung it around in an arc.

The person who'd hauled her upright swore. Realizing she had a flashlight, Amber switched it on and shone it into a pair of flinty eyes.

It was the man with the twisted ring and the buzzcut. His lips peeled back as he lunged forward. She saw blood on his cheek and something in his eyes that made her breath ball like ice in her throat.

When he lunged again, she stumbled backward. He'd have caught her if his feet hadn't gotten tangled up in Gage's pack. He went down hard and struck his head.

Amber didn't hesitate. On her knees, she found her own bag and searched the room for Gage.

What she saw through the smoke and falling bodies were the two servers yanking each other's hair, the Merle wannabe plastered to a wall holding his guitar like a shield, and every other man in the place throwing punches at anyone who staggered past.

Seriously?

"Go." She didn't realize Gage had come up behind her until he lifted her to her feet and pushed. "Thirty seconds and they're on us."

"Who…" she began, then stopped and ran for the door.

"This way." Outside, he swung his pack up and nodded toward a dark truck with monster size tires. "Up and in, Snowbird."

She crawled over the console and dropped down on the passenger seat. *No key,* she realized. But Gage had that covered. He yanked a handful of wires from under the dash and quickly made the connection.

"I heard gunshots." She pivoted, tried to look everywhere at once. "Did you shoot the guy who hit you?"

"Nope, I left him trading punches with the man you didn't recognize. Hold on."

She braced while he swung the wheel and fishtailed away from the curb. Even so, her back and shoulder slammed into the door.

"Is this—ouch—their truck, the one that was following us?"

"Was theirs. Now it's ours."

"You know that won't stop them."

"I never figured it would. The bar fight'll slow them down some."

"While we drive a hundred miles in a stolen truck?"

"Pretty sure we won't be going that far. At least not right

away."

"Why—ouch—not? Shit!" She had to use her hands and feet to stay in her seat.

She couldn't have said what drew her gaze over and down when he took the next corner, or why she noticed the wet stain on his T-shirt. But she did, and her heart gave a stuttering double beat. "That's blood." Her eyes snapped up as fear rushed in. "My God, you've been shot!"

Chapter Six

They had to stop. Logic and the steady trickle of blood flowing from his side demanded it. Gage had no idea if the bullet had passed right through or lodged itself somewhere between his ribs. All he knew was that the pain was a bitch and he was going to plant his fist in McCabe's face next time they met. *If* they met. Which wasn't where he wanted to go at this point.

"Head's starting to spin, Amber." He used his mirrors to check the road behind them. "You have to drive. I'll give you directions."

"I'll drive," she agreed. "After I inspect that wound."

"Great. Are you a doctor and McCabe neglected to mention it?"

"I took a survival course in South America one summer after college. It included field training for medical emergencies."

"Like bullet wounds?"

"People get shot, Gage, often by jerks with rifles who can't tell a deer from a dinosaur. Go somewhere off this road and let me at least take a look at the damage."

She sounded calm. Edgy, but in control. He swung the truck onto a side road, bounced through ruts that had him seeing stars, and finally braked in a small clearing near what smelled like a bog.

He climbed out so she could examine the entry wound by flashlight. *Too much blood,* he realized immediately and went down on one knee.

She pulled up the back of his jacket. "There's no exit hole."

"Yeah. Figured that."

"You won't make it a hundred miles, Gage, and we can't go back to Halo. What's near here?"

"Abel's fifteen, maybe twenty miles east."

She drew his jacket back down. "What or who is Abel?"

"Abel Bodine. He trained me. He was search and rescue before taking on the cop life."

Standing, Amber rooted through the back of the truck. "I want to say that name sounds familiar, but I'm not sure why. There's no chance he's on Fixx's payroll, is there?"

"Doubt it." Breathing was becoming more difficult. And his head was pounding. "He brought down three like Fixx when he was on the force. Got medals for bravery and achievement. What's that?"

"A steel-toed boot." Wrapping it in a sweatshirt, she handed it to him. "Press it against your side while I find something to hold it in place." She worked up a smile. "Feel free to swear."

"I've pretty much got that covered." The words had been running like a litany through his head since they'd left Halo.

"This'll do." She drew out a thick rope. "Keep pressing on the entry wound."

The litany changed as pain arrowed through his entire upper body. Then she twisted the rope, and he hissed in an accusing breath.

"Jesus, Amber. Any tighter and you'll cut off my blood flow completely."

"That's the plan." She tied the rope, caught his chin, and looked into his eyes. "Or as close as I can come to it. Can you stand?"

He didn't answer, just let her help him to his feet. Which sent waves of dizziness through his head.

How the hell much blood had he lost?

It took two attempts for her to get him into the truck and three to figure out how to change gears without stalling the engine.

"Let me guess. You've never driven a five-speed."

She yanked on the stick shift. "My Daddy's old Dodge truck four times and Gareth Fixx's cherry red Lamborghini once. The car slept in a body shop."

"Because Gareth drove like a bat out of hell?"

"No, because even the smallest scratch bothered him. I thought he was normal and nice at first. Turns out he's as anal as his father."

"Just not as ambitious."

"Not ambitious in the same way. Where do I go, Gage?"

Her hands were rock steady. Her jaw was set and her breathing level. All good signs in Gage's opinion.

"Reverse out of this swamp," he told her. "Check for any kind of movement, and head north."

"But I thought—"

"Away from Halo and back toward Black Creek. They won't expect you to take that direction. They'll be looking south or west, maybe east."

"Which is what we want, right?"

Gage fixed his mind on Abel Bodine even as he worked his cell phone from the pocket of his jeans. "Gonna give you a really twisted route, Snowbird. Follow it. You see any sign of Fixx's henchmen, do what you can to lose them. McCabe figures you for a survivor. Survive."

She rocked the gear shift into place, checked for oncoming traffic. "That's not exactly what I was hoping for in terms of encouragement."

"Best I can do." And a helluva lot more than he'd thought he could manage with his brain turning lopsided somersaults and his throat filled with gravel.

He gave her the phone—pretty sure he did anyway—and heard her reply. Gorgeous, but with a mouth like a longshoreman when challenged. For some reason, and despite the pain, the realization amused him. Under other circumstances, he'd be thinking hot sex and a very different use for that incredible mouth of hers.

They bumped and bounced through the mud and the rocks and the dark, dense woods. He began to drift. That couldn't be good.

When he moved his hand, fresh blood seeped over his waistband.

...

Every firefly transformed into a headlight in Amber's mind. Or would have if she hadn't clamped down on the bulk of her panic. She could have a meltdown later, after she untangled herself from the fifth wrong turn in thirty minutes and arrived at Hickory Lake, home of Gage's cop trainer, Abel Bodine.

As she maneuvered along yet another boulder-clogged road, she ran the man's name through her head. Why did it sound familiar? Was the near-recognition a good or bad thing?

Her heart stuttered when Gage's cell phone rang. "Perfect," she muttered. Then she read Tom Vigor's code name and breathed a little easier.

Pressing speaker, she answered. "Hey, Leroy Brown. Got

stuff happening here."

"Don't tell me too much," her WPP contact warned. "Are you alone?"

"No."

Tom gave one of his deliberate dumbass laughs. "Men just can't leave you be, can they."

"I think this one probably would if he could. Some other men seemed interested earlier, but I—well, we—discouraged them."

"So all's well then."

"Except for a bit of blood. His," she clarified when Tom made a choked sound. "We're good. Sort of. Heading for help…I hope."

"You need more of that than you get, you let me know."

"I will." She reverted to code. "Gonna need a personal trainer, Leroy. Someone who can rescue me—us—from this nightmare."

"All nightmares end, even the real ones."

"Searching for the end, Tom."

"I know it, Snowbird. I'll keep in touch. You do the same."

As always, hearing her contact's good old boy drawl settled her. To a point, and only for a minute.

She glanced at Gage beside her. Sexy as hell and passed out, but thankfully still breathing.

More miles clicked by. His friend's place must be close by. Yet even as hope passed through Amber's mind, the right front tire dropped into a hole the size of a small crater, causing the truck to buck and her head to slam against the side window.

"You drive like Judy Blue."

Gage kept his eyes closed when he spoke. To Amber's relief, his voice didn't sound as bleary as it had when he'd faded out earlier.

She rubbed her throbbing temple. "Okay, I'll bite. Who's

Judy Blue?"

"Third girlfriend, senior year. She had a screw-you attitude. I wanted in on it. Any headlights behind us?"

"No. So far, all the traffic's come from the opposite direction. No one's turned to follow us." She started down a steep hill. "If Fixx's men are back there, we're going to trap ourselves in this gulley."

"One road in, Snowbird. Anyone comes down who shouldn't won't make it out again. Won't even make the lodge."

She sent him an unbelieving look. "Your friend owns a lodge? As in guests?"

Gage's lips curved. "He calls it a lodge. Sounds better than a cabin. No guests. Just Abel. And maybe one of his two ex-wives, or his stepdaughter."

"Does he know we're coming?"

"I sent a coded email. He'll figure it out and show. Kill the lights."

She did, and barely avoided plunging the truck into a ditch. He told her to park behind a small outbuilding that smelled strongly of grain and woodsmoke. However, when she hopped from the driver's seat, smoke of a different kind assailed her.

"You didn't mention your friend's a pothead."

Gage winced as his feet hit the ground. "He wasn't—not on the force anyway. Ideas change. He was a whiskey man when we worked together."

"Still is by the smell coming from that shed. I hope he's conscious when we get inside."

"If he isn't, pump my gun. He'll wake up soon enough. Some reflexes are instinctive no matter what condition you're in."

Amber dipped lower so Gage could sling an arm over her shoulder without raising it. "You're not exactly bolstering my faith in this guy. Do you really want someone who's intoxicated plucking a bullet out of you?"

"No worries, Snowbird. He'll probably want you to do that part."

She grunted out a breath as he leaned the bulk of his weight on her. "You so need to work on that reassuring attitude. Which door?"

"Whichever's closest."

She spied one and got him over to it. Luckily, the knob twisted freely and the door creaked open.

The smell of smoke was more pungent, but not overly fresh. A light, possibly from a fire, flickered in the room ahead of them.

"He's your friend," Amber said. "You call out to him. I don't want to be mistaken for a deer."

"It's all bears around here."

"Reassuring attitude," she reminded him and shifted her grip on his waist.

They made their way toward the front room. Amber's eyes adjusted quickly to the darkness. By the glow of a dying wood fire, she made out a shape on the sofa.

As they entered, the shape uncoiled itself and stood, swaying. "Got company, Wanda," a female voice said.

"Heard 'em."

When a lamp clicked, Amber found herself staring down the barrel of a sawed-off shotgun.

The woman holding it stared back, coldly and without expression. Then she lowered the shotgun a fraction. "Well, will you look at what the cat dragged in? Half dead, but still yummy enough to bite." A nasty smile split her face. "You want I should bite you, Gage, and finish you off? Or d'you wanna leave that tasty morsel for your new lady friend." Her gaze shifted to Amber. "Where'd he'd dig you up, honey? Strip club or honkytonk bar?"

"Hell, she ain't no barfly." The other woman, a pretty blond, sneered. "She ain't no stripper, either. Too snotty looking to wrap herself 'round a pole."

The spell holding Amber's voice in check broke. She sent the blonde a quick look, then returned her gaze to Wanda. "At the risk of sounding snottily forward, do you think you could help me find a flat surface before Gage and I both collapse?"

"What did I tell you?" The blonde rocked on her feet. "Gotta be strong to work a pole."

Amber let the obvious comeback slide and regarded the still smirking friend.

"What's the story, Gage?" Wanda lowered the shotgun all the way. "Short version'll do."

"Bar fight, bullet, beautiful bystander. Where's Abel?"

"Louisville, last I heard. But then, I'm just his black sheep stepkid, right, so what do I know? Ma's living thereabouts. Could be he's trying to woo her back. Got a thing for her he can't dig out of his craw. This here's Mandy. She's my partner."

"This here's Lily." Gage sagged and took Amber with him. "She's mine. Need that surface now, kiddo."

"You sure do at that. Over here, then." Wanda used the shotgun to indicate the sofa Mandy had recently vacated.

A short, stout woman with hacked-off brown hair, Wanda whipped off her T-shirt and stuffed it under Amber's makeshift compress. "That's a lotta blood you're wearing, handsome. You a doctor?" she asked over her shoulder.

"No." Amber rolled her aching shoulder once Gage was on his back. "But with help, I should be able to cope."

"I can skin a rabbit. Is that helpful?"

Not quite what she'd had in mind, Amber reflected. However. "We'll need a knife, forceps or something like that, sterile cloth—plenty of it—and the strongest whiskey you can find."

"Got sour mash."

Fresh brewed and with a powerful kick, Amber imagined.

"It'll do," Gage said. He regarded her half lidded. "Start cutting, Lily."

Now it was Amber's turn to swear in silence. Or partial silence, she realized when Mandy snorted. "My daddy's a trucker, and he don't cuss like that 'round women. 'Less he's hammered, which he mostly is."

"I'll remember that next time I pass a big rig on the road." Amber re-secured her ponytail. "Where's the bathroom?" And the nearest window, she thought, because she truly did not want to start cutting on Gage. Not with her thoughts jittering and every last thing she'd learned during her survival course currently scuttling to the corners of her brain.

Once the tools were in place and Gage had several shots of sour mash under his belt, Amber took a deep breath and removed the makeshift tourniquet.

The blood flow had slowed considerably, but that didn't make the task at hand any less difficult.

She'd cut into Rachel's leg three years ago when her sister had been bitten by a snake. A vastly different scenario, considering she hadn't been forced to go deep back then. But she could do this. Because she had to.

Mandy's sense of humor proved to be malicious. She played AC/DC at full volume while Amber hunted for the elusive bullet.

"Dirty deeds," Wanda muttered. "They'll come back to haunt you every time." She shone a flashlight over the entry wound. "That bullet went deep. You sure you know what you're doing?"

"What *I'm* doing, yes. If it'll work is another question."

Ten endless minutes passed. Gage didn't make a sound. A clock ticked over the fireplace, and AC/DC mellowed to

Garth Brooks.

Finally, in the middle of a down-and-out song, she located the bullet and exhaled. "Got it."

Wanda hung over her shoulder. "One piece?"

"I think so." She drew it out. "Yes. Jesus."

"So you're okay then if I go and puke?"

"Sure— What?"

"This wasn't no rabbit, sweetie." Straightening, Wanda headed for the bathroom.

When Amber looked up, she saw Mandy perched on the hearth, filing her nails.

"Why'd he get shot?" She sounded more bored than curious.

Amber's smile was thin. Very carefully, she used a sterilized needle and nylon thread to stitch the wound. "He cheated at five card stud. Pissed his opponent off."

"Guy had a gun? Bang, bang?"

"Like that."

Headlights sliced across the shaded window.

"That'll be Abel." Mandy blew dust from her nails. "I'm guessing he struck out with Wanda's ma. He won't like finding me here. Figures Wanda can do better."

In Amber's opinion, jumping down a rabbit hole would be infinitely preferable to being in that place right then. But, of course, reaction was setting in, and God help her, her hands were beginning to tremble.

She finished applying the bandage to Gage's side just as the front door opened. A big man in a stained cowboy hat and worn boots strode in.

"What the hell's going on here?" he demanded. "Go away, Mandy. Who are you?" He scowled at Amber. Then he caught sight of Gage and snatched off his hat, slapping it against his leg. "Well, ain't this a kick in the crotch. God's sake, Morgan, what've you done to yourself now?"

"Bar fight, bullet, beautiful bystander." Mandy sashayed past him en route to the bathroom. "I'll leave you three alone and tend to Wanda's weak stomach."

"I got your email." Abel glanced again at Amber, frowned, and returned his attention to Gage. "You spelled most every word wrong. I knew that meant trouble, probably of the female variety."

"Yeah, well." Gage hissed in a breath through his teeth. "Some of that trouble's been handled. Your sour mash packs a punch, by the way. You're skirting the law brewing that stuff, Abel."

"I turned in my badge a good while back." The older man cocked his head at Amber. "Why do I figure I should know you?"

"She's a stripper. " Mandy's voice sailed down the hall, accompanied by a wet snicker.

"So, friend of yours then," Abel called back. Crouching, he smacked Gage's hip. "Fill me in, and don't skimp on the details."

"Send Wanda and her friend for milk and eggs and I will. Until then, Lily's a stripper."

Abel rolled his eyes, raised his voice. "Okay, you two. Take a drive."

Mandy sauntered back in. "How's about we take a walk instead, check out your latest batch of booze. I'm always up for a taste test. Come on, Wanda. Your stepdaddy wants us gone."

Wanda returned, looking pale but smug. "Told you Ma'd say no. She's moved on, old man. You need to do the same."

Abel waited until the door closed before he gave Gage's hip a second tap and rose. "Long story there, crappy ending. You ever been to Baltimore?" he asked Amber.

She let her head fall back. "Maybe."

A thick finger stabbed the air. "Renata Chase. You're the

spitting image of her. D'you know Renata?"

Grinding her teeth, Amber glanced at Gage, who'd pushed himself up onto his elbows.

Gage shrugged. "Go ahead, if there's something to tell. You don't know McCabe. I do. There'll be more reasons than he chose to explain about why he gave me this particular assignment."

Although she hated to admit she half understood that, Amber regarded Abel and forced herself to relax. "Yes, I know her." Her cool eyes met his. "At least I did until I was thirteen. That's when she ran off with another man. Renata Chase is my mother."

· · ·

Owen Fixx hated the desert. And that, he knew, was precisely why Mockerie generally chose it for their meetings. Out in the middle of dusty nowhere, far from the Las Vegas lights and as often as not in a dead zone for cell phone reception.

His boss was a bastard.

He paid well, though, Owen reminded himself, and until recently, life and the business had run along smoothly.

"You're late."

Invisible in the darkness, Mockerie spoke the instant the Mercedes door opened.

Owen regarded his watch. "Maybe thirty seconds."

"A lot can happen in thirty seconds." Mockerie strolled out of the desert night, hands in the pockets of his denim jacket. "Bullet only takes a few nanoseconds to enter a person's body. I should know. I've put many a bullet into many a body."

Mockerie's own late wife included, Owen reflected. Poor, deluded Rowena, thinking she could outfox a reptile like James Mockerie.

He searched the ground at his feet. There wasn't much to see. A few boulders, a little scrub, a pair of prickly cacti. However, snakes lived there. They might've seemed to be asleep in the cool night air, but they were always ready to strike.

"I want news." Only the lower part of Mockerie's face was visible under his broad-brimmed cowboy hat. "Something I can sink my teeth into. Have you involved your son or nephew in the search?"

"Luka to some extent. Gareth, too…"

"Wishy-washy?"

Owen clamped down on an urge to plant his fist in Mockerie's mostly hidden face. "Gareth works well within the confines of the business. He's not a killer."

"And his feelings for Alexa Chase continue to have weight."

He'd called her his muse, but then Gareth had been born with a poetic soul. "She's uncommonly beautiful. Exotic, in fact. Men being men tend to be susceptible to that, as we both know."

Removing his hands from his pockets, Mockerie toyed with the ring on his half finger. "What about your brother?"

"We haven't spoken for some time. He's aware of the situation." Still leery of rattlesnakes, Owen took a step away from a clump of rocks. "I have good people working on this, James, not including the pair who got burned in Black Creek, although I put their inefficiency down to Alexa Chase's sharp mind. My ex is being held, and another pair of men I sent reported they might have a, pardon the pun, fix on my former sister-in-law. Their message was garbled, but I believe they spotted her in or near Halo, Mississippi."

"Spotted. Not apprehended?"

"I didn't get the whole story. One way or another, we still have Georgia—Rachel—whatever the hell her name is at the moment." Owen paused there. Features he was usually adept at masking must have betrayed him, because Mockerie stopped twisting his ring and chuckled.

"I sense something more here. More I won't like and you're therefore reluctant to share." He returned one hand to his jacket pocket. "Nanoseconds, my friend."

Owen half wished a rattlesnake would slither out and take aim at Mockerie's leg, but no such luck. Above his head, a star shot through the blackened sky. Owen's blood flowed like sludge. "Alexa Chase isn't alone."

A vein pulsed in Mockerie's neck. "By that, you mean she has protection."

"Yes."

"McCabe." Mockerie fairly spat the name.

Nodding, Owen watched Mockerie's hidden hand. "Odds are. It doesn't change anything. McCabe's protection list is comprised of burned-out has-beens."

"Or so he'd like us to believe. Who's with her?"

"Does it matter?" But when Mockerie's bared teeth appeared, Owen realized it did, very much. "I'll find out. I'll find her. I trust my people like I do my own family." Which wasn't something he should have said. However, duress, sweaty palms, and Mockerie's hidden right hand would loosen the toughest man's tongue.

"I'll wait a bit longer," Mockerie replied after a long pause. "You want to produce for me, Owen. And bear in mind, I'm not a patient man. It's Alexa and Georgia Chase on those long tables, or you and your family. Take your pick; don't take your time. McCabe is not going to win this game."

Whatever that meant. And frankly, at that moment, Owen didn't want to know.

The instant Mockerie vanished from sight, Owen returned to his SUV and placed the required call. When the ring was answered, he said simply, "Beat the answers out of her if you have to. I need to find Alexa Chase now."

Chapter Seven

Amber watched Gage off and on through the night, in between bouts of sleep and dreams that were both erotic and dangerously compelling. Sometimes Gage was Gage, a man sent to protect her. Other times, he was more of a dark threat. One she wanted to take on but knew she could never have. How could she drag any man—*anyone*—into the Witness Protection Program with her?

But seeing him, relaxed in sleep, she was sorely tempted. The touch of his fingers on her face lingered in spite of her best efforts to ignore it. How would his hands feel running over her body? How he might taste if she set her mouth on his and…

Amber came fully awake with a jolt and a rush of heat in her lower limbs. Her skin was warm and flushed, her insides tangled into hungry knots. *No more*, she told herself. Gage was here to help her. Anything else was out of the question. The dreams that followed were far less pleasing. They involved Fixx, her sister, and a bunch of faceless gunmen.

Another man hovered on the fringe of them. McCabe

was a mysterious and thorough man who resided on the outer limits of the US Marshals office. Apparently, he'd been well aware that Gage's trainer was acquainted with her mother—that they had in fact gone to high school together.

"It's McCabe's style," Abel remarked as the first rays of dawn streaked the sky outside. It relieved Amber to see that Gage was up and sitting in the kitchen. "Find any speck of common ground and use it." After flipping a pair of over easy eggs, Abel took a pull on the beer he evidently preferred to orange juice. "Your mama was a beauty, Amber. Like mama, like daughter, I guess."

"To a point." Sick of a topic she'd done her utmost to sidestep since she'd blundered into it, Amber sat at the chrome kitchen table and rubbed her temples.

Gage sprawled in a chair across from her. He looked annoyingly good for a man who'd been shot. He looked annoyingly good in any case, but unshaven and tousled just made him that much more tempting.

He took a long swallow of black coffee. "I don't think they're a close family, Abel. You might want to change the subject."

"Hell with that. Iran." A little dreamy eyed, Abel tested the name of her mother's birthplace on his tongue, savoring it like fine wine. Then he clued in. "Not close…why? Renata was a wild and stunning creature."

"She still is," Amber said. "Moving on. Where did Wanda and Mandy disappear to?"

Abel waved his spatula. "Wanda's RV's parked back in the woods a piece. Been sitting there for the past three months. She'll pull out when the mood strikes, or when Mandy gets sick of the back of beyond and hankers for the bright lights of Nashville. You've been a bit short on details as regards the lady here, Gage, and why she's currently under your wing."

"The less you know, old friend."

"The healthier I'll stay. Screw that. You get yourself shot, come and bleed all over my lodge, I find out lady here's the kid of a girl I knew back when, I cook you breakfast, and off you go, leaving me to scratch my head and wonder. Me an ex-cop, who had the hell in a handbasket chore of training you. You've decided I should be okay with crap for an explanation for my own sake, did you?"

"I'll tell you what I can when I can."

"For all our sakes," Amber added and tried not to react when Abel slapped a pair of plates in front of her and Gage. She peered closer. "Uh, what's that black stuff?"

"Sausage. Fell apart in the pan." Abel took another pull on his beer and eyed her along the length of the bottle. "How many people you got after you?"

"Two that we know of. But there'll be more." Gage reached for a slice of charred toast. "Do what you can to smother your curiosity, Abel. We need a truck."

"You've got a truck."

"It's not ours, and I don't want to drive it any longer than necessary."

"Why not?"

"It has blood in it."

Abel snorted. "You're full of shit, former Lieutenant Morgan. But for the sake of an old friendship and the lady's pretty face, I'll let you borrow my Ford. She may be an old gray mare, but she's better than she used to be. Tough, steady, and dependable as hell. Like me."

Amber womanned up and tasted the eggs. They were rubbery, but edible. She ate two slices of toast, drank her juice, and filled two large thermoses with coffee for the trip.

With his boots propped on the table, Abel polished off what they'd left on their plates and nodded at the peg that held the truck key. "I still say your ma was one beautiful vixen," he reminisced around a mouthful of black sausage.

"Which truck do you want to drive?" Gage asked once they were outside and heading for the shed that housed Abel's still.

"We're taking them both?"

"Can't leave a stolen vehicle here. Abel might be crusty, but he's a friend. Wrong people find that truck, he could wind up dead. Or Wanda could."

Or Mandy, Amber reflected, then she sighed. "Mornings are definitely not my best time. Is Abel's truck an automatic?"

"Doubt it."

"Then you choose."

"Better the devil you know. I'll take the gray mare. Stay right on my ass. You hear or see a problem, use the flashers. Thirty miles should do it. We'll ditch your vehicle at Fire Hollow and head for Hidden Valley."

She walked backward so she could study him. "You sure you're up for this, former Lieutenant?"

When he grinned, her heart gave a little bump. "Got white lightning in my pack. I'm good."

"You are so not upping my faith in law enforcement officers."

"It'll come. Assuming we don't get blindsided and die before we reach our destination."

"Right." She pointed at the stolen truck. "Hotwire it for me and we're out of here."

With the engine revving, he brought the route to Fire Hollow up on his phone. "Just in case," he said. "You hear from anyone about Rachel, or from Rachel herself, signal me."

"I will. You sure you're good to go?"

"White lightning," he reminded her and slammed the door, smiling.

"Perfect," Amber muttered. "At this rate, we'll be dead

before we get to Hidden Valley." Which wasn't a positive thought, so she found a pleasing country radio station and turned up the volume on Carrie Underwood.

The thirty-mile trip didn't pass easily, but it did pass without incident. After they stopped, Gage drove the stolen truck into a thicket of brambles and berry vines. He didn't look happy when he climbed back out.

"Fucking thorns are everywhere." He yanked a pair from the arm of his jacket.

"Are you bleeding?" Amber inspected a red stain on his T-shirt.

"It's berry juice." Gage removed her probing hands. "I'm holding together just fine. This isn't the first time I've been shot."

"Good to know." Amber shoved her hands in her pockets. She didn't want to touch him anyway. "Which direction…" Frowning, she looked down. "My phone's ringing." She pulled it out of her right pocket and regarded the screen. "It's Rachel."

"Might be, might not." He made a head motion. "Answer it."

"Alex? Are you there." Her sister sounded simultaneously vexed and teary.

"I'm here," Amber told her. "Where are you? Do you know? Use our new names, Rachel."

"Oh, who the hell cares about our new names. I don't know where I am. They won't let me see. You have to do what Owen wants. They told me if you do, you won't be harmed, and neither will I."

"'They' being the people who kidnapped and are holding you?"

"Yes. And they have guns and knives and big ugly faces, but they won't hurt me because Owen loves me, I know he does. You screwed him around, is all. He's pissed, but if you go back to Las Vegas and tell him what you gave to the FBI, he'll let it go."

Amber breathed out her frustration. "Rachel, you know that's ridiculous. It's very likely Owen has everything I gave to the FBI back again. You also know he has someone doing his dirty work on the inside. The only way for him to deal with this problem is to kill me. End of threat."

"He won't kill you." Rachel sounded fierce and certain. "I won't let him. At least… Oh, damn, this isn't going to work, is it? You're right. Someone in the FBI is working for Owen, and no one knows who that person is… Hey, you asshole!"

A man's voice came on the line. "It's your sister who's the asshole, sweetheart. You come in or she's dead."

"Wait a minute you son of a—" Someone cut Rachel off, undoubtedly by force.

Eyes closed, Amber struggled for control. "You hurt her, and Fixx will never know what's in my head that might threaten him."

"Maybe not, but she'll still be dead, and you'll have to live with that, sugar pie. For as long as you can anyway."

There was a click and the line went dead. Amber's ears rang, mostly from fear, but partly from anger. "Shit." She jerked her hand and the phone down. "The worst part of this is, I don't really know anything that could hurt Fixx. The information I collected was nothing but a jumble of numbers and files and— What?" she demanded when Gage squeezed her upper arm.

"That click we heard didn't come from your phone."

Everything inside her turned to ice. "From where then?" Raising her head, she followed his gaze. And saw a man twenty feet to their left, pointing a rifle right at them.

...

Gage had seen old before, but never anyone as ancient as the man who'd faced them down a long and badly shaking rifle barrel.

"We're lucky he didn't shoot first and not bother with questions," Amber remarked ten minutes later. "Next time we ditch a truck, let's try not to do it on land belonging to a man who has a still in his barn and a highly suspicious nature. Don't you just love it when a day starts with a non-literal bang like this?"

"Sign says the road's washed out ahead," Gage murmured. "We'll have to backtrack."

"Across the man with the still's land?"

His lips twitched. "Maybe."

Amber sent Gage a placid look. "Okay, I want to go home. That's it. That's all. Just home to Wyoming where my father spends half the year with his photo albums, his memories, and his pipe—not the kind used for tobacco."

"Your father's a pothead?"

"Among other things. He took up the habit after my brother, Elijah, went to Afghanistan. He died six months in. Roadside bomb. There was only Rachel and me after that. Our mother was long gone and, soon enough, so was our father."

"So you want to go home why?"

"Let's say I want to go back to when Rachel and I were really young. And innocent..." She trailed off. "Gage, that call. Fixx *will* hurt her. He'll wait a while, dangle her in front of me like a carrot on a stick, but if he figures I'm not going to bite, he'll do it. Despite what she believes, he doesn't and never has cared enough about her not to."

"Which is why we're going to Hidden Valley."

"Hiding out in a commune isn't going to help me find my sister."

"You need to learn to trust people, Amber. I wasn't

planning on hiding there. It's a brief respite, nothing more. We need a plan and as many facts as we can gather."

"About Fixx?"

"And James Mockerie. Fixx wants you, but it's Mockerie who wants you dead. It's his answer to any and all problems. Torture it, kill it, make what's left of it disappear."

"That's sick."

"That's Mockerie. It's how he built his empire. If your problem started and ended with Fixx, going into the WPP might have worked. He'd have searched for you for a good long while, but time would have passed and the more it did without threat to him, the less vigilant he'd have become."

"Lovely." Amber folded her arms. "It would have been nice if Tom or anyone had mentioned that fairly important detail."

"Yeah, well, government agencies delude themselves as much as any single person."

He saw her shiver. "If Fixx's men have Rachel, then Mockerie must know about it. You used the word torture. How long before he decides to employ it?"

"I don't know." Gage slowed as they approached the town. "Like Fixx, he'll probably see some value in keeping her alive."

She exhaled in a huff. "That wasn't the question I asked."

He regarded her briefly. "You want honesty? Not long. So, we head for Hidden Valley and figure out a way to get her back that doesn't involve getting all of us killed."

"Sounds like that's going to take more magic than planning."

Gage chuckled as they passed a sign that proudly proclaimed the Fire Hollow Pickle Festival to be in full swing. "It's not magic we're after, Snowbird, it's technology." He bypassed the first pickle stands. "Look for a gas station, then use my phone and Google the quickest route to Elbow,

Mississippi."

She took the cell he handed her. "Let me guess. We're going to visit another one of your friends."

"Not sure I'd call him that." His grin in profile revealed nothing. "Once you've found the place, you need to hunt out your gun."

Exasperation won out. "For God's sake, Gage, what's in Elbow that requires us to go in fully armed?"

His grin widened. "The biggest mother of a bear you've ever seen."

· · ·

He stopped on the edge of town to buy bandages, Tylenol, and two jars of pickles. Although he claimed he was fine, Amber could see the pain on his face. Regardless, she remained in the truck. She'd long since given up trying to follow his logic. First two jars of pickles, then half a mile farther on, two bottles of white lightning from a boxcar bar with the name Spike nailed over the door. The bottles he brought back to the truck had no labels and they smelled like diesel fuel.

While Elvis played on Abel's aging truck stereo, she shook one of the cloudy, dark bottles. "You keep talking about bears. Are there many around here?"

"Some." He dry swallowed four of the Tylenol pills, then regarded the phone she'd propped up on the dash. "Amber, that's not…"

"It's the quickest," she interrupted. "The route I'm sure you'd prefer takes twice as long."

"Better roads to the north."

"Not the way you drive."

"Pot, kettle, Judy Blue."

She grinned. "Your third girlfriend, senior year sounds a lot crazier than me."

"I doubt that. But she did drive a little red Corvette." Gage shrugged. "Her daddy had a thing for Prince."

"Like you have a thing for Elvis?"

"The King rules. Always has, always will. What's your musical era?"

"Everything. Except Tanya Tucker, and that's not her fault."

"What about Rachel?"

The first drops of rain splashed on the windshield. "Katy Perry."

"Yeah, I probably could've guessed that."

Amber ran her palms along the legs of her jeans. Every nerve in her body was jumping. For Rachel more than herself at that point. "She's not a bad person, really. Just spoiled, and reckless because of it. Youngest kids sometimes are."

"Often are."

She slid him a shrewd look. "There's an intriguing statement. Do you have siblings, half siblings, anything?"

"Not that I know of."

"Or want to know of?"

"That, too."

"So you're a lone wolf."

"I'm good with my own company."

"Yet you grew up in a commune."

"Think monks and meditation. Plenty of 'me' time. My childhood wasn't fascinating or even particularly interesting. And your knowing about it won't help us locate your sister. I heard a train whistle in the background when she called."

"A distant one," Amber agreed.

Rain began to fall harder. Gage flipped on the wipers and studied the sky. "How did Rachel seem to you?"

"A little scared, but overall pissed off. Impatient."

"Odd reaction, don't you think, considering her situation?"

Was it odd? Amber rolled her head to relieve the tension in her neck muscles. "You're thinking she should have been terrified, or at least fearful."

"She called one of the kidnappers an asshole."

Which wasn't at all out of character. However... Doubt and a different kind of fear snaked through Amber's belly. "She's not part of this, Gage. She wouldn't do that to me." Would she? No. Absolutely not. "She's not unfeeling—only a little selfish."

Gage checked his phone again, and made his way along a winding road that might have been a highway fifty years ago. "You can stop dredging up reasons to hate me. I don't believe Rachel's working with Fixx or his men. What I'm suggesting is that she might know one or more of them."

The tension in Amber's neck grew to mammoth proportions. "Know." She closed her eyes to blot out the streaming rain. "As in someone on Fixx's staff?"

"Did Rachel have a personal guard, an assistant, even a maid, when she was married to Fixx?"

"Yes." Two faces appeared in Amber's head. "Lauren Crowe and Helmut. Helmut was her personal trainer. Lauren was her stylist and sometimes her general assistant."

"Tough?"

"Yes. Lauren climbed rock walls and did triathlons when she was young. Helmut was, well, buff."

"What about Fixx's nephew, his son, his brother? What's their deal?"

"Gareth's not involved in that end of the business—not the coercion or the roughing-people-up stuff. Neither is Fixx's brother, Tony, not really, but I imagine he'd do whatever needed doing for the right amount of money. Tony's an acquirer. Get a thing, toss it aside, move to the newer and better thing. Luka likes watching people squirm."

"He'll climb fast in Mockerie's world, given the chance."

"He'd have to climb over his uncle to do it. Fixx isn't stupid, and he won't be easily displaced. But Luka could be holding Rachel. Any of them could be, though I'd put Lauren low on the list. And Gareth..." She shook her head. "I don't see that, either. Uh..." She pointed at a weird cluster of vehicles that included an old streetcar, a moldy Winnebago, a school bus wearing a coat of camo, a tractor, and a rickety shack made of dented metal. Most were topped with leaning towers and satellite dishes. Amazed, she could only stare. "What and why?"

Gage arched a brow at her. "You said we'd need magic, Snowbird. Well, here it is." When something moved behind the shack, he lowered the window, whipped out his gun, and fired three shots at it. Without taking his eyes off the shack, he murmured, "Welcome to Grizzly Adams's hideout."

...

Gage sensed he was losing her. Or she was losing whatever small amount of faith she might have possessed in him. Unfortunately, normal had never been his style, and while Amber might just have been starting to understand that, McCabe had known it for a very long time.

"Stay behind me," he said as they climbed from the truck. He checked his side, saw no blood, and flexed a careful shoulder. Despite the Tylenol he'd taken, pain still radiated from chest to hip. "Bear's not the most hospitable of men."

"So shooting at his house—I assume that shack's his house—was what? Some form of intimidation tactic?"

He took her hand to hold her where he wanted her. "I rang the doorbell. If he's home, he'll see us."

"He'll see two rain-soaked people slogging toward his front door. One has his gun out in full sight. The other has hers in her pocket. Sorry to tell you, I'm not getting the magic here."

Three shots whizzed past, and she immediately stopped trying to walk abreast of him.

"Good start." Amusement laced Gage's voice. "Bear says, 'Come in.'"

Chapter Eight

It wasn't bad. It wasn't much, but Amber had seen worse. Bear's furniture ranged from old and worn to sleek and modern. Broken in most cases and probably someone's castoffs; however, everything appeared to function. The clutter came in the form of electronic equipment. Cables, wires, and computers crowded around no fewer than forty monitors. Amber recognized about half of what she saw. The rest? No idea.

Then, of course, there was Bear himself. He weighed somewhere in the region of two hundred and fifty pounds and had to stand at least six foot seven. He towered over her by close to a foot, yet, oddly enough, he didn't diminish Gage at all. Interesting. And not a thing she wanted to notice right then.

All hair, beard, tattoos, and body piercings, Bear lounged at a round table surrounded by four computers. He had a bowie knife in one hand and his other resting on the barrel of a .30-30. The scowl on his face appeared perpetual.

"I don't like women," he stated flatly. "The prettier they

are, the more trouble they cause. I can tell by looking at yours, you just brought a passel of it into my home."

Gage wandered around the room, checked out the vast collection of modems and screens. "You want us gone, we'll leave. The lady's got a problem."

"They always do, and I reckon this lady's got more than most." He turned his shark-like stare on her. "You made Mockerie mad."

Surprised, Amber snapped her gaze to Gage, who kept his own on a flashing monitor. "Bear likes to know people's business. Gets him in deep sometimes."

"Word's out on you, Amber Kelly." In a move much faster than she would have anticipated, he sat up and stabbed his knife into the top of the table. "Mockerie's pissed and Fixx is on the hunt."

"Mockerie's also got at least one person on retainer at or connected to a government agency. Possibly the FBI and/or the US Marshals office." Gage tapped on a keyboard, found an Elvis song, and started him singing about suspicious minds. "That someone has access to a whole lot of information. Names have surfaced, but so far we have no proof. In my experience, it tends to be the devil you don't know who's doing the damage. I'm thinking high level with major clearance. Any ideas on that score?"

Bear settled back in his hard chair. "Lizzie Barton's a high-level bitch. Drives a spiffy little Alfa Romeo and owns a tidy collection of diamonds."

"Where does she live?" Gage asked.

"Depends on the season. She'll be heading to Florida in the next week or so. For the moment, it's D.C."

"What's her clearance?"

Bear snorted out a laugh. "Better than yours or mine. Not many doors between her and the oval office."

"Yeah. Well." Gage continued to scroll through Bear's

computer. "Who else?"

"Your man McCabe's close to the top whether he should be or not. And there's Ichabod Drake. He was a US Marshal. Now he's FBI. Used to be WPP before Amber's guy took over. Flipside of that, Amber's guy was FBI before he became a US Marshal. And we all know old connections never really die."

Amber's eyes widened in disbelief. "You know about Tom Vigor?"

Bear yanked his knife free, toyed with it. "Know about lots of people, lady. Your Tom's son worked with our Gage. Me, as well, in passing. We called him Tommy Two-step. I'm referring to the son here. He danced around any rules didn't suit him. No harm in it, we were told. He's a PI these days."

Amber ran her hands through her hair, held it briefly off her face. "So you're telling me that my WPP contact's son is a private investigator. As in, he finds people."

"Not always people, but yeah, he could. If it eases your mind any, young Tommy never two-stepped over any serious lines that I know of."

"That you know of." Amber sat down on a wooden stool. "I wish Tom would have told me his son was a cop turned PI."

"You already knew the cop part," Gage pointed out.

"But not the nickname or the PI thing."

"Tom's your contact, Amber. For emergencies only, I might add. His wayward son's a separate deal."

She dropped her hand, gave a half laugh. "Great. Now Tommy's wayward. This just gets better and better."

Strolling over to crouch in front of her, Gage caught her chin and drew her head up until it was level with his. "Tommy's not connected to the federal government, and he's not materialistic."

"He likes horses," Bear said.

Gage grinned. "So do you."

"And you."

"Not my own doing. I was just dating a woman who had a thing for horses."

"Right, blame it on a female captain who liked race tracks and your pretty face."

Amber rolled her eyes. "Excuse me, but as fascinating as this conversation is, can we go back to who in a position of authority might be slipping information to James Mockerie and/or Owen Fixx? All I know is that the information I collected and passed to the FBI vanished."

Bear spun his knife like a top. "Who'd you pass it to? Give me a name."

"I don't have one. They used a courier."

"Describe him."

"Five ten, white male, athletic build, sandy hair, cut really short. Arctic blue eyes…" At Bear's grunt, she paused. "You know him?"

The big man studied the tip of his knife. "Well enough to know he's clean."

"And you think that because?"

"He shot and killed two of Mockerie's people. That places him squarely on Mockerie's blacklist. Guy lives with his granny, Chrissakes, and volunteers at a soup kitchen every Wednesday night. He's straight."

Unable to sit, Amber stood and paced.

"Don't go too close to the window," Bear warned. "You, either," he said to Gage, who merely grinned at him.

"Yeah, I do remember a thing or two from basic training. "I want to know Fixx's status, Bear. And Mockerie's, if you can access it."

"You want me to try and hack one or both of them?"

"Them, or someone close who might possess information that'll help us. My gut tells me we're not more than a few steps ahead of Fixx's men."

"Your gut's been wrong before, Gage."

"Many times. I still want you to check it out. Amber and I can take a walk while you dig."

"Walk in the pissing rain? Pretty lady here might melt."

Rather than take offense, Amber smiled. "Wicked witches melt. I haven't descended to that level yet. I want my sister back, Bear. Then I'll happily—well, not happily, but I'll disappear again and hope the second attempt works better than the first."

"First was working just fine until your sister took off with her hillbilly lover." Gage removed a yellow slicker from the wall and held it out. "Says to me that Mockerie's inside man or woman hasn't accessed the WPP site. See what you can unearth," Gage said. "I've got two bottles of Mississippi whiskey in my truck and a jar of sweet pickles, if you're interested."

Bear laughed for the first time and revealed three gaps where teeth should have been. "This life of lonely ain't all it's cracked up to be." He moved a massive shoulder. "Best woman in Elbow only has two working brain cells." Standing, he handed his bowie knife to Amber. "Gift from me to you. Go on out and take a look at my Ram-erado. I custom built her this past summer. Got systems on board and a mother of a powerful engine. Sounds like a locomotive." He tossed Gage the keys. "You don't feel like driving, just sit in there and make out or something. I don't like people watching me work. Give me two hours and the whiskey."

Amber waited under an overhang while Gage retrieved the moonshine. Part of her wanted to risk calling Rachel's cell phone, but what good would it do, even if by some miracle the call went through.

"Probably lead Fixx's assholes to Bear's door," she murmured. A sudden thought hit and stalled her breath. She brought her gaze up to Gage's when he returned. "My phone has GPS. Fixx's men could be tracking."

"They'd need your password to do that."

"Rachel knows it."

"Yeah, I figured that. That's why I disabled your GPS after we left the amusement park."

"You… How?"

"You zoned out for half an hour. Took a nap," he clarified when she huffed out a breath.

"I don't take naps." She regarded her phone. "How did you get in?"

"I was a cop, Snowbird. That's a standard issue phone. Meant to be used for emergencies only. You have the passwords they gave you." He grinned. "I have McCabe."

Although it probably shouldn't have, amusement tickled her throat. "So, not a mind reader then."

"It's all about resourceful thinking."

"And connections."

"Those, too." He held up the bottles. "I'll take these to Bear, find out where his truck shed is. We can hang out or make out while we're there. Choice is yours."

"Okay, banging my head against a wall now," she murmured. Her heart had no business tripping over itself just because the idea, God help her, had a marginal amount of appeal. Or, yes, fine, maybe more than marginal. Maybe full-blown, in fact. Gage was gorgeous, as far as men who were jaded ex-cops went. And what self-respecting woman didn't like bad boys with issues?

Of course, strictly speaking, she could probably classify Bear as a bad boy, and she certainly wasn't attracted to him. But making out in trucks was for hormonal teenagers… And dammit, the thought of doing it had her heart beating even faster now.

She breathed in and deliberately out. This had to stop. Now. Before Gage came back and read her.

"He's good." Shoving the door open, Gage joined her. He regarded the forbidding sky. "This should be a fun walk. Truck shed's a quarter mile away."

Amber pushed her hands inside the pockets of her borrowed slicker. "Are you sure Bear doesn't mind doing this?"

"Are you kidding?" Gage took her arm. "This is Christmas for him."

"How do you two know each other?" Rain bounced off the yellow rubber and slithered into the neck. "Was he a cop, too?"

"Nope, CIA."

Surprised, she stared up at him. "Why did he leave?"

"He didn't like his boss." Gage grinned. "You want details, I'll give you what I can. The grin sparkled in his eyes. "Right after we make out."

...

By the time they reached the shed, he was soaked but not really unhappy about it. The cold and wet put a damper on his libido. No way did he want to complicate his life by getting involved with a beautiful fugitive. Mary Ellen was the way to go. No commitment, no expectations, no morning after, nothing but sex and a beer.

Gage considered as he shoved the shed door open and let Amber precede him inside. It was Mary Ellen, right? Mary Ellen? Mary Ann. "Shit."

Amber glanced back. "Problem?"

"Only if we can't find a light switch."

"I hear a generator. I also smell oil, gasoline, and grease. This is Bear's workshop. I'm guessing there'll be light. Maybe even a small still."

"No still," Gage said. "Smell gives it away, and Bear

doesn't care for company."

"Yes, I figured that when you rang his doorbell." Amber located a chain and tugged on it. "There. See? Light. Forty whole watts of it. He must have a master switch somewhere."

"Maybe, but since I don't plan to work on his truck, this'll do. I can see his Ram-erado just fine." Gage circled the odd-looking vehicle. "It's a Dodge Ram crossed with a Chevy Silverado. Guy has way too much time on his hands."

"At the moment, I wouldn't mind some of that."

Amber felt Gage watching her as she wandered through the shed. "You're tired of running."

She picked up a wrench, examined it. "I was tired of running back in Black Creek. This?" She waved the wrench. "This is insanity. How many people do you think are after us?"

"Twenty, thirty."

"And two of them found us. Lucky them."

"I doubt if luck had a whole lot to do with it. Just a theory," he said when she stared at him. "Far from solid, and no, I'm not going to fill you in. It'll only piss you off."

"You think someone followed me from Black Creek."

"I think you're smart and resourceful and you did everything you could to get out of there alive."

"But Fixx is smarter and more resourceful, meaning he has more resources, and he already had people in the area by the time whoever's holding Rachel called me at the bar. I had to run, though. But there's the GPS tracking thing, and that wasn't smart. Also, Rachel might have talked. Pain, threat of disfigurement—she could have caved. Or maybe one of his insiders, whoever and whatever that might be, had information. Except you said you don't think he has access to WPP files. This is very confusing, Gage."

"Off the scale," he agreed.

She shivered, hopefully from the cold. "Can we get into

Bear's truck, start it, and get warm?"

For an answer, Gage opened the door and, circling her waist with his hands, helped her up and in.

The engine did indeed sound like a locomotive—a very old, very rough one that backfired from time to time.

"Serious horses under that hood," Gage remarked. "None of this is your fault. You know that, right?"

She pulled off Bear's slicker and shook her hair loose. "I could have said no when I was approached. It's a sentence unto itself, and I've used it before, many times."

"With the FBI?"

"That's a point. God, Gage, I was so calm and centered in Las Vegas."

"You're calm and centered here."

"No, I'm not. I look and act that way, but inside, my mind's buzzing. Constantly whipping thoughts around. And being with you isn't helping me combat that."

"Why?" He grinned. "Because you don't like taking orders? Or because you want to make out with me?"

Punch him or laugh. It was a tough choice. Amber took the less aggressive path and, tipping her head at him, smiled. "Maybe a little of both. But then, they say patients often fall in love with their doctors, so who knows which feelings are valid and which aren't?"

"Making out doesn't require feelings." Reaching over, Gage caught a strand of her hair and played with it. "It's a jungle thing."

She teased him with her expression. "Primal instinct?"

"I'm a guy, Amber. I'm a sucker for the most basic sexual lure."

Her situation with Fixx wasn't the only form of insanity, Amber reflected. On the other hand, she could be dead by tomorrow, so why not indulge her senses?

One quick taste, she promised herself and let him use the

hair he still held to draw her forward. Rain wouldn't melt her, and neither would a kiss. Quick and simple and… "Oh, what the hell," she murmured.

She caught hold of his jacket as he hauled her across the seat, and took his mouth with a hunger she hadn't realized she possessed.

Hadn't realized *he* possessed, either. The taste of him exploded in her head the instant his lips met hers. There was heat and need and far too many other sensations for her to untangle.

The self-control she'd prided herself on possessing splintered. She wanted more than just a kiss, much more than a taste. She wanted to explore his mouth, then take that exploration deeper, lower until she'd seen and felt every part of him.

He used his tongue to probe her mouth. She used her teeth to nip. His hands slid from her shoulders to her arms, then up again to cup her head and hold it steady for a more thorough invasion.

"Definitely going crazy." She drew back ever so slightly, couldn't seem to find air in the truck. Could a person suffocate from desire? "This shouldn't be happening."

"Yeah, well, life'll screw you around sometimes." Gage kissed her cheek. Then he captured her mouth again and made her head spin.

A dozen rockets burst in her brain. One after another, like the blast of a high-powered rifle.

Her fists clenched on Gage's jacket as reality crashed in. She tore her mouth from his. "Those aren't rockets."

He was already moving. "Stay down. Stay with me. Right with me."

More shots blasted through the air. Amber hit the ground and remained low. A small army of Fixx's men was all she could think.

"Look right," Gage said from in front of her. "They're up on that knoll. We'll have to circle back to Bear's shack."

Amber didn't argue, didn't hesitate. She pulled the gun from the pocket of her hoodie and ran with him.

Bear was firing back. Bullets flew every direction. A stream of them whizzed past Amber's arm and zinged off the side of the old tractor.

"Stay down," Gage told her. He used his body as a shield so she could make it to the camo-painted bus. "Keep moving right to the far end."

She did as he instructed and peered around the back door at the side of the shack. "Do you think they spotted us?"

"Doubt it." Leaning over her, Gage followed the bullet spray coming from both directions. "They probably think we're inside."

"Which we should be, helping Bear."

"He'll hold his own."

"Maybe, but I can't let him die for me."

"I know." He kept following the line of fire. "Okay, get ready." Five endless seconds passed before he gave her a small push. "Go."

She identified the door and ran for it. "Don't be locked," she begged it. Twisting the latch, she shoved. And tumbled into the shack when it gave.

She landed hard on her hands and knees. Gage helped her up and pushed her forward. "Where are they?" he shouted at Bear.

"Every damn where, far as I can tell." Crouched at the side of a tall window, Bear used his rifle to point. "One, two, three, planted like bull rushes. Dumb assholes. They should be moving."

"There could be others already moving." Gage went down on one knee next to him.

Bear shook his head. "*Were* others. I took out three

sneaking round the side." He fired again. "Those ones up on the hill are too scared now to budge."

Amber eyed the assault rifles standing in a long row beside him. Nudging Gage's shoulder, she said, "They taught me how to use a rifle. I can help. I might not hit anyone, but I can at least add to the firepower."

Bear thrust a weapon at her. "Go for it. Just remember, these things kick like a bitch."

In front of her, Gage took aim. "Your slip's showing, asshole." And he fired five shots in quick succession. Amber saw a man stagger out from behind a tree and drop.

"Two to go." Bear pounded Gage's knee. "All together now. Make noise."

Amber eased over to a smaller window and pulled the trigger. The kickback would have sent her onto her butt if she hadn't been braced for it. Bear was right. It hurt like hell. And made her angry enough to keep right on firing.

"Okay, I got the one on the right in the arm." Bear switched rifles. "He'll haul ass back to his truck. Dickheads like him always do."

"You hope." Gage fired again. "There. Movement at two o'clock."

"And ten," Amber noted.

"Looks like the reinforcements are here." Bear bared his teeth in an anticipatory smile. "This is me enjoying myself. You two take off. I'll keep these pricks busy."

"We can't just..." Amber began.

But a head jerk by Bear was followed by a, "We have to," from Gage. "You sure you're good?" he asked the big man.

"Basking in sunshine. Disk on the table might tell you a little. I didn't get far before company showed up. Now stop distracting me and get the hell out of my place. And don't make 'em chase you. That'd piss me off enough I might come after you myself. You might not know this, but there's a fat reward out on your lady friend. It started on the underground network, but it's my guess the news will spread like wildfire."

Gage shouldered an extra rifle. "Any reward being offered by Owen Fixx is bound to be as phony as hell."

"Which is partly why I ain't turning her in." Bear ended the sentence shooting and cursing at the chicken ass bastards in the bushes.

Amber didn't want to leave. It felt cowardly and wrong. They'd get away. He might not. She dragged her feet. "I can't live with the thought that someone died for me, Gage."

He pulled her along. "Bear's a survivor. He'll be fine."

She twisted the wrist he held. "You don't know that, and neither does he. This isn't Christmas. This is bad guys with an arsenal of weapons and a ton of motivation to keep right on shooting until they make their way inside."

"You don't move, I'm going to pick you up and carry you," Gage warned her. "You need to trust me, or we'll all be dead in a minute."

Amber took one last look at Bear, firing away fast and furious, and gave in. "But I'm going to hate myself for this."

"If that's what it takes."

They made it out the side door and back to the bus. Amber stayed right on Gage's heels. She noticed he made a point of positioning himself between her and any potential shooter. By the time they reached the truck, her ears were ringing with rifle fire.

"On the floor," Gage ordered.

"Thanks, but I'd rather see what's coming at us." Gun in hand, she positioned her forearms on the dash and watched for anything out of place around them.

Gage drove in a zigzag pattern for two miles. Then he picked up her cell phone and dialed Rachel's number. The call was answered immediately.

"S'at you, sugar pie?"

"Sugar pie's busy." Gage winced as a renewed shaft of pain arrowed through his ribs. He bumped across the highway and started down a dirt road. "So are several of Fixx's men. I don't know how happy your boss is going to be when he finds out they're shooting up the home of a former CIA agent while we're heading into the hills."

"You're shitting me, pal."

"Maybe, maybe not. In any case, they're back there shooting, and sugar pie and me are laying down some serious distance between us and them. Just thought you'd like to know." He broke the connection, tossed her the phone. "Don't say it."

She regarded her cell as if it were a snake. "Crazy." Dazed, she blew out a breath. "Good crazy, but still. I thought about phoning her earlier. I didn't really think I'd be able to get through. Why did they let her keep her cell phone?"

"It's to their advantage to have the lines of communication open. In this case, it was to our advantage, as well. Bear did us a favor, I did one back. It might or might not work."

Picking up the disk Bear had burned for them, Amber turned it over. Closing her eyes, she forced her muscles to relax. "One way or another, I guess we'll find out."

...

Gage kept his foot down hard on the gas. He hadn't intended for Fixx's men to get anywhere near Bear's mini compound. Those guys were better than he'd expected. Which suggested that Fixx was using some of Mockerie's people as well as his own.

He carved a labyrinthine path up into the mountains. The air grew darker, his stomach growled, and his side hurt like a mother. But Hidden Valley was the goal, and he didn't intend for trouble to follow them there.

"Where are we?"

She'd been sleeping. The heavy rain, lack of food, and Elvis crooning early ballads had lulled her into a much-needed state of rest. Deep enough in, he hoped, to recharge, because their nightmare was far from over. If Mockerie's people were indeed involved, he wasn't even sure it had actually begun.

"Did I— Ouch." She rubbed the back of her head, sat up a little straighter. "Have we been driving on this rocky road to hell the whole time?"

"For about an hour. We're almost there."

"Good. Where? Never mind. Hidden Valley. Please tell me it's really well hidden."

"It is."

"You're not just saying that?"

"Think Hole-in-the-Wall, Butch and Sundance, then add in mud structures, herb gardens, potting kilns, and farm animals roaming wherever. Also a winery and a whiskey distillery, but I'm not sure the last thing's legal."

"Okay, I'm forming a picture. It's kind of intriguing. Who runs the place?"

"Krista."

"That's it? First names only?"

"Pretty much."

Twisting around, she located her pack, drew out one of the travel coffee mugs. "This'll be cold, but no caffeine is ever bad."

"Don't say that to Krista."

Amber flipped the top up, drank the cool coffee, and felt better. "What's Krista like? Is she a hippie?"

"She's German and quirky. If it doesn't match, she wears it. Her son's name is Knute."

"Is he quirky, too?"

"He's resentful." Gage held out his hand for the mug. "He won't like seeing me with you."

"There's good news. Let me guess. Anything or anyone you have is something or someone he wants. Like that?"

"Exactly like that."

"Tell him about the killers who are after me. I bet he won't want your someone for long."

"Look in a mirror, Amber."

Amusement rose as she watched him drink. "Men place too high a value on physical appearance. Take Owen Fixx, for example. He hired me because he thought I was pretty. I had far less experience than two of the other people who applied for the hotel manager's job, yet he chose me."

"Didn't you have an in with his son?"

"Gareth's not an in. He's a, well, a rival of sorts, I suppose."

"Father and son rivals? Is that sick, or am I going in the wrong direction?"

"It's a little sick. And sad."

"Who usually wins the sick and sad battles?"

"Gareth. It's complicated between them. Between all of them, really. Luka's jealous of Gareth and of Fixx's brother, Tony. Tony would like nothing better than to knock Fixx on his ass and take over his end of Mockerie's business, while Gareth wants to write a hit song, prove to everyone that he has his own unique talent."

"You said he was anal."

"He is. They all are. Rachel's not so much anal as needy and neurotic, but she has a high opinion of herself and she's very beautiful. Somehow, she fit right into the family fold." Amber linked her fingers together. "Gage, we will go after her, won't we? Needy or not, self-centered or not, she's my sister, and any bravado they or we hear is nothing but an act. She's scared. Being nasty is her way of masking it."

"We'll go after her." Gage squinted into the premature darkness. "Rain's not helping me spot the landmarks. Look for a hickory tree dead split by lightning. It'll be on your side."

Amber leaned forward to rest her arms on the dash. She pushed the hair from one side of her face. A spectacular face that was starting to haunt him, Gage reflected grimly.

"I see plenty of trees. No cell phone towers or power lines. Please say there are flushing toilets and showers, hot or cold."

"Composting toilets and showers that run rain water."

"Not my first choice, but I can make do. Food?"

"Depends on your palette."

She narrowed her eyes at him. "Meaning?"

"Nothing in particular. Is that the dead hickory?"

She started to answer, but wound up skidding sideways into the door when he swerved left.

Righting herself, Amber stared at the windshield. "Is it my imagination, or did an arrow almost come through the glass?"

"Not your regular arrow." Gage flashed the headlights three times. "It was a crossbow bolt."

Still searching the trees, she rubbed her arms. "Does anyone you know believe in normal greetings?"

"One or two." He nodded right as they rounded a rough, tilted bend. "There's the gate."

She peered through the rain and murky dusk. "Where is it? All I see are tangled vines and bushes..." She did a double take. "Which are parting."

"Just like the Red Sea, minus the biblical implications. This parting is done by people. Comm link," he said when she frowned at him. "Short range, battery operated. A little communication tech is necessary to keep Hidden Valley hidden."

"That's very...comforting."

Gage continued to check the twisty road behind them. The low-tech aspect might have been a comfort to her, but the glimpse of distant headlights he'd caught earlier in his rearview mirror definitely wasn't.

...

Rachel's thoughts ran in a loop, from people with guns to a scuzzy traitor to her ex-husband Owen.

The sparkling lights of Vegas had dazzled her. Owen had courted her. Married her. Given her anything and everything. She'd had a stylist cum assistant cum bodyguard in Lauren Crowe. The Crowe hadn't been her friend, but she hadn't threatened her, either. Lauren had taken too much testosterone in her triathlon days to attract Owen's attention.

Helmut had kept her toned. That six-pack of his had been a true thing of beauty. And his Swedish accent had been to die for.

Once upon a time.

She'd trusted Tony. She'd also flirted with him, but only a little, because, well, because sisters-in-law did that, didn't they?

And Gareth and Luka might not have been the best of friends, but they'd always been nice to her. Gareth more so than his cousin. Luka had a mean streak. Hadn't let her see it very often, but when he had, Rachel couldn't deny she'd felt a fearful tingle in the pit of her stomach.

No matter. She figured everyone around Owen—family, friends, and employees—for assholes at this point. Someone had actually had the audacity to stroll into this god-awful motel room, yank her hair, and give her a hard slap that had scratched her cheek.

"Probably leave a scar," Rachel fretted, fingering the mark.

The doorknob turned, and she snatched her hand down, levered up on her elbows on the bed.

"There's food if you want it," the man who'd grabbed her at the filling station drawled around a wad of spearmint gum. "No point fussin' about things you can't change, honey lamb. Ain't no point turning those doe eyes on me, neither."

"She turns them on everyone, male and female."

Rachel's insides simultaneously froze and boiled at the sound of a second voice. She raised a protective hand to her cheek. "You keep away from me. Owen won't—"

"Give a damn what I or anyone does to you, Georgia. Not one good goddamn."

Pouting wouldn't help. Neither would tears or a tantrum. And defiance would only get her slapped again.

"Do you want food or not?" the person, once trusted and now despised, asked again.

Rachel's lower lip wanted to wobble. She stopped it. "What kind of food? I don't want anything healthy, or Southern."

"I'll see what the chef can rustle up. Don't hold your breath you'll enjoy it."

The door closed, and Rachel lay back down. She let the wobble grow, closed her eyes. "Bitch," she whispered with venom. And giving in, she allowed the tears to come.

Chapter Nine

"No talk. You stay put, stay quiet, and eat. You're too skinny." Krista, a short, stout woman with the remnants of a strong German accent, waved her wooden spoon at Amber. "You." She stabbed the spoon in Gage's direction. "Explain why you came here and scared my little Robin half to death. She's not used to people who drive so close to the gate without warning." Her voice gentled. "You got trouble, Gage?"

"Always." He dug into the heaped plate in front of him on Krista's round kitchen table.

The house was made of mud and stone; the floors were hand-painted tile. Paper-covered lights hung on braided chains and sported colorful tasseled ends. The kitchen smelled like stew and bread and rosemary.

Maybe incense, too. Amber couldn't separate all the scents, and she was too distracted to try with Krista's spoon flapping wildly back and forth mere inches from her head.

"Eat more," Krista warned her again. "What's your trouble, Gage?"

"You're a foot away from hitting that trouble with your

mixing spoon."

"You're not his lady friend?" Krista seemed genuinely surprised.

"I'm...no." *Keep it simple.* She glanced sideways at Gage, who gave a little smile. Maybe she'd let him handle the details here.

He regarded the motherly woman whose striped socks didn't match. Not each other or the oversize patterned sweater she wore. "Is little Robin acting as lookout for uninvited guests?"

"Until midnight, yes. The cards I read this morning said 'beware of approaching danger.' I take my cards seriously."

"I know. And in this case, they're not far off."

Krista pushed a glass of something green and milky toward Amber. "She doesn't feel dangerous to me."

"Krista reads auras," Gage said. "It's a gift."

One Amber wouldn't mind possessing at that moment. "I'm not dangerous," she told the older woman. "Not really. Not deliberately."

"She means the trouble that's chasing her isn't of her own creation."

It was, in a way, but Amber had no desire to get into a philosophical discussion with an aura-reading stranger.

Gage mouthed the word "eat" to Amber. Out loud, he asked, "Where's Knute?"

Krista's lips turned down in disapproval. "He's at the kiln, making new plates to replace the ones he broke this morning. We had a large group breakfast out at the long tent. It was his turn to clean up. His eyes and brain went all sideways when Jenny sauntered in in the altogether. Jenny forgets to put her clothes on sometimes," she said to Amber. "It happens. Knute tripping over his tongue shouldn't. Jenny's half his age, and her mind's mostly elsewhere. How big is the trouble?"

So much for keeping it simple. Amber sampled the stew.

The texture was odd, but it was tasty enough. "It's a long story that starts in Las Vegas and ends in Tennessee. My former boss, who's not a nice man, wants to kill me because I collected damning evidence against him and gave it to the FBI."

"Who in turn made the collected evidence disappear." Gage shrugged. "The story's not just long; it's old as hell."

"Bad people exist in all levels of government. I'll read the cards for you later, Amber. Maybe we'll see something that could help you and my danger magnet, Gage... Oh, this thing."

Her comm link was beeping. Gage stopped eating and held out his hand for the device. "Hey, Robin. Gage. Yeah, real long time. Is there a truck hanging around out there?" He walked away.

Krista planted the tip of her spoon on the table and stared Amber down. "Nourishment stimulates the brain. How long have you and Gage been running?"

"Only two days. It feels like weeks. We've stopped once or twice to sleep and clean up."

"My tea helps digestion." Krista tapped a steaming cup in front of Amber's plate. "Won't help break down pork, which is why we don't keep or eat pigs. Except for Peter, Paul, and Mary."

"As in the sixties folk trio?"

"Knute named them. Gage wanted to call them Elvis, Jessie, and Priscilla."

"So you only eat pigs you've named?" Somehow, that didn't strike her as fair.

"No, we keep pigs we've named. We never consume any of our pets."

The conversation had taken a very strange turn, Amber decided.

"Gage used to name all the animals that lived on or

passed through the commune in the hopes that none of them would end up in a pot. He was an interesting young man, my Gage. Very different from Knute. Sadly, the two of them never got along. I believe there was a strong rivalry between them, mostly of Knute's doing. Pah! And they say jealously is a woman's curse."

Laughing, Amber relaxed. "Krista, I'm really sorry we had to come here. The people who are after me are a lot more than dangerous. They kidnapped my sister, and I know for a fact they're deadly. They'll kill anyone who gets between them and me."

"You must know a great deal about your former boss's crimes."

"If I do, I'm not aware of it. My boss doesn't believe that, but it's true."

"Maybe you know more than you think. Do you understand hypnosis?"

"It doesn't…"

Krista's spoon hit the table with a thwack. "Don't say it doesn't work on you. Has anyone ever tried to hypnotize you?"

"Yes." Amber met her piercing stare. "It was suggested that some of the information I'd gathered against Owen might be accessible. But the attempt to retrieve it didn't work."

"You didn't let it."

"Yes, I did. Or I tried to. I was open to anything that meant my sister Rachel and I wouldn't have to run and hide. It's one thing to separate yourself from the world. It's a whole different thing to have that separation forced on you."

"Drugs?"

"They used a few. I didn't like them, and all I felt afterward was sick."

"Chemicals." Krista's voice held a strong measure of distain. "The devil's candy. Unnatural and unholy. My way is better."

"What way is that?"

"I have other, more humble brews, natural concoctions. Do you like my chicken stew?"

"What? Yes. It's delicious"

"It's squirrel."

Amber regarded her plate. "That's...interesting."

"The biscuits have crushed grasshoppers mixed into the grain."

Although her stomach seized, Amber summoned a serene smile. "Even more interesting. I hardly tasted them. What's in the tea?"

"Chamomile and well water. Unstrained, of course."

Setting her fork down, Amber arched a brow at her hostess. "I grew up in Wyoming. My grandfather had a cattle farm. There was branding time, calving season, cougar attacks. I mucked out stalls and even slopped the pigs on occasion. Very little affects my appetite. Or did until now."

A slow smile crossed Krista's lips. "Was it the squirrel?"

"Grasshoppers."

"And now you think you'll vomit."

"I might have as a kid, but not anymore. I'll employ one of my defense mechanisms instead."

Krista's spoon hit the table again. "There, you see? I tell you things that make you feel sick, and you find a way to deal with it. You have a strong mind. A little exploration might make the reasons for this deadly pursuit you are involved in come clear."

Were the reasons not to try important? She considered, then sighed. "I suppose any knowledge is good knowledge at this point. If nothing else, maybe I can figure out where Rachel's being held."

"In that case"—Krista set her wide hands on either side of Amber's head so she could look into her eyes—"we should begin at once."

...

After his conversation with the Hidden Valley lookout, Gage left Amber in Krista's capable company and struck out for the potting kiln.

Full darkness had descended, and the commune lights were few and far between. But Gage knew exactly where the shed was located. He also knew, or suspected, that Knute wouldn't be anywhere near it.

"Bastard," he swore as he jogged across the grounds. "You've got way too much of your old man in you."

Then again, Gage thought, so did he. His ornery shit of a father had come one step short of naming his only kid Sue before he'd stuffed his Johnny Cash tapes in a pack and taken off to pursue whatever it was alcoholic, pool-playing assholes pursued on their winding path to nowhere. At least his mother had had the balls to dump him in a place where he'd be raised safely without someone's fists itching to pound him to a pulp.

Screw old memories. He needed to keep the bigger picture in mind, and this particular picture was all about Amber. At the moment, the smaller one depended on him successfully restraining his temper if Knute tried to lay into him.

As expected, the shed was empty and the potting wheel unused. Much as he hated to do it, he forced himself to crawl inside Knute's head while he scanned the crop of buildings scattered around the commune.

His gaze came to rest on a ramshackle barn used primarily for storage those days. The roof needed work, the walls were unstable, and only things that didn't matter ever made their way inside. Or so the story'd gone back when he'd lived there.

Shadows and the smell of old hay and manure hung heavy in the air when he stepped through the door. A few animals, undoubtedly rodents, scuttled across the dirt floor ahead of him. Gage stood still and listened to the waves of silence, until finally his patience paid off and he caught a murmur of voices. Three of them, all pitched low and all tight with strain.

A smile tugged on his lips. They knew he was there. Not there in the barn necessarily, but on the grounds, in the vicinity.

He moved toward the rear of the structure. Three voices became two. A door creaked closed. He smelled smoke, forbidden in Krista's world. Then he heard another creak and the voices ceased.

No way to avoid the screech of hinges when he opened the feed hatch and ducked through the opening into a long, sectioned-off room with similar hatches at either end.

Knute jumped, spun, and thinned his lips. "You don't waste time, do you, bro?"

"Not generally." Gage let the hatch fall shut. "Were you and your friends having fun?" He glanced at a pair of jacks on a rough slab of barn board. "Five card stud, Texas hold 'em, or strip?"

"Piss off." Kicking the board with a booted foot, Knute sent the cards flying. "If you really need to know, and you really don't, we were playing fish."

"Not your usual high stakes game."

A thick, stocky man, Knute might have been shorter than Gage by a couple of inches, but he probably outweighed him by twenty-plus pounds. Right then, his fists were clenched and, even by lantern light, his neck was turning visibly red.

His blue eyes glittered. "Word has it you brought trouble to our valley. I don't appreciate that. Neither will my mother after the dust settles and she sees what's what."

Even knowing Knute as he did, Gage was surprised. "Word travels faster than it used to," he remarked easily. "Have you got your mother's house bugged these days?"

"Yeah right." Knute snarled. "I talked to Robin, is all. She's spooked on account of the vehicle that keeps creeping past her and the gate."

Gage studied him. "What makes you think I brought that particular problem here? Don't forget, I was a cop once upon a time."

"And I built furniture."

"Yeah?" He could almost smile at that. "For how long?"

"Seven, eight years. Left, made money, got bored, came back. Still build and sell when the mood strikes. Who's the woman?"

"No one you need to know—not if you want to stay healthy."

"So, either she's got Ebola, or she's living on the wrong side of the law. I'm thinking you value your life too much to risk the Ebola thing, so she must be a fugitive." His ruddy face broke into a smile that fell just short of cruel. "An image comes to mind. What was her name? Lydia? Man, you always could pick 'em."

Shoving his hands in his jacket pockets, Gage strolled away. He wasn't going to get sucked into that. No fucking way. "You're lucky I'm years past the nut-kicking stage of adolescence. This isn't the past, this is the now, and what's outside that gate didn't wind up there because of us."

"To hell with that, and you." A scowl appeared. "You think only a cop or a US Marshal can figure things out? Well, I'm neither, but I've got a lot of things figured you haven't got a clue about."

"Oh, I've got plenty of clues." Gage watched Knute's knuckles closely. "What I don't have yet is a sense of where you and your card playing friends factor into the overall scheme of it. As I recall, there are a lot of hidey holes scattered throughout the commune. Caves, tunnels, even a store room or two."

Knute's features and tone turned suspicious. "You been poking around already, or is this you guessing?"

Gage merely offered him an unrevealing smile. "Talk to me, Knute. I can't afford to have trouble come crashing through the gate. And I sure as hell don't have time for games or old resentments."

"Right then." Smacking his right fist into his left palm, Knute stepped forward, bared his teeth. "Let's get straight to it then, shall we...bro?"

...

Amber allowed her mind to drift. Krista had taken her to a room full of mats and floor cushions. Soft blue lights glowed from no particular source and turned her hostess's features into a weird, elongated mask.

Two people, a man and a woman, hummed in the background. Amber couldn't see them, but she heard their clothes rustling and smelled two different kinds of incense.

"Relax and empty your mind," Krista instructed. She lit something in a pot and swung it like a pendulum in front of Amber's nose. "This is to center yourself, body and soul. The teas you drank in my kitchen were to illuminate your mind and open all the closed doors inside it... You like Gage, yes?"

"What? Yes. I guess. He's very..." Sexy. Hot. Reminding herself that anything she might have felt for Gage had no part in this, she settled on, "Uh...efficient."

"Pah." Krista batted the lie aside. "You want him. He has a great body and a beautiful face."

Amber thought she heard one of the hummers sigh. She did the same inside. Heat rose in her cheeks. "Okay, fine, he's more than efficient. But I don't see how that relates to me accessing some obscure tidbit of information in my head that might help me locate my sister."

"It doesn't." Krista continued to swing the simmering pot. "I was simply curious. He's been my child from boyhood, after all."

"He's not a boy now." Amber set her palms on the floor for balance. "I feel strange. Like my mind's spinning in crazy circles."

"Place your former boss's face in one of those circles and hold it there. See it. Use it. Remember all you did to discover what was bad about him."

"Everything was bad."

"What was worst?"

The humming stopped, but the circles in Amber's mind continued to swirl and overlap. "He sold drugs and weapons for another man. The drugs were smuggled in from South America. Overseas sometimes, but he preferred to deal with the people in Colombia and Panama. One of his late wives came from Bogota. Her brother wanted her dead. He gave my boss a bonus shipment for making that happen. My boss didn't mind. Plenty more where she'd come from."

"And now what is buried in your mind begins to come out."

"Maybe." The circle of Amber's thoughts spun faster. "I glanced at some of the files before I copied them, to be sure they were relevant. Certain words registered, but maybe I was too worried about being caught to put them together on a conscious level." A dark haze slithered through her head. "What am I saying? Why don't I know what I'm saying?"

"You know exactly what you are saying. And you know more than you realize. What about the business itself?"

"He owns property in Nevada and New Mexico. A man named Carlin did something for him, or with him. I can see the name Carlin, and I know there was a deal either done or pending. I'm just not... I had to get out, take what I could with me. I probably switched off the memory app in my head—that's what my WPP contact suggested after the fact. I might have done it too late, but it wouldn't matter anyway at this point. My boss and his think I know stuff, therefore, I need to be eliminated. Simple equation, even simpler solution."

The air in the room altered, freshened briefly. Amber heard Gage's voice, muffled and distant.

"What the hell are you doing, Krista?"

"Getting her to remember. I didn't force this on her. Your lady friend has a strong will and an even stronger won't. Information is buried inside."

"That's great. Or it would be if there was anyone she could trust enough to relay it to."

"She can trust you."

"Again, great, but who can I trust on her behalf?"

"You work for a man you believe in."

"He's not at the top of the ladder, Krista." Amber felt Gage's hands grasping her upper arms. "Wake up, Snowbird. There's more trouble here than you know."

"You should give her more time," Krista reproached. "You're always in such a hurry. You need to slow down and see what might be important."

"I'm sorry to tell you this, Mama K, but you need to refocus. There's been a vehicle cruising around the bend and on past the gate to the commune since before Amber and I got here. I caught a glimpse of it while we were driving. I think it's an unmarked cop car."

"Police have cruised past us before and will again."

"The cops inside aren't looking for Amber."

"Who then?"

"You need to ask Knute that question." Crouching, Gage used the side of his finger to tip Amber's chin up. "Are you awake?"

"More or less." The haze in her head was beginning to dissipate. "I feel buzzed, but okay. Why are cops hanging around?"

"Because someone in this commune isn't here to experience a more powerful way of life. He, she, or they have a tidy little operation happening that isn't strictly legal."

Through a shimmer of residual sparkles, Amber saw Krista's features harden. "Is someone growing marijuana?"

"I imagine many are, but that's not the problem. There are two old barns on the west end of the property that are being used as storehouses for stolen goods. Everything from electronics to a damn fine Hummer."

"Those barns are falling down. They're dangerous. A year ago, I had signs put up forbidding anyone to go inside them." Removing the scarf from around her neck, Krista tied it over her hair. "You have told me, Gage, and I now will see for myself how bad this situation is. Can you tell me who is behind the thefts? Is it Knute?"

"I don't know." Gage winced as he stood and drew Amber to her feet. He checked his side for blood and saw none, but the pain was like hot knives through his ribs at that point. "We got into it before I could find out. He took off after I planted a fist in his throat."

Krista shook a stern finger. "I warned you not to fight dirty."

"He kicked me in the balls."

"You're a US Marshal. You should have seen it coming. Knute has never fought fair." She turned her attention to Amber. "Remember what you have drawn from your subconscious, and use what you can of it to help your sister. Is there more I can do for you, Gage, before I go and drag my son back here by his ear?"

"I need a laptop."

"I don't have one. Few of us do. Maybe you can find something useful in one of our barns."

"Or I could talk to Scrap."

"Or that. You go your way, I'll go mine. I might need your help to refocus the attention of the police."

Gage examined Amber's eyes. "Cloudy but clearing," he remarked, then said to Krista, "That's not very ethical, considering."

"It will be in the end. Tonight, you need to sleep. Talk to Scrap."

Her sandals flapped against the soles of her unmatched socks as she left the room.

Amber desperately wanted to sink back onto the floor and do as she'd been instructed. Sleep. Instead, she let Gage shake her one last time before she forced her way out of the clingy haze and returned to the present.

"There's no place like home," she said, rolling her head in a slow circle. "Why is there always such a vast distance between concept and reality?"

"The mind paints pictures." Gage took one last look into her eyes. "Those pictures tend to be somewhat abstract. We'll do as Krista suggested and wait until morning. I'll take you upstairs. Scrap gets up early. Just be aware, he doesn't like unexpected visitors dropping by asking for favors."

Amber pushed her feet into her boots. "Tell me honestly, Gage. Do you know anyone who's remotely normal?"

"Knute's relatively normal."

"Knute kicked you in the balls."

"After I kicked him."

She slid her arms into her hoodie. "I sense we're going to wear out our welcome here very quickly."

Gage said nothing, just took her up a narrow set of stairs to one of the second floor bedrooms.

Capturing her chin, he looked into her eyes. "You'll be

fine tomorrow, Amber."

"Will I?" She swayed against him, smiled when his expression darkened. "Gotcha thinking."

"I'm always thinking when I'm with you." His fingers stroked the sensitive skin of her jaw and throat. "You're a dangerous woman on too many levels to count. A smart man would have ditched this assignment at the first sight of you." He lowered his head. "Looks like I'm not very smart."

When his mouth covered hers, every thought in her head turned to mush. Her insides softened, then began to sizzle. However, before it could get out of hand, Gage stepped back. "Not smart and not going to take advantage of what Krista's done." He gave her another brief, hot kiss. "Sleep, Snowbird. We'll talk to Scrap first thing in the morning."

Sighing, Amber opened the door and went inside. She spotted a robe and floppy slippers in the spartan room. Her pack sat beside a long single bed. Still feeling floaty and strange, she used the bathroom and climbed under the covers.

Naturally, she dreamed about Gage. Which was better than having nightmares about Rachel being tortured or Owen Fixx on a rant.

...

The next day dawned cloudy and damp. Gage knocked early. He barely gave her time to shower and dress before he dragged her down to the kitchen and out the door.

"Muffin, orange." He handed her one of each.

"You're all heart." Shoving them in the pocket of her hoodie, Amber secured her hair in a sleek ponytail. "Having Krista wander through my mind last night was weird."

"I can imagine."

"She called up memories I didn't realize I possessed and made things even muddier than before. I appreciate the attempt, but I'm not sure how helpful any of what I remembered is going to be."

Gage shrugged. "I have Bear's computer disk in my pocket. We'll see what he has for us." *Be positive*, Amber reminded herself. She had to believe Bear was still alive and that his efforts hadn't been wasted. Efforts he'd made while she and Gage had been tangled up in a kiss that refused to let itself be shoved to the back of her mind, no matter how hard she struggled to get it there.

The landscape roughened as they made the wide turn from the woods that surrounded Krista's home to the eastern edge of the vast commune.

"Krista's husband owned the entire valley when she met him," Gage revealed. "He was a recluse. One look at Krista in her heyday and he fell. He died ten years later and left everything to her. Krista started the commune when Knute was two years old. It means more than the world to her. It's her life."

Amber avoided a ridge filled with water. "We need to help her lose the cops."

"We will. Tent's that way." He nodded to a dirt path on the right. "Don't step in a snare."

"Jesus." She stopped dead. "Your friend sets traps?"

"Only for the unwary." Gage grinned, took her hand. "You need to cultivate a sense of adventure."

"Right." She hopped over a fallen branch. "Because my life's so dull and boring at the moment. Are we going to be dodging bullets again?"

"Not unless something's happened to spook Scrap since the last time I was here."

"Which was how many years ago, exactly?"

"Quite a few. Cultivate the adventure, Amber, and lose the paranoia."

"Uh-huh, because after being shot at and having an

arrow fly across the windshield of a truck I was traveling in, why shouldn't I think twice about approaching the home of a snare-happy recluse at the crack of dawn with mist swirling around, thieves in the vicinity, and I'm guessing a cop still outside the gate? No need to worry, just stroll right up and..." She blinked, stared at the object in front of her. "Bang the gong?" She regarded the round metal object that had suddenly materialized through the fog. "You are not serious?" A laugh escaped. "Why do I say that? From rifles to gongs. Maybe I should just go to Fixx and explain."

"Mockerie." Gage unhooked the hammer from a splintered pole and struck the gong. The sound reverberated through the morning air. A lone light inside the raised tent revealed movement. When the flap eased up, the figure of a man bent low peered out at them.

"S'at you, Gage?"

"Last I checked." Gage pulled Amber forward. "Got a friend with me."

"Any friend of yours, man."

Amber told herself not to gape, but really, all she could think was "Chong." A little older, a little grayer, but bearded, barefoot, and dressed in full hippie regalia.

Inside the tent, also decked out like a 1970s hippie den, Scrap studied her through a pair of wire-rimmed glasses.

"Great skin," he said at length.

"Thank you." Amber resisted a strong urge to step back. "Your place is very eclectic."

"It's a hole." Scrap continued to inspect her. "Classy, Gage. Has taste. I'm feeling some fear underneath the polish. Got people chasing you. Bad dudes. Serious shit. Sucked you into the mire now. You're thinking maybe I can help her crawl partway out." His smile revealed two slightly chipped front teeth. "That about the size of it?"

Gage shrugged. "Pretty much."

Still a little unsure, Amber looked past Scrap's shoulder. "Is that a comm link on the table back there?"

"Sharp as a tack." Scrap punched Gage in the arm and swept a hand toward his makeshift kitchen. "Got bacon on the hotplate, eggs and booze somewhere hereabouts. Got two ears, mostly working, and one or two other things might serve your purpose."

"Got a laptop?" Gage nudged Amber forward. "I have a disk that needs reading."

"All in good time. I want to look at your lady over a steaming hot omelet. Krista made the plates. I'll make the steaming hot."

"What kind of omelet?" Amber refrained from stomping on Gage's foot when he continued to push her forward. "It won't have any squirrel or grasshoppers in it, will it?"

"Nah, I don't use crap like that. I'm a vegetarian. Even the bacon's not real." A huge grin split his bearded face. "I rely on the local fungi for my cooking. You getting my drift here?"

"Unfortunately." She kept her tone pleasant and her expression neutral. "We're having a mushroom omelet, right?"

"Sharp as ten tacks," Scrap decided. He winked at her.

Amber glanced back at Gage, who merely smiled.

Sighing, she murmured, "Let the magic begin."

Chapter Ten

Mockerie used Owen Fixx's hotel office to do his contemplating. And to work through the fierce rant that accompanied it. Throwing things hadn't been his habit for years, but the urge lingered. Hell, sometimes it burned. With his feet propped on Owen's desk, he turned a fascinating crystal orb over in his hands, tested the weight of it, then gritted his teeth and launched it at the far wall.

The crystal shattered beautifully and destroyed a small Picasso in the process. The double destruction made his minor rant much more satisfying than expected.

On to business.

Using his own specially programmed laptop, he Skyped one of his government insiders. McCabe and his US Marshal cronies might think they only had one turncoat in their midst, but it went a little deeper than that. Mockerie considered the newest member of the turncoat team a coup. He hadn't anticipated success with that particular acquaintance, but as he well knew, money talked—and walked and danced and sang.

He kept the conversation short, no extraneous details required. Alexa Chase, currently known as Amber Kelly, was on the run with one of McCabe's more unpredictable marshals. That sucked, but unpredictable was Mockerie's middle name. That should've given him some kind of edge.

"So where do we go now?" he asked his contact. "Owen's been driving the usual route, and it hasn't generated the results I'm after."

The office door opened, and Owen Fixx stepped inside. His instinctive scowl came and went so quickly, a less perceptive man might have missed it. Unfortunately for Owen, Mockerie missed nothing. He continued his conversation.

"Give me something here. Tell me about the agent who's protecting her."

"Sources are sketchy on him. He was LAPD in a former life. Possible crappy childhood. I'm looking into that. Surreptitiously, of course."

"Don't dig yourself into a hole. Just let me know when you hit pay dirt."

"You'll be the first. My lines are open, should the need to use them arise."

Mockerie broke the connection, kept his eyes on Owen's face. Looking around, circling the room. Then pow. He saw the damage. And, oh, the horror that invaded those Ken doll features. The outrage, the delightful implosion.

"Oops." Mockerie smiled. "I hope you have insurance."

Owen breathed in through his nose. "I do." And out. His fingers wiggled at his sides. "Are you here to look over my shoulder?"

Mockerie's smile widened. "Let's just say I'm adding some more of my resources to yours. She's been far too lucky for far too long. Hurt the sister."

"The woman's not stupid, James. Hurting Georgia won't entice Alexa to turn herself over to us. She'll know how it'll go from there. She'll die, her sister will die, and that'll be the end of it, for all of us. Except it's not the end she wants, and you can bet the guy with her..."

"Gage Morgan."

"Won't just let her come charging in to a suicidal situation."

Mockerie's patience began to wear thin. The urge to throw something weightier than a blown crystal orb reasserted itself. Tempering it, he picked up Owen's gold letter opener. "Bait a trap then."

"She'll recognize it for what it is. Or Morgan will."

"Doesn't matter. Emotions often trump logic, and for whatever reason, she seems to love her sister. Bait an inescapable trap."

"And if it doesn't work? Do I bait another and another?"

"The right one will do." Mockerie slid the letter opener through his fingers. "If it fails, it wasn't the right one. I'll bait the next. And I'll use a pair of corpses to do it." Tossing the letter opener up, he caught it by the blade and launched it at the ruined Picasso. It landed between a pair of distorted eyes and brought a pleased smile to his lips. He turned his gaze to Owen's face. "Point made, I trust."

...

Scrap's omelet wasn't magic, and it sure as hell wasn't good. It tasted like tree bark boiled in dirty water, and his elderberry juice was even less palatable.

Gage ate and drank for form, and he had to admire Amber for doing the same.

Krista called via her comm link to say she'd dealt with her surly turd of a son. But he'd zipped up. He wouldn't give her any more details about the thieves than Gage already knew. No surprise there. Their best bet lay in the hope that the cops who'd been cruising past the commune would grow tired of the hunt and go home when their nightshift ended.

After breakfast, Scrap perched his feet up on a mauve hassock and smoked a meditative cigarette. "Laptop's in the cupboard over the wastewater bucket. Careful you don't drop any of the cords into the bucket when you lift it down." He moved his cigarette between Gage and Amber. "You two had sex yet?"

"No." Gage opened the cupboard, rummaged.

"Why not? Are you gay?" Scrap asked Amber.

She grinned. "No, I'm just off men. My last relationship ended really badly. In fact, my whole life changed because of it."

Gage located the laptop and wedged it out of the cupboard. Thankfully, it looked quite new. "We all have our horror stories, I guess."

Scrap snorted. "Me, I got a mess of them. That's why I'm here. Is it working, Gage?"

"Enough for my purposes." Once the computer loaded, he dropped the disk in and leaned on the counter to see what Bear had unearthed. "Looks like your boss has a thing for high- and low-end establishments, Amber. Slick and moneyed in Las Vegas, cheap and utilitarian in New Mexico. He's looking to buy up a collection of boutique hotels in L.A. Has a man who does his dealing for him. Guy owns a bunch of piss-pot motels that stretch from Georgia to Arizona."

Amber swung her head around. "Is the man's name Carlin?"

"Could be. Bear came up with the initials RC." Gage pushed upright, removed the disk. "Piss-pot motels are often situated within spitting distance of railroad tracks."

"The train we heard during Rachel's call," she murmured. "Did Bear hack this information from Fixx or Mockerie?"

"I'm seeing the name Tony Fixx, so it's door number one.

Fixx is an old-fashioned bank to Bear. Mockerie's firewalls are more likely to resemble Fort Knox."

Rising, she rubbed the heels of her hands together and, in as much as she could, paced. "Okay, so, we have a clue. Piss-pot motels going from Georgia to Arizona. Train tracks. They wouldn't have taken her very far, would they? And she was probably en route to New Orleans or Miami with Jess Murkle when they caught her. We need a map. Can you...?"

"No internet here." Scrap blew a series of thick smoke rings. "I mostly keep the generators running, and repair the one and only truck in the commune. Even so, it coughs and wheezes like my ninety-five-year-old granddad."

"Ours sputters when it idles."

"Untamed engine," Scrap said.

"I guess. Bear's sounds like a locomotive, and it backfires."

"Well-tuned engine." Angling a stream of smoke through the last two rings he'd blown, Scrap closed a canny eye. "Cop car outside'll be smooth as a baby's butt. Pansy ass vehicle overall, but then that's the condition of the whole police department hereabouts. Even an untamed truck shouldn't have a lick of trouble outrunning it. You hearing me, man?"

"Loud and clear." Gage checked his side for blood, found none. His ribs hurt, and a few other parts were still feeling the effects of Knute's boot. All in all, he was good to go. And had better go before more than that lone cop car cruised by.

Scrap gave them a bottle of elderberry juice for the road, then returned to his cigarette and solitude. The light in the tent went out behind them.

Amber glanced over her shoulder as they made their way along the path. "He's certainly different."

"Yeah," Gage agreed. "He is. Tell me more about your relationship with Gareth. You've never really gone into it."

"No."

"Why not?"

"Because that was a bad interlude in my life, and it makes me uncomfortable to go back over it. Why don't we talk about you instead? Why did you stop being a cop?"

"I got tired of the life."

"Bullshit. Something happened. It pissed you off or made you sad or freaked you out, but you didn't get tired of it. Getting tired of things is for people like my sister."

"Who should be your priority," Gage pointed out. "My reasons for turning in my badge aren't open for discussion, with you or anyone. And don't give me that look. Guilt doesn't work on me."

"I'm not trying to make you feel guilty. Difficult as it might be for you to believe, I respect people's privacy quite highly. Bear in mind that you started this question and answer session, not me. I'm fine talking baseball, politics, or how to placate a cranky conventioneer."

"Fair enough." The pricks of guilt laced with self-directed irritation subsided. He was starting to give a rat's ass, and that bothered the hell out of him. He needed to erase the taste of her from his head before it took root there and screwed him up all the way.

He spotted Krista walking out of the house with Knute in tow and found his irritation relaxing into amusement. "Now there's a picture I never get tired of seeing. Knute looking well and truly chastised."

Amber squinted into the mist. "While you were gone last night, Krista told me a little bit about the relationship between you and Knute when you were younger. From what she said, I think Knute's jealous of you, always has been. The question is, is he jealous enough to talk to the police out there about us?"

"Yes, but he won't."

"And you know that because?"

"His friends are thieves, and helping them matters more

to him than screwing me around. Plus, he hasn't seen you, so he doesn't realize what it is I've got, metaphorically speaking, that he should want."

Amber shook her head. "I must be incredibly tired. That almost made sense. Are we going to say good-bye to Krista, tell her what it is I'm sure you're planning to do?"

"She'll only hit me with her spoon and insist we stay on as planned. Better to leave, no good-byes, and let her deal with Knute."

Amber regarded the mud and stone house that was Krista's home. "I want to thank her for helping me unlock things I didn't realize I knew."

"You can thank her later, when this is over." Gage took a firm grip on her hand. "The sooner we leave, the less chance of anything unpleasant splashing the people here." He produced a comm link from his jacket pocket.

"Scrap's?" Amber asked.

"Nope. Knute's."

"He's going to hate you, Gage."

"He already does." He raised the device, spoke to Robin's replacement. "Frank? Gage. Let me know when the cop passes by heading south. Give him a good lead, then have the guys open the gate." Dark humor rose inside. "I'm in the mood to have some fun."

...

Amber suspected more things were unfolding than Gage had admitted to her. He'd planned for them to stay at the commune. That hadn't worked out. Because of the local police? Somehow, she doubted that. Maybe the cops figured into it, but Amber sensed there was something else at play there.

"You're driving differently now," she remarked as he

maneuvered the truck along an overgrown track barely wide enough to be called a road. "And when we stopped for gas twenty minutes ago, you wouldn't let me come into the station. I wanted a candy bar, Gage."

"I bought you a candy bar."

"Exactly. You bought it." Amber eyed him in annoyed suspicion. "What's going on that you're not telling me? And for God's sake, don't say 'nothing'. It's my life that's in danger here. Well, okay, yours too, but I don't like being out of the loop."

He fixed his gaze on the narrow road ahead. "I'm trying to make sure any tail we might have picked up can't follow us. If you want to help, we're coming up on a town large enough to support decent cell phone reception. Use my phone. Text Bear and ask him to send us a list of RC-owned motels located close to any train tracks. Tell him to focus on central and southern Mississippi, in some kind of a line between Black Creek and New Orleans."

The moment she had reception, she began the required text.

"You have an idea, don't you, about the person or people who are after us?"

"I think we've had distant company for quite a while. I'm not sure where or when it started. At first, I was fine with it. I had an idea to use it, draw the bastards in and see what was what. Then I talked to Robin and I realized we'd been followed to the last place I'd ever want trouble to appear." He slid her a level look. "A vehicle other than that police car passed by the commune gate."

Amber's thumbs paused over the keypad. "Are you saying you tried to lose a tail, but you couldn't? And I'm going on the assumption that losing tails is something you're really, really good at."

"It's one of my better skills. Finish the text, Amber, and

watch for traffic behind us."

She fumbled over the spelling of Mississippi, made a second attempt, and finally thought to hell with it. Let Bear figure it out. "If you're deliberately attempting to lose Fixx's men, and you think it isn't happening, you must have some idea about when and why. Should I be going back to the idea that something I have is bugged?"

"It's possible, but no." His gaze flicked to the rearview mirror. "Shit, I saw something."

Amber's insides turned to liquid, but she kept texting. "I only have my pack and a box of Krista's herbal tea. We borrowed the truck from Abel, stopped and saw Bear, then went on to the commune." Dammit, why couldn't she spell New Orleans properly? "Do you know when we picked up this tail, and are you absolutely sure the vehicle you saw behind us isn't a local farmer? I mean, people other than us use back roads."

"I'm only at the idea stage right now. But money's a big motivator, and you heard Bear. There's a fat reward out on you."

"Which is why I can't buy myself a candy bar. Okay, text's done and sent." She swiveled to face him. "What do we do now? Just keep driving aimlessly and watch for anything that might or might not be hostile?"

"We're not driving aimlessly. We're heading for the border. But first." He took his phone from her, checked the GPS. "We're going to trade this old gray mare in for another set of wheels."

"Trade it," Amber repeated. "In the middle of nowhere. How many friends do you have in remote places, Gage?"

His grin in profile told her nothing. But what else was new? The man was a magical mystery tour unto himself.

"It's not who I know." He eased them across a shallow creek and up a hill that slanted at least fifteen degrees to the left. "It's who McCabe can contact in the vicinity."

"Jesus." Exasperation made her want to tear her hair out. "This nightmare's getting stranger by the minute. I saw a flash. Might be metal or a light."

"Yep. It's a few miles back, but whoever's behind it is definitely following us. And that leaves only one option."

"We hide and ambush them?"

"No." He sized up the terrain outside. "Bundle up, Snowbird, and gather your things. We're walking from here."

"What? No. That's crazy." But she caught the pack he tossed at her. "They'll find the truck. They'll know we're on foot. Vulnerable."

"They won't find the truck."

She opened her mouth to argue, suddenly realized what lay in front of them, and grabbed his arm in alarm. "Gage, you are not going to ditch Abel's truck in a lake."

"It's not a lake, it's a pond. A deep one, full of mud and slime and possibly a little quicksand."

"Are you serious?"

"All part of the adventure, Amber. Have you got everything?"

"Everything except my sanity." Shoving the door open, she climbed out. "I hope you know what you're doing."

"Me, too," he said. Reaching inside, he set the truck in gear. It rolled through sludge, over rocks and branches to the edge of the pond. Slowly, slowly, it tipped into the muddy water. Then, with a series of sick glugs, it disappeared from sight.

...

Gage knew he was taking a risk. But that flash of light hadn't been more than a few miles behind them, and he only had one more ace up his sleeve. McCabe might have had a few more if that last one of his didn't work. Unfortunately, communication was becoming difficult, and he wasn't entirely sure his ace wouldn't turn out to be a dud.

"Give me a hint, Gage." She sounded out of sorts, but thankfully not out of breath. "What's our destination? An underground cave, an old riverboat owned by a friend of yours that might or might not be seaworthy?

"Whose seaworthiness are you questioning, my friend's or the riverboat's?"

She shot him a look that cut through the light mist. "Take your pick."

"No boats, no caves. Scrap has an ancient but functional Winnebago. He stores it far enough away from Hidden Valley that Krista won't find it. Every once in a while, he hikes out of the valley and thumbs a ride to Whisper. It's a town on the Mississippi-Tennessee border. A friend of his stores it for him in a hollow on his property. Scrap gave me the keys to the storage shed and the Winnebago."

She glanced at a clump of huckleberry bushes straight ahead. "We're going to try and outrun Fixx's men in a Winnebago. I think I'd feel better in an old riverboat."

Gage hitched his pack higher. "It's inconspicuous."

She gave a half-hearted laugh. "That's not even remotely possible—not unless it's wearing a cloak of invisibility."

An old-fashioned road map told Gage to head south. He nudged her through a break in the dense bushes. "Tell me this," he said. "Put yourself in the position of Fixx's men. Would you be looking for yourself in an ancient-as-hell RV with peace signs painted on the sides?"

"The Mystery Machine?" She halted to stare. "That's our getaway vehicle? A Scooby-Doo replica that probably tops out at thirty miles an hour?" She reached into his jacket pocket, removed his phone, and held it out to him. "Contact your boss. Maybe he'll have a fresh idea for us."

Gage took the phone and hid his amusement. "Does this mean you're losing faith in me?"

"The Wizard of Oz had a better plan to return home."

"You're mixing your metaphors, Snowbird. Stick with Oz, and imagine we're on the Yellow Brick Road. Fixx is holding your sister in the Wicked Witch's fortress, and our mission is to break her out."

"I don't think throwing a bucket of water at Owen Fixx or his henchmen is going to do it here. And, frankly, I'm still working on the whole Winnebago idea. How are you going to explain to Abel that you ditched his truck in a pond? Or is that your way of saying you think he's working for Owen, that he bugged the truck before he loaned it to us? Damn." She paused, plucked a sprig of huckleberry from her ponytail. "He could have bugged it, couldn't he? Fat reward, connections within the law enforcement community. The only plus is, he knew my mother."

"Abel wasn't alone at the lodge. Wanda was there, and Mandy."

"But they're not in law enforcement. Are they?" When he didn't answer right away, she sighed. "Great. One or both of them?"

"Wanda did encryption work in Biloxi. She quit the job a year ago. I don't know why or under what circumstances. Mandy's the X factor. No idea what her deal is or was."

"What about Bear? Do you trust him or not?"

"He helped us get away."

"So did Abel, and you seem to be doubting him."

"I'm not doubting anyone. All I'm doing is throwing out possibilities. The only head space I'm in is my own. Talk to me more about Fixx."

Amber skidded down a muddy hill. When the ground leveled off, she sighed. "It would never have occurred to him that I'd do what I did. That anyone would. He's a ruthless man, and as I've already told you, arrogant as hell. But his employees are very well paid. There are benefits, even for the most menial positions at the hotel. I had a great job, with phenomenal benefits. I can't remember one time when I approached him with an idea that he didn't tell me to go ahead and do it, and don't give the expense a second thought. So there's that side of him—the conscientious employer—and then the other, the one with no or very selective compassion. He strikes me as a person who's incapable of loving anyone but himself. From the research I did, I'm convinced he had his first three wives killed."

"You must love your sister a lot to worry that she'd have ended up like her predecessors."

The annoyed sound Amber made caused Gage's lips to twitch. "Just testing, Snowbird. At the risk of sounding cynical, I don't get the strong impression Rachel would do for you what you're doing for her."

Amber pulled another sprig of huckleberry from her hair. "She wouldn't. That's not the point. I love Rachel because she's my sister, but that's where it ends. I don't actually like her at all. We're not friends. We were once when we were young, but not anymore. Maybe it makes me as selfish as her that I realize I'm mostly doing this because I couldn't live with myself if I didn't. I also have no idea why I just told you that. I must be really tired. Are we anywhere near Whisper and Scrap's Winnebago?"

"Another few miles," Gage told her. Something inside him softened slightly. Giving in to it, he took her hand. "How about I talk for a while. I'll tell you about the time Abel and I chased a murder suspect into a mother of a brush fire. We lost the suspect and our bearings and wound up hanging from a helicopter cable as it hauled us up over the fire."

"And then?" she prompted when he stopped.

"And then." He lifted his eyes to the cloudy sky. And

then, draping an arm over her shoulder, he kissed the top of her head. "The cable snapped."

...

Amber couldn't see how the storage shed housing the Winnebago managed to stand given the rotten state of the foundation. But she thanked God and the universe for the fact that there were mineral hot springs less than half a mile away. She was treated to a tiny slice of heaven on what felt like the road through hell.

Her skin was clean and tingling, her hair damp, and her clothes clean. The Winnebago was a horror, but the engine ran and there were hookups for shower, toilet, and sundry appliances.

Gage only cared that none of the warning gauges lit up and the gas tank was half full. Men, Amber concluded, possessed extremely low expectations.

They'd be heading into Mississippi, but not until the sun set and he heard from Bear. He decided to hike in for takeout Chinese food supplied by a store/restaurant on the edge of town. He told her to shoot anyone who came near the shed while he was gone. So Amber sat in a patch of grass near the falling down door, and let the breeze dry her hair and her mind drift while she drank a cup of what she called Krista's memory tea. The tea and her mind took her back to the time prior to her relocation to Black Creek.

"I don't want to divorce him." The tantrum Rachel had thrown back when the whole identity change thing had happened burst vividly into Amber's head. "I hate you, Alexa. Why couldn't you leave things alone. Owen's not a monster. He loves me. You're just being a bitch because it didn't work out for you and Gareth."

Alexa who still hadn't quite thought of herself as Amber,

had tried to calm her sister down. "Owen Fixx has been widowed three times. Every one of his wives' deaths was deemed accidental. The only lawsuit launched against him by any of the families never made it to court. He bought them off, Georgia."

"Rachel," the WPP officer in attendance had corrected her. "Use the names you've been given."

"I want to go home," Rachel said through clenched teeth. "Why can't you get that into your robotic head? And don't give me that big sister look, Alex— Okay, fine, Amber. I want to talk to someone who understands feelings, not some replicant refugee from Blade Runner."

"You'd want to talk to me, then." The door to the stuffy little office had opened, and Tom Vigor had entered. He was a big, strapping man with a voice as commanding as his appearance. His hair and mustache were both white and shaggy, and he walked with a slight limp.

"Gout," he said when Rachel mutely glared. "Got my knee shot out, too, a while back. Healing's a slow and painful process."

Rachel had spun away. "Just what I need. A hillbilly hick—no offense—a robot, and a divorce I don't want." Flouncing around, she plopped down in a chair, arms folded. "I'm not happy."

Unruffled, Tom laughed. "I sensed that from the other side of the door, Rachel, and I'm sorry as I can be about what's happened. But truth be told, your sister did both you and the FBI a big old favor where Owen Fixx is concerned. It's not her fault the information she gathered went astray." He glanced at his thin-lipped man across from him. "You can go now, Sidney."

"With pleasure, sir," the suited young man replied. He summoned a quick, false smile. "Good luck to both of you. I hope your new lives work out well."

The door clicked closed. Rachel stuck her tongue out at it. "Have a nice day, Mr. Roboto."

Tom laughed again, and the sound of it coming straight from his belly settled Amber's turbulent thoughts. "Don't you mind our Sidney now," Tom soothed. "He's going through a nasty divorce at the moment, probably isn't feeling as friendly toward females as he otherwise might."

Rachel slapped the arms of her chair. "Screw Sidney. He's in the middle of the very thing I don't want. I'm not going to…"

"Amber!"

Jolting back, Amber snapped her head and the gun in her lap up. "Sidney." She blinked and her vision cleared. "Gage. How did you…? Where did I…? Holy crap, what's in that tea Krista gave me?"

Gage crouched, caught her chin, and examined her eyes. "You can't do this. Zone out in plain sight. Krista meant well, but she doesn't fully understand the danger you're in." He tipped her head back. "Who's Sidney?"

She wrenched free of his grip. Too close, her brain cautioned. Too many feelings swirling inside. Too damn sexy for his, or her, own good. Backtracking to his question, she pressed her index fingers into her temples. "Sidney was with the WPP—some kind of middle man. He walked into a hot little room where Rachel and I had been sitting for almost two hours and told her flat out she'd be getting a divorce, that the wheels were already in motion. He was very…clinical. Tom defended him, but I remember thinking he was a government stereotype down to the ground. He wouldn't let Rachel talk to her assistant, Lauren, or to Helmut."

"Her trainer."

"Yes. And of course Tony, Luka, and Gareth were totally out of the question."

"Making Sidney a prize asshole in Rachel's eyes."

"Her description was more colorful, but like that." Still seated cross-legged, she gripped his wrist. "Gage, something moved in the trees behind you. To my right."

The last word barely made it out before a pair of bullets embedded themselves in the shed. Gage shoved her down, grabbed his gun, rolled in front of her, and came up firing.

Screw that. Wriggling sideways, she laid flat on her stomach and aimed her own gun at the trees. She had no target, but she could see the spot where the shooter or shooters had to be hidden.

She targeted the first thing that moved, heard a quick, sharp cry of pain and fired again.

Gage got in front of her, continued to shoot. Five more bullets flew toward them. "He's down," Gage shouted. "He's firing, not aiming. Stay on the ground."

Amber glimpsed another flurry of motion. Were there two people? Were both of them wounded?

More shots rung out. Gage returned the fire. So did Amber when she could squeeze the trigger without fear of hitting Gage.

Her clip ran out, and she dropped her hands. The extra ammunition in her backpack might as well have been a thousand miles away.

Another cry reached her, and suddenly everything went quiet. Only the frogs and crickets made any sound at all. And, of course, there was the blood pulsing in her ears.

She levered up on her elbows, then worked her way into a crouch behind Gage. "Is this them setting a trap?"

"Either that, or we hit them and they're dead."

"How many did you count?"

"Two. They travel in pairs. I'm going to stand, Amber. I want you to stay down. The weeds'll give you cover."

She grabbed his jacket before he could gain his feet. "Are you crazy?"

"Not yet," he said. Then, reaching down, he cupped her head and brought her mouth up to meet his.

The kiss scorched. It also stole the breath from her lungs, leaving her just dizzy enough that when her mind stopped swimming, he was gone.

She couldn't see him, so she knew he had to be circling, using the underbrush for cover. Her heart, which had been banging against her ribs only a moment ago, began to skip every other beat.

This was insanity. Silent insanity, but still.

Amber counted through the quiet. She was on the verge of standing when she saw Gage walking toward her, shoving an array of guns into his pockets and his waistband.

"We got them," he called out. "They're dead."

"They." She dropped her head onto her arms, felt the weight on her chest slide away. "I am so not used to this. I know they were Owen's men, but how did they follow us here? We ditched the truck five miles back."

He helped her to her feet. "It has to be something were carrying."

"Something I'm carrying." She regarded the gun in her hand, sighed, and held it out to him. "I guess this is as good a place as any to start."

Chapter Eleven

He went over everything. Her gun, her phone, her boots, her clothes. He even examined the cosmetics.

"Mocha Haze?" A brow lifted as he held up her lipstick tube.

She took it from him in a weary gesture. "There's nothing unusual inside, Gage. I bought most of this stuff in Black Creek, where stock is limited and sold by a couple who've run the drugstore for thirty-five years."

"What about your jewelry?"

She twisted off a thumb ring and one from her middle finger. "White gold filigree, both given to me by my grandmother." From her pack, she produced a delicate ankle chain and a pair of earrings. "These plus the pair on my lobes constitute the sum total of my current jewelry collection."

"You travel light," Gage noted. "Lingerie not included.

She snatched away the bra he was holding up and told herself not to laugh. Nothing about this situation was funny. There were two dead men fifty yards ahead, plus their truck, which was thankfully well hidden in the trees.

"Are we just going to leave the bodies where they are?" she asked Gage as he checked out the lining of her backpack.

"No, and if you're smart, you won't ask for details."

Amber wondered if perhaps she hadn't asked for enough details. When he finished with her pack, she tipped her head at him. "That's my stuff done. What about yours?"

A new smile played on the corners of his mouth. "You think Owen Fixx bugged something I'm carrying?"

"He might have."

"Or I might have?"

She met and held his stare. "Apparently, it's no secret that there's a healthy reward out on me. You're human, Gage, and by your own admission, cynical as hell. Fixx's men keep finding us. Why is that? I'm not sure if you're incredibly clever and deceitful or exactly what and who you say you are. If it's the first thing, I'm in serious shit, which I am no matter how I look at it, since all the weapons are currently on your side of the RV."

Still not quite smiling, he tossed her a gun and two full clips. "I'll wait while you load. I'll even stand up and walk into the kitchen unarmed. I don't fully expect even that to convince you, so if you want McCabe's number, it's on my phone."

She slid a clip into the empty chamber. "Talking to McCabe wouldn't prove anything. I know him less than I know you. What's his background, credential-wise?"

"He's a US Marshal with—let's call them special privileges. He gets the tough assignments. Beyond that, there aren't many people who know exactly what his privileges are.""Are you sure he's not working for Fixx?"

"Mockerie." Shrugging, Gage poured two mugs of fresh coffee. "McCabe would mingle with the great white, not the tiger sharks. I checked my own belongings, too, Amber. You can believe that or not. If you don't, you're free to take the truck hidden in the bushes and disappear. Go where a Winnebago can't follow. I'll even give you a list of RC-owned motels. They're dives, but they work for a night or two on the road."

It was quite the speech, and it gave Amber time to study his body language. Nothing about his movements or his facial expressions suggested he was lying.

The smile barely quirking his lips became a chuckle. "You can read me all day, Snowbird. I don't have many tells. I'm told a muscle in my jaw used to jerk when I was tense, but that's old news. I can play poker with the best of them these days."

"Comforting prospect." She considered for a moment. "How big is the reward on me?"

"Five hundred K."

Disbelief had robbed her of speech. For a stunned moment, she simply couldn't form a coherent thought. When her head cleared, she huffed out an incredulous breath. "Bear turned his back on half a million dollars?"

"It'll be six hundred thousand before you know it. The price is going up by the minute." Gage pressed a mug of coffee into her hands. "Another few days, you might be tempted to turn yourself in."

The shock wall surrounding Amber's brain shattered, and she shot him an exasperated look. "So much money," she murmured, "for a few jumbled pieces of information that are already back in Fixx's possession. Or Mockerie's. Whoever. I know I'm repeating myself, but nothing about this makes sense. If I could remember what I stole from Fixx's computer files, I'd have relayed it to a whole team of people by now. Surely not everyone in the US Marshals' office and/or the FBI is corrupt. You trust McCabe. Why didn't he come and talk to me after the information disappeared?"

"Not his department, not his deal."

"Tom Vigor then."

"Same answer, for him and Sidney."

Her smile fell just shy of a grimace. "Sidney's not someone I'd get chatty with. Definitely not somebody I'd trust. By the book and not a hair out of place never feels totally real to me."

"Is he attractive?"

"To Rachel he could be. Why?"

"No reason."

The coffee turned bitter on her tongue. "Rachel didn't sell me out, Gage. Not to Sidney, anyway."

"To Fixx then?"

"No." She thought, but remained firm. "No. Even if she had, she doesn't know where I am."

"You're forgetting the lure, the phone call. The appeal to big sister for help."

"Your way of twisting things around sucks." Leaving her cup on a low table, Amber climbed to her feet to walk off her irritation. And, as much as it galled her, to mull over what he'd said.

"I'm not trying to annoy you." He came back around the counter. "I just want to be sure. I want you to be sure. You want to find Rachel. Help her. But you need to be absolutely certain that her cry for help is genuine and not a ploy to draw you in."

Arms folded, Amber tapped her elbows with her palms. "Rachel's not working with Fixx. I know my sister. Her voice wobbles when she's frightened. She can't fake it. I've seen her try. She's a crappy actor, and I heard a distinct wobble."

"Maybe she's been practicing."

Amber hissed in a breath. "Stop doing this. Rachel's not involved, beyond the fact that she's been kidnapped. What surprises me is that she hasn't used her wiles on the men who are holding her. She has amazingly effective wiles."

"Maybe not all the people holding her are men."

"We know at least one of them is. We've talked to him. She'd need only one to succumb."

"Trade six hundred K for hot sex?" Gage moved toward her. "Could be a hard sell. Lucky for you, I'm not motivated by money."

"And I'm not swayed by kisses."

"Hot kisses," he corrected, still closing.

Scorching hot, but she didn't intend to admit it. Or let him get any closer. She circled a small table. "Don't push me, Gage," she warned. "I fight dirty when I'm backed into a corner."

"I'm not backing you anywhere."

"You're walking toward me and the door's behind you."

"Guns are behind you. Loaded and within easy reach." He kept his eyes fixed on her and made her throat go dry. "You want me to stop, all you have to do is say no. Otherwise..." Reaching out, he trapped her hand and eased her up against the wall. "We need to get this out of the way so both of us can think. Because right now, we're going in circles."

He was right. This was wrong, but Gage wasn't. The circles he'd mentioned were spiraling inward and making her dizzy. She couldn't think when she was off balance. And, God help her, he had the sexiest mouth she'd ever seen.

"Tell me to stop, Snowbird, if that's what you want."

She felt his breath on her face, inhaled the scent of soap and leather and man. "You're the scariest bodyguard I can imagine, Gage Morgan. I truly think I'd have been better off with Sydney Greenstreet. Or WPP Sidney for that matter." Taking hold of his jacket, she touched her tongue to her upper lip and watched his eyes begin to smolder. "Word of warning, pal. There's a side of me you know nothing about. Back in college, I learned how to make men beg." A slow smile curved her lips as she tugged him closer. "You're in serious, serious trouble."

...

Mockerie tapped his pen on Owen's desk. Tapped it, rolled it, slid it through his fingers while he contemplated. When Owen entered, Mockerie began to draw on the blotter. The despised model-perfect features tightened into a wince for a nanosecond before smoothing into his usual bland smile of acceptance.

"Tan Italian leather," Mockerie remarked. "Nice surface to write on. I see you're carrying a bottle of fine whiskey. Are we celebrating something momentous?"

"Soon. I have a plan."

"Better than the previous one, I trust."

"We didn't play the first one right. Morgan's good. I keep losing men."

"Meaning we've suffered another loss?"

"Two of my people haven't checked in for eight hours. They're long past due. I'm thinking elimination."

"So am I." Mockerie's head remained down. Only his gaze rose. "Though not necessarily in the same context. Bump the reward up to a million, pour me two and half fingers…" He rubbed his own half finger. "And fill me in."

"About the losses I've suffered, or my plan?"

Mockerie drew a guillotine with a lopped-off head lying on the ground beside it. "My patience is wearing extremely thin at this point." He gave the head a tortured expression. "Loss of life is unimportant. Spell out your plan, in detail. And bear in mind that while I'm in the mood to see hot female blood being spilled, hot male blood works almost as well."

It pleased him to watch Fixx's hand tremble before he turned. His voice, however, remained steady. "I think it's time we gave technology a rest and focused on the golden carrot we have tucked away in hiding."

"That's hardly a new plan." Mockerie tossed back all two and half fingers without removing his gaze from the other man's face. "It's been our fallback from the start."

The tiniest bit of impatience leaked through. "Then we're at the point where we need to use it."

"Excellent. However, didn't you just finish telling me that Gage Morgan was extremely good at his job?"

"He's only as good as Alexa Chase will let him be. She loves her sister." Owen sipped his drink. "The carrot needs to dangle on a longer stick, James. It also needs to move."

...

She wouldn't let this get out of hand, Amber promised herself. She'd kissed men before and managed to hold them back. The difference here was now she had to hold herself back.

Gage made a thorough exploration of her mouth. His tongue dipped and teased and ignited every one of her senses. He was a shot of whiskey that set her throat on fire, then exploded like a fiery bomb in her belly.

Whatever her intentions when she'd started this, they lay in shards at her feet. He was sin, pure and simple. The kind of man she'd made a point of avoiding to focus on her career.

To hell with it, she thought. While Gage's mouth was doing amazing things, his hands slid to her hips and eased her forward to meet his.

The scattered heat in her belly coiled into knots. Her nerves leaped, her mind turned to mush.

His lips left hers to skim across her cheeks and forehead. His palms came up to span her waist and her rib cage. She pressed herself against him while his thumbs stroked the sensitive skin beneath her breasts.

Too much clothing, her bleary brain reflected. *Too many layers.*

He pulled off the decorative band she used to secure her ponytail and threaded his fingers through the heavy length of it.

Men always loved her hair, which she supposed was why she tended to pull it back. Shaking it loose, she savored the feel of his hands tangled in it.

The shadows in the RV shifted with the changing clouds outside. The room turned a soft shade of purple. The air warmed. Or maybe it was her blood heating up as her needs mounted.

She dragged her mouth free. "I can't think. You're messing up my head."

The sexy half smile of his appeared. "Never think about sex, Amber. Just go with it and enjoy."

"I am enjoying. I just like to know the person I'm enjoying it with."

"Not one of Fixx's or Mockerie's minions." He kissed the corners of her mouth. "That's the best I can give you at the moment."

Was it enough? Amber ran her tongue over his lower lip, made a sound of pleasure in her throat. Maybe—for the moment.

She nipped the side of his mouth. "Kiss me again and I'll see how I feel."

"Not a problem," he said and, cupping her face, dived in so deep her senses felt completely swamped.

The shock of it had her easing back. "Okay. Wow!"

Grinning, he shifted his grip. "Pretty sure we can do better than wow."

But before he could capture her mouth again, his eyes slid sideways and he halted.

She frowned, dug her fingers into his shoulders. "What?

Is someone outside?"

"Shhh."

"But who…"

He covered her mouth with his hand. "I heard an engine."

She stopped moving and listened until she heard it, too. Far, far in the distance, she caught the rumble of a high-powered engine. Then, just as it began to grow louder, the engine cut out.

Five seconds passed, then ten. "We're close to town, aren't we?" Amber whispered at length.

"Town's north. It's all back roads to the south. That truck was on one of them."

"We were south of here a while ago."

"I know."

"Do you think someone's looking for the dead men?"

"Could be."

"Gage, your monosyllabic responses are far from reassuring. Do we need to be worried?"

He set her aside, bent to retrieve his guns. "We need to go."

Rather than object or question him further about the truck or its owner, Amber swept her hair back into a ponytail and wound the band around it. "Do we have a direction? A destination?"

"The Heart of Dixie Motel. Five miles north of Harper's Bend, Mississippi."

She repacked her bag, quickly, slipped the rings back on her finger and thumb. "The first RC-owned establishment on our list, I presume."

"First of twelve." He gave her a brief but still rather heated kiss. "Cross your fingers we get lucky."

He didn't say it, but Amber knew they needed to move fast. However they were doing it, Fixx's men always seemed to be right on their heels. At some point, he was going to get tired of sending men out to die. He might not kill Rachel right away, but he'd have no compunction about shooting her and passing that news on to his former sister-in-law.

Strapping herself into the passenger seat, Amber breathed around a deep shudder. And wondered bleakly how many more people would be dead before this was over.

Glancing at Gage, she closed her eyes. How many, she thought, and who?

Chapter Twelve

"Here we are. The Heart of Dixie Motel." Gage slung an arm over Amber's shoulders. "Right next to the Heart of Dixie Bar and Grill, complete with pool tables, two bucking broncos, and a whole lot of bathtub whiskey in the front and back rooms."

"Not going to ask," she told him. "Are we checking in or just checking it out?"

"We have an RV, such as it is, Snowbird. Wouldn't checking in look the tiniest bit conspicuous?"

"Maybe we're sick of our crappy old RV, an RV that only has a single bed in it, by the way. At least one of us should do the decent thing and offer to sleep in the Winnebago while the other does the motel thing."

Gage merely smiled and propelled her toward the bar. He was taking a risk bringing her into a bar, but leaving her alone seemed even more dangerous somehow. Six of one, he supposed. Anything they did or didn't do was bound to have a consequence attached to it.

Lively country music spilled through the door, which

had been propped open by a crushed beer can. Someone had vomited in a nearby bush, and someone was passed out under a window. A drunk man lay spread-eagle while a woman in high heels and bright pink pants shouted at him.

"I have to say, you take me to some of the most interesting places. Bullets flying, thieves lurking, drunks lying prostrate in the weeds, and bathtub whiskey flowing like water. Oh, and look, there's mud wrestling, too." She motioned at a makeshift ring set five feet away from and slightly lower than the musicians' stage. "Maybe we should find a back booth."

Amused, Gage flexed his arm over her shoulders and forced her to halt. "Afraid you'll be drawn into the muddy fray?"

"Frankly, yes. Sorry if that disappoints you, but my hair-pulling, grappling-with-an-intoxicated-female days are far behind me."

Now he laughed. "You grappled with intoxicated females?"

"Once. Back in college. Her name was Keely, and she had a really perky blond ponytail. Someone—not me—used it to yank her off her feet. She came up swinging, knocked two other women flat, then turned her wrath on me.'

"Were you intoxicated?"

"Totally. But I took kickboxing in high school. She swung, I kicked, she landed on her ass. The bouncer marched in and threw all of us out. Gage, almost every man in here is wearing a hat. I can't see any faces. Are we going to stand out?"

"Not especially. It's amateur night at the Heart of Dixie Bar and Grill. We could be here to participate."

"Great. Do you sing?"

"About as well as I tap dance. You?"

"I'm Reba in the shower. Minus the water and steam, I'm probably more like Stevie Nicks."

"Who was hot as hell in her prime and still is, which goes

to prove it's not all about vocal talent."

"I'm sure Stevie will be delighted to hear that. The man in the ratty brown cowboy hat is watching us."

Gage squeezed her shoulder. "He's staring at you, not paying much attention to me. Here he comes."

The man in question had a bottle of beer in his hand and a curious expression on his face. Ignoring Gage, he ran his gaze up and down Amber's body. "You kin to Lorraine Bixby? Cousin or something?"

"She doesn't have any family," Gage told him. "We're on our honeymoon, just up from Miami."

"S'at so?" Finally, the man acknowledged his presence. "What y'all do down there in Miami?"

Keeping his expression pleasant, Gage replied, "We're cops."

The man snorted. "Why?"

Amber grinned at him. "We like guns."

"Well, hells bells, so do I. Wouldn't be a cop on account of it. I'm guessin' the honeymoon story's crap. If so, are you here on vacation or a manhunt?"

Gage sized him up. Pudgy with soft hands and a gimpy right leg, and he'd been standing at the dark end of the bar, scoping the room. "Do you own this place?" he asked.

The man chuckled. "Matter of fact I do. How'd you figure that so quick?"

"It's what I do."

"Huh." The man regarded Amber. "What do you do, cop-wise?"

"Missing persons." She offered a smile and a subtle body movement that would have made a corpse sit up and take notice.

The man's eyes glittered, bringing a curse to Gage's throat. He didn't like the interested look on the guy's face, not a damn bit. Which pissed him off almost as much as the feeling itself.

"You on the hunt for someone now?" the man asked.

"Got a line on a young woman," Amber said. "She's a drug addict, on the run with some friends. Three, maybe four of them. Her MO is to hole up for a while, stay out of sight, until she thinks it's safe to surface."

Okay, that was a damn obvious deception. Gage squeezed her shoulder again. "We're not working tonight, Ginger. Remember that."

She took hold of one of his fingers. Didn't bend it back, but he figured she was tempted. "Thanks, Fred, dear. I keep forgetting that. Tell me, do you have any vacancies?" she asked the still-dazzled owner.

"What? Oh, yeah. Plenty. Twelve rooms, nine vacancies. Bar's where we make our money. You, er, fixing to stay a spell?"

"Only at the bar." Gage freed his finger, then moved his arm so he could catch hold of Amber's ponytail. "A drink, a meal, and we're back on the road. Got an old friend we want to see about twenty miles out of town."

"Harry, you get your butt over here," a woman with platinum-blond hair and black roots shouted from behind the bar.

The man's vision cleared in a snap. A scowl took its place. He swallowed a large mouthful of beer. "That's the wife yelling at me. Pretty woman walks in, she goes all green-eyed and suspicious. Y'all take care. First drink's on the house."

"Thank you, Harry," Amber began, but Gage cut her off by tugging gently on her ponytail.

"Yeah, thanks, Harry." His brows went up. "Washrooms?"

Harry wagged a finger to the right of the stage.

His eagle-eyed wife scarcely spared a glance at Harry as he made his way back to her through the crowd. Her gaze was locked on Amber, and it got meaner the closer her husband drew.

"Shit." Gage shoved Amber ahead of him. "She has her phone out."

Amber twisted her head to see. "Is that bad?"

"She's pointing at it and you. Harry's waving her off. Now she's stabbing the screen."

Swinging to face him, Amber caught all his fingers. "Are you saying there's a wanted poster out on me?"

"There's something." And Gage kicked himself that the idea hadn't occurred to him sooner. "My guess is Fixx and/or Mockerie put the word out about you to the criminal element first. But that word can be broadened substantially in today's world. Social media is a powerful tool. All they'd have to do is post a picture of you, say you were Fixx's sister who's gone missing, and offer a large reward for any information leading to your whereabouts."

Fortunately, he'd parked the Winnebago a good half mile away, far from probing eyes.

"There's a side door." He pointed straight ahead. "Go. Meet me at the RV."

She nodded, took the keys he gave her. "What're you going to do?"

"Create a diversion. I'll be right behind you."

She muttered something unflattering before they parted. He watched her jog toward the RV, made sure no one was following her, then ducked back inside and scanned the corridor walls. He spotted the red fire alarm, flipped up the casing, and pulled it.

The shriek was deafening up close. It cut through the music and noisy chatter. He hoped to hell it broke Harry's wife's train of thought.

As people poured through the exits, Gage took a moment to see who emerged from the motel rooms. The doors opened one, two, three. A pair of kids stumbled out of number three, a sixty-something male in his boxers ran out of number two, and a middle-aged couple in nightclothes shuffled from number one. They congregated under a lamppost, removed from the bar crowd. In the absence of any flames or smoke, they seemed anxious to return to their rooms.

Harry and his wife were the last to leave the bar. His wife had a phone placed to her ear, but every wild gesture she made appeared to involve the building. In the distance, Gage heard a siren. Thanks to a group of heavy-handed drinkers, chaos continued to ensue. For that moment, Harry's wife had weightier things on her mind than a raven-haired beauty whose face was very likely plastered across several social media sites.

Should have checked that out earlier today, he berated himself. He could have contacted McCabe and had him search for and pull any photos of Amber. But too little too late would likely be the catch phrase in that case. He'd have to revert to keeping Amber out of sight as much as possible, even in backwoods towns.

She had the key in the ignition and the engine idling when he joined her. "Anything?" she asked with head bent over the phone.

"Rachel's not here." Gage checked the mirrors, saw nothing, and eased the RV out of its hiding place. "Did you locate anything on the social media sites?"

"Lots." Amber passed him her cell. "I didn't have to dig very hard to find any of them. I'm Fixx's beloved stepsister and worth a cool million tonight. How flattering is that?"

"McCabe can wipe the pictures and the offer."

"It'll only pop up again someplace else. I want to say this surprises me." She took her phone back. "But it really doesn't. Fixx has all kinds of nasty tricks up his sleeve. He screwed Gareth up once. Owen wanted his son in the business. Gareth wanted to pursue his music. His father had him blackballed within the musicians' community. Under a false name, he flat out accused Gareth of plagiarizing another artist's songs."

"Gareth must have been pissed."

"He was. I gather he went into his father's hotel office shouting threats."

"How did he come out?"

"According to Luka, amazingly calm. Still waters," she said. After a last look, she shut down the site and plugged her phone into the lighter to charge it. "How long will it take McCabe to eighty-six the photos, et cetera?"

"He'll already be on it. I emailed him on my way back to the RV."

"A million dollars." Pressing on her eyelids, she gave a humorless laugh. "How high do you think Fixx will go?"

"Extremely, if he's smart and doesn't want to die himself. Mockerie has limited patience. How many million would it take for your sister to be tempted?"

He saw her indignation rise. Then he watched it bleed away. "I don't know," she admitted, and that time, she pressed the heels of her hands to her eyes. "A million might tempt her. I hope it wouldn't, but it might."

"And you still want to find her?"

"I said she *might* be tempted, not that she *would* be. She cares a lot about money, but believe it or not, there is more to her than that."

Unfortunately, McCabe's research, which Gage had tapped into, suggested there wasn't. All indications were that Rachel loved money and men above all things. From the Owen Fixxes of the world to anyone and everyone who could get her what she wanted.

Gage arranged to hook into the electrical outlets at a service station near Tupelo. They took turns using the washroom to clean up. Being a gentleman for once in his life, he let Amber have the bed while he made do with a foldout chair and a footstool. Before he slept, though, he needed to see what was what. So he took Elvis outside and let his iPad play while he contacted McCabe again.

"Pictures and reward offer are wiped," were the first words out of McCabe's mouth. "Are you safe? Is Amber?"

"She's asleep. I'm outside with the King and a Bud Light. You need to give me something here. We've got Fixx's or Mockerie's bastards chasing us all over hell and back. She's stuck on rescuing her sister, and I'm only half convinced the sister isn't trying to draw her in."

"Has Amber spoken to her?"

"In a limited way. Amber says the pleas for help are real. Maybe they are. Rachel seems to be a background player at this point. Fixx is relying on tails for the moment. One of them almost caught up to us at Mama K's."

"Shit."

"My sentiments exactly. She's carrying something, I can't figure out what, where, or when she acquired it. It wasn't in a vehicle. I ditched Abel's truck in a mud bog."

"He'll love you for that."

"You'll get him a new one. What have you got on Fixx's family members?"

"No more than Amber's probably told you."

"What about Sidney, Tom's slick counterpart?"

"Sidney Hollingsworth. Name sounds snotty, but he's a child of welfare and abuse. He clawed and scratched his way out of a nasty New York ghetto. Drives a Porsche Carrera these days."

"Interesting. Have you talked to Amber's actual contact?"

"Hell yes. Guy's been living in my office. He's also planted false information both in Black Creek and at the hotel where Amber used to work. Could be those false trails are what's keeping the numbers on your tail down to a manageable level."

"Define manageable."

He heard the grin in McCabe's voice. "Look at it this way, Gage, she's gorgeous, she's in trouble, and she's not a homicidal maniac. Keep your eyes open, and don't let little sis play her."

"Do my best." Gage took a long pull on his beer. "I want Almira Gulch next time."

"Next time," McCabe promised.

Gage disconnected, took another drink, and listened to the cacophony of riverside insects and animal life. One by one, he eliminated chirps, croaks, and hums. Until only one thing remained.

It was the sound of a powerful truck engine revving in the dark.

...

They kept to the back roads and managed to check out two more RC motels. Amber learned to skulk and creep. She even gritted her teeth and peeked through several unshaded windows. She saw two naked grandfathers, a couple who'd snuck a pit bull into their room, and a man who might have been a shoplifter emptying stuffed Owen Sheffel bags onto his bed.

Intriguing discoveries, but no sign of Rachel or her captors anywhere.

Her phone rang while she waited for Gage to check out the last room in the second motel. She answered at once. "Rachel! Where are you?"

"I got away." Her sister's voice was low and urgent. "They

left me alone with a guy named Benny. I bonked him on the head with a whiskey bottle."

"Who's Benny?" Amber began, but she shook the question off. "Never mind. It's not important. Where are you?"

"I don't know. Near a road. I hear traffic. I think there's a lake somewhere around here, too. I smell water."

"That could be the river." As she talked, Amber jogged around the motel with the hope of intercepting Gage. Stars glimmered overhead, so she took care to stick to the shadows. "Can you give me something else?"

"No. I'm scared to move."

Amber tried another tack. "Do you know where you were, where they were holding you?"

"No." The tears came. She heard them in Rachel's voice. She also heard the telltale quiver of fear. "If they find me, they'll take me back, and I'm afraid they'll hurt me."

Meaning they hadn't yet. Amber spotted Gage and waved him forward. "Who was holding you, Rachel? Was it Owen?"

"No! He wouldn't. He's not a monster. We should go to him. You come and find me, and we'll go to Las Vegas, both of us. We'll make him listen."

"That won't work." Amber put the call on speaker for Gage. "It doesn't matter what you want or even what Owen wants. It's James Mockerie who's running the show, and he wants us dead."

"I know that name. Mockerie. Why do I know it?"

"He's Owen's boss. Now stand up and head toward the road. Don't let anyone see you; just locate a sign and tell me what it says."

"Won't they be looking for me on the road?"

"I said find a sign, not flap your arms at oncoming traffic."

"I hate you for doing this to me." Rachel's tension bled through a line that cut in and out. "It's cold, I'm wet, I think

I disturbed a skunk, and the ground's all soft and icky. Oh, wait. There's a sign. Stupid place to put it. I need a flashlight." Amber heard a *click*. "Good thing that asshole Jess smoked. It says Bitterroot Lake."

Amber glanced at Gage, who entered the location into his phone. "Just a minute. We're Googling it."

"Who's we? Oh, yuck, something slimy fell on my head." A short, sharp scream followed. "It's a slug, a big, creepy slug." She burbled out a sob. "Get me out of this nightmare. Alexa—Amber. Make it go away."

"Love to," Amber said under her breath. "Do you have a location?" she asked Gage.

"She's seventy-five miles due south of here. Unfortunately, the roads run anything but straight between us and her. As a point of interest, there aren't any RC motels in the vicinity."

"So, either they weren't holding her in an RC motel or..." She raised her phone. "Rachel, did you hitch a ride with someone?"

"Well, duh. I wanted to get away. That was the point, right? You'd be a bad fugitive, Amber. God, I hate slugs." The quiver returned. "Driver got all winky and crude after a while, so I told him I was fourteen and a preacher's kid. Running away because my mean bastard uncle who's a sheriff beat on me when I wouldn't put out. That did the trick. It was all 'here's your hat, what's your hurry' once he heard the word 'sheriff'. Who're you with, Amber?"

"His name's Gage. He can help, but you need to stay where you are, at Bitterroot Lake. Are there cabins or homes there?"

"Some cabins. They're all dark, no cars outside them. What should I do? I'm cold, and it's starting to rain."

"Tell her to try and break into one of the cabins," Gage said. "But only if she's sure no one's there."

"*She* heard that," Rachel snapped back. "Tell whoever he

is, whatever he is, that she's—I'm—not an idiot. I'll make sure the cabin's empty. Just hurry up and get here before someone figures out where I am and wraps me up in a stinky blanket again."

The line went dead.

Gage slid Amber a level look. "You're sure she's not part of this?"

No. Or, well, yes. Maybe. In the end, Amber sighed. "I'm not sure of anything at this point, but my instincts say she's as frightened as I am."

"Guess we'll have to go with that. Let's move, Snowbird. We've got a long drive ahead of us."

Amber adjusted her ponytail. "Long," she agreed, "and probably loaded with pitfalls."

Chapter Thirteen

The drive was difficult on twisty back roads. Gage let Elvis fill the air while his mind ran a dozen different scenarios.

Beside him, Amber slept and looked annoyingly gorgeous doing it. He was tempted to pull off the band that held her hair back, but that would be pure self-indulgence, and he didn't have time for it. Or the inclination to venture any deeper into an emotional minefield he should never have set foot in from the start. *Stupid,* he told himself. He knew better than to let his feelings rule his brain. If nothing else, Lydia had taught him that gut-wrenching lesson.

He braked at a fork in the road. Old highway or interstate? Did it matter?

The throaty truck he'd been hearing behind them continued to maintain its distance. Similar to the way he and Amber had been holding each other at arm's length. Kissing her hadn't alleviated a single sexual urge. And if he didn't find a way to manage those urges, they could both wind up dead. To say nothing of what might happen to Rachel.

He didn't want to do it, but a fuel gauge with a needle

resting on empty forced him to pull into an all-night service station. He filled up on McCabe's dime, and bought two coffees, a couple of subs, and a large candy bar. He made a point of using a deep Southern accent and telling the cashier he sure as hell wasn't looking forward to spending the winter aboard an oil rig in the north Atlantic.

The young man sympathized and wished him luck.

Amber woke up when he slammed the door. She blinked, attempted to focus. "Where are we?" She looked around. "Gas station? Is there a restroom?"

"Probably, but you can use the one behind us. There's plenty of water in the reservoir."

She made a frustrated sound. "I'd say I hate you if you weren't helping me." She regarded his iPod. "Do you have Dolly Parton on there?"

"No."

She checked her own phone. "I do."

"And hearing that's supposed to make me want to keep helping you?"

"Her music's happy, Gage. I need some happy right now."

"Elvis did happy music."

"Only in his movies. If you have 'Blue Hawaii', I'll listen, otherwise, I want Dolly." She tilted her head at him. "It was a woman, wasn't it? A female who made you become all reticent and introverted."

"I'm not an introvert, Amber, I just like my own space."

"Do you have friends?"

A smile ghosted across his lips. "One or two."

"Are they cops?"

"Most are. Not all."

"I assume you met Scrap at the commune. What about Bear?"

"I met him in the Army. We served together for two years. You already know where I met Abel."

"Your mentor."

"Teacher. The word 'mentor' is too close to the idea of hero worship, and I don't worship heroes."

"So, you're a God-fearing man."

"God and some men. Drink your coffee, and eat your sub. I'm not about to discuss my fears and philosophies with you."

"Fine. How far are we from Bitterroot Lake?"

"Twenty-one miles."

"That's not far. You just turned onto a highway, right?"

"An old one. Not much traffic. Unfortunately."

"Why?" She immediately checked her side mirror. "Is someone behind us?"

"A shadow for the moment. Not a major concern. Did you hear something pop a minute ago?"

"No." Learning forward, she squinted into the blackness behind them. "I don't see lights, Gage. And I didn't hear a gun."

"I said a pop, not a bang. RV's riding low on my side in the back. We blew a tire. And if you knew Scrap, you'd know he won't have a usable spare."

"Uh, I'm not sure that's going to matter."

Amber pointed at the road ahead, where no fewer than eight motorcycles were angled crosswise from shoulder to shoulder. The riders, Gage noted, hovered near the ditches. All of them appeared to be brandishing knives.

Reaching for his gun, he muttered, "Just fucking perfect. Somewhere along the line, we traded the Yellow Brick Road for the Highway to Hell. Hold on, Snowbird."

She shot him a doubtful look, but braced herself. Gage hit the gas, felt the RV leap forward. As long as they were on the road, he might as well knock down the gates of Hell.

Still laying into the gas, he lowered the window, took aim, and fired. The bikers jumped back, the front of the RV struck metal, and the night exploded.

...

Amber had never met a true renegade before. It was weirdly sexy. Terrifying, but a definite turn-on. Which proved more than ever that she was losing her mind.

Pieces of motorcycle flew in every direction. The RV's windshield cracked, but didn't shatter. Gage seemed to know exactly where to hit the line, because when she looked in the mirror, the entire row of bikes appeared to be out of commission.

She stared for several moments before offering a relatively calm, "Were they after money?"

"And jewelry. Anything of value. They call themselves the Night Raiders. I live and work in Tennessee. The raiders have been problematic there and in Mississippi for a few years now."

"Did you wound any of them?"

"Got a leg and a couple of arms. The bikes are more seriously injured than they are. Right rear's still flat. We can't drive thirty miles on it. Google an auto wrecking yard in the vicinity of Hamelin, Mississippi."

"One that's open after midnight and conveniently run by vampires." Leaning back, she slid him a quick, sarcastic look. "I can't imagine how many of those places might exist."

He smiled. "Google it, Amber."

Still a bit stoked, she did as he asked and pinpointed two local businesses. "Jack's Truck Junk and Leon's Auto Wreckers. Take your pick for what it's worth. They both closed their doors at five p.m."

"I like the idea of Truck Junk. How far?"

She regarded the screen, motioned left. "Off the Highway to Hell, maybe a mile east. The yard's bound to be gated,

Gage."

"Yep."

"Meaning you know how to pick locks?"

He smiled again. "Keep thinking about your sister."

"Shouldn't we check for a spare first? Scrap might surprise you."

"I checked before we left. There's a tire, but the tread's bare, and it has a two-inch hole in one side."

"Your friends have the most interesting mindsets. Go left again."

Another half mile brought them to a wooden gate held shut with a rusty but stout padlock.

Gage wasted no time. He clicked on a silencer and shot out the lock. Then indicated the flat. "We need a tire, the same size as this one, on a rim."

Amber's phone beeped while she was wandering through the crowded yard by flashlight.

"I broke a window and climbed into a cabin," Rachel said without preamble. "It smells like cow dung inside."

"Don't turn on any lights," Amber warned her.

"Don't worry. Nowhere around here is on any kind of grid. This sucks, Amber. I am so dirty. Are you and whoever almost here?"

"We're working on it. Has Owen contacted you since you were abducted?"

"No, and they wouldn't let me call him, either. Maybe I should try from here."

Amber spotted a tire, kicked it. Then she realized what her sister had just said and she stopped. "Rachel, you need to listen to me. Owen Fixx is an unfeeling bastard who kills without a second thought."

"No, he isn't. He doesn't." Rachel huffed out a weary breath. "Criminal or not, I was happy with my jackpot win, Amber. I really was. All you had to do was say no to the FBI.

You could have looked the other way and married Gareth. Then win, win, we'd both have been living the high life. We still could, if… Oh, to hell with it." She sighed. "Just hurry up and get here before one of those assholes finds me. Hurry, Amber, please."

Gage walked toward her along a narrow path between stacks of trucks that creaked and groaned and occasionally threatened to topple. "I found a tire. There's an air pump outside the office. Were you talking to Rachel?"

"She wants us to hurry."

"Was she wobbling?"

"No." Amber slipped the phone into her pocket. "I'm thinking she's in shock. She's angry with me for not marrying Gareth." Her gaze rose as one of the overhead creaks grew louder. "We should go. Does Scrap have a jack, or do we have to steal that, too?"

"We're not stealing anything. I'll leave enough cash to cover the damaged lock and the tire. It's getting windy."

She shivered. "I noticed… No, I'm fine. You don't have to do that."

Ignoring her, he draped an arm over her shoulders. "This is for warmth, not a quick grope in the dark."

Not that she'd have minded a quick grope, but…no.

"We're doing this for Rachel," she said out loud. "It has nothing to do with you or me or potential sex in a crappy RV."

"Point taken. I'll give you my jacket. After I change the tire, we'll drive the thirty miles and see what's waiting for us at Bitterroot Lake."

She accepted the offering, zipped it up. "She's not involved… Whoa, wait, what was that?"

Amber looked up quickly as one of the creaks above them became a loud shriek of cascading metal.

She glimpsed an avalanche of motion a split second before she hit the ground, with Gage on top of her and stars glittering like diamonds in her skull. When the shriek faded to eerie silence, nothing moved in the wrecking yard. Not the fallen metal, not her, and not Gage.

...

Twenty minutes later, Gage's head was clear enough that he could swear at McCabe and the world in general while Amber cleaned a cut on his forehead. Junkyards were accidents waiting to happen. He should have paid more attention to the dangers around them.

"Sit for a minute." She went into the RV's kitchen to look for a bandage. "You don't think we should do this, do you? Go to Bitterroot Lake."

"I think we'll be walking into something and it won't be pretty. Look what we walked into right here, and this had nothing to do with Fixx's people."

She inspected the cut above his eye. "Give me an alternative, then. Tell me what we can do besides what Fixx expects."

"Not a damn thing. We play the hand we're dealt and hope to hell we're quicker and smarter than he is." Gage stood and waited for the pain in his side. When it didn't materialize beyond a quick twinge, he reached for his jacket. "I need to use the air compressor. Tidy up what you need to in here. Then we'll change the tire and leave. Maybe I'll come up with a brilliant idea before we get to Bitterroot Lake."

Or maybe he'd go with the one already swimming in his head.

While the air compressor hummed, he emailed McCabe. For some reason, his mind wanted to slide back to a more bizarre period in his life. He stopped the weird descent, but not without a fight. Amber wasn't Lydia. And who knew, Rachel might turn out to be halfway pleasant, as well.

Unlikely, but people had surprised him before.

He saw Amber moving around inside the Winnebago and made his decision. He used the keypad, waited for the ring.

"Come on, you know it's me." Partway through the third ring, he heard a rough laugh.

"It's already done, old friend. Nothing left to say or do on my end. I know where you are, and you know where I am. I'd say mission accomplished, except we both know it isn't." Another harsh sound rumbled from the speaker. "Have a nice trip, Gage. I'm guessing I'll see you and your lady in hell."

...

They slept, because neither of them was functioning at full capacity. Four hours and a whole lot of doubts and questions later, Amber was back in her seat in the RV, searching for road signs that would point the way to their destination. Dolly's "Coat of Many Colors" played on her iPhone. Oddly, the music didn't make her happy right then.

"You've veered over the center line twice in the last fifteen minutes," she said to Gage. "Are you sure you didn't hit your head harder than you told me back in the junkyard?"

"I've been shot in the head before and survived," he replied. "The steering on this thing is loose as hell. You can try driving it yourself if you don't believe me."

"Crankiness after the fact can signify a concussion." She smiled a little when he sent her a dark look. "Okay, fine. What do you mean you've been shot in the head?"

He shrugged. "Shot, grazed, whatever. There were bullets involved. A bit of falling debris is no big deal."

"Hmm." Amber spotted a sign. "Bitterroot Lake, five miles. The exit should be coming up soon. Have you had any brilliant ideas about how we can get Rachel out?"

"There are no brilliant ideas in situations like these. There's calculation, which is usually wrong, theory, which is seldom the right one, and pure dumb luck. You have to figure we'll all wind up dead. However, since I don't have a viable alternative, we're going in. Does Rachel understand what we want her to do?"

"Stay low, keep quiet, and do exactly as she's been told. She wants out. I think she'll cooperate."

"All the way?"

"I hope so."

"Call her then," he said, "and let's get this done."

Amber used her speed dial.

"Amber?" Rachel shouted into her phone. "Why is this taking so long?"

"Don't talk, just listen, okay?" Code, she reminded herself. She had to stick to it, for all their sakes. "Remember when we were kids, and you and Elijah and I wanted to get away from the screaming at home? I need you to do what we did back then, but add in our midnight escapes during the hottest part of summer. All that heat and humidity. It was like being underwater. And when we got there, we were mermaids, free and unburdened in a world where no one could yell at us."

"Oh God, I hate all this coded gobbledygook the Witness Protection people taught us to use. I don't know how, but I understand what you want me to do, and I'll do it."

"Good. We're almost there. You'll see our headlights in a few minutes. Be ready. Do exactly as I told you, and trust me."

She ended the call before Rachel could blurt out anything that would give Gage's plan—in as much as Amber actually understood it—away.

When Gage parked the RV, she turned to confront him.

"You haven't told me everything, have you?"

"No." He stuffed weapons in his waistband and pockets. "If I had, you'd be arguing with me, or trying to modify part of it, and we don't have time. Rachel needs to do as she's been instructed. Nothing more, nothing less. And you need to stay close behind me."

Which made no sense to Amber and only served to widen the cracks in her belief that any of them would survive this night. Unfortunately, since she had nothing better to offer, she trailed him through the dense woods toward the cabin Rachel had described to them.

The shadows shifted as filmy layers of cloud passed over the moon. "Less light would be good," Gage remarked. He had a gun in each hand and three more that Amber knew of in his belt. "Do you see anything? Anyone?"

She shook her head, realized he couldn't see her, and whispered a soft, "No. Unless…" Had she spied a movement on the far side of the cabin? "Straight ahead, Gage. Was that someone?"

"Chances are." He went down on one knee, waited. "Trust me," he said when she opened her mouth to speak. "This is all about faith, timing, and your sister's willingness to follow through. We know this is probably a trap with Rachel as the bait."

It required a huge effort, but Amber knelt behind him. This wasn't quite what she'd envisioned, rescue-wise. She assumed his intention was to pick off Fixx's men back here, before moving in and helping Rachel.

Her sharp eyes spotted a definite movement. One, then two, and behind them, a third. "Near the twin pine trees," she told him. "Can you see those three men?"

"Yeah." He raised both hands. "A little more to the left, guys. And…"

He fired both guns simultaneously, with no gaps between

shots. The rapid blasts reminded Amber of an Uzi. She saw the first man fall, and the third. The second almost made it to the shelter of a giant sycamore, but Gage's bullet took him down.

He dropped his weapons. "Reload those." He motioned downward. "And keep an eye on the woods behind us."

She did both things. And caught the sound of someone creeping through the bushes. Snapping the clip in, she shot twice. The bushes stopped rustling as the creeping man staggered backward and fell into view.

"Shit." Her hands started to shake. "Shit. I think he's dead."

"That's the idea, Snowbird. I got two more on the west side of the cabin."

"How will we know when they're all…gone?"

"That'll be the dumb luck part."

A scream cut through the darkness.

"Rachel." Amber whipped her head around. She started to rise, but Gage yanked her down.

"If she shuts up, she'll be fine."

However, instead of quieting down, Rachel screamed again. "Get away from me, you bastard!"

Bodies streamed toward the cabin. Gage shot, but the first two made it to safety. "Christ."

"Don't touch me!" Rachel shrieked. "I don't care who you are."

Rifles went off. Rachel continued to yell. "Dammit… ouch! Aren't you…? Oh God, Amber! I think I did it wrong."

More rifle fire exploded.

"You assholes! Rachel screamed. "Wait until Owen hears about this. You won't… Amber, help me. I messed up!"

"Run." Gage pulled Amber to her feet.

"But…"

He grabbed her hand. "Rachel screwed herself, Amber.

All she had to do was listen and think, and she didn't."

Amber took a last desperate look back, then gave up and ran toward the RV with Gage.

"What happened?" she demanded once they were inside. "Did one of them get past us and grab her?"

"In a way. Son of a bitch. Watch your mirror." He floored the gas pedal. "Tell me what you see."

"Nothing," she said. She peered more closely. "Wait, there's something back in the trees. I see two sets of lights."

He braked so suddenly, she had no time to brace. She rammed her shoulder into the dash.

"Get your pack," he said. "We're switching vehicles."

She reached for her backpack and phone. "Have you lost your mind?" She saw an empty truck to his right, but still. "What if you can't hotwire it?"

"Then we're dead. Go."

She shoved the door open, jumped out, and ran for the truck.

"It's not a new vehicle," Gage said once they were inside. "It won't have antitheft everything." Yanking wires, he got the engine running. "Hold on tight."

Amber twisted back and forth in her seat, struggled to keep the headlights behind them in sight. Gage, she noticed, wasn't using theirs.

"What's this for?" she asked when he tossed her his phone. She regarded the already lit screen. "Who am I calling?"

"Just hope he answers."

"Who?" Since Gage had already speed-dialed the person in question, all she could do was listen.

A litany of curses burst from the speaker after the third ring.

"What went down?" Gage demanded, swinging the wheel hard. "Are you hurt?"

"Bullet sliced my arm. My nuts hurt like a bitch."

Amber blinked. "Bear? What in God's name are you doing here, or anywhere near here?"

"Getting myself kicked, scratched, and spit on. Your sister's an effing wildcat. And I'm sorry, Amber, but I lost my grip when one of those flying bullets carved a half-inch groove through my bicep. Your sister spooked and ran. Fixx's people grabbed her. Knocked her out cold."

Amber said nothing. What could she say?

"How did you get away?" she asked instead.

"It's what I do. I killed two, but there was a swarm of others behind them. And you better know they're not gonna let a few dead guys put a damper on their enthusiasm. Word on the criminal underground—and don't ask me how I know—is that the reward's spiked to two million. You want my take? Mockerie's past the detonation point. When he goes off, the fiery bits are gonna rain down like shrapnel. Only word someone like him knows in the end is 'dead'. That's how he wants you. Dead and buried. And you'd better hope he wants to do it in that order."

Chapter Fourteen

Pain was having a field day in Owen's head. Any minute, it was going to start leaking from his ears. On its heels would be blood. James was going to kill him. Slowly, though, and without a sliver of compassion.

He had his phone on speaker. His head rested on his folded arms atop the office desk as he spoke to his second. "Explain again, in detail, how more than a dozen fully trained mercenaries missed the target and landed us right back at square one."

"Morgan picked them off," the caller informed him coldly. "There was another guy in the mix, as well. He had Rachel. It must have been his responsibility, or burden, to pull her out of there. We had her bugged, so we knew something was up. We just didn't know the specifics of Morgan's plan. And we sure as hell didn't count on a wildcard built like a gorilla on steroids to be part of the deal. Be grateful we got the bitch back."

Owen raised his head high enough to swallow a mouthful of whiskey. "Why should I be grateful? I'll be lucky to make it through this night alive. Raise the reward. Two and a half million, no questions asked, Swiss bank account, et cetera. If nothing happens, we'll go higher. Maybe Morgan will turn."

"And maybe hell will freeze over, or the big boss will sprout wings and a halo, but I'm not holding my breath."

Owen emitted a humorless snort of laughter at the mocking tone. "Gloat away," he slurred. "Big boss gets well and truly pissed, you'll be as dead as I am."

"No chance." There was a lengthy pause, followed by a slightly less cocky, "Why would he kill me? I'm only the messenger, the keeper of the goods."

"I'm sure that'll be taken into consideration... Not. Do yourself a favor, lose the attitude and figure out where the fuck Morgan's taken her."

"What about Rachel? Kill or keep?"

Owen took another deep swallow. "Keep. For now. I have to call Mockerie. Or... Crap, no I don't. He's climbing the stairs from the casino as we speak. If you don't hear from me again, watch your back."

"You're insane," his second said in disgust.

"Must be in the genes," Owen mumbled.

He ended the call, took a final drink, and sat up to watch the doorknob ahead of him turn.

...

By three a.m., Amber was too exhausted, emotionally and physically, to think in a logical manner. She and Gage managed to steal a few hours of sleep. Not that it really helped. Bear's name and face ran through her head like a bad movie skipping back over the same snippet of film.

Owen had Rachel. Again. Bear had been shot, and she and Gage were driving God knew where on roads that probably hadn't been used since horse and buggy days.

She drank cold coffee to wake herself up, then thought to hell with it and hunted up a bottle of whiskey. She poured three inches into the empty coffee cup, sniffed it, and downed a third of the fiery liquid.

"Pour me some of that," Gage said wearily.

"No."

"Amber…"

"I'm not listening and I'm absolutely not talking to you." She drank again. "I don't know all the reasons why yet, but it involves Bear, that stupid code thing you had me try and make Rachel understand—which she mostly did, by the way, except for the naked and wrapped in a blanket part. I'm not sure she got that. We used to run to the lake when our parents fought, wrapped in towels. Skinny dipping was empowering somehow. But that was then. She might not have understood why she shouldn't wear her clothes outside the cabin."

"Tracking devices." Gage glanced over as she tossed back the rest of the whiskey. "They're incredibly sophisticated these days. If she'd left all her possessions—clothes, shoes, phone, everything—near another cabin as you tried to explain to her earlier, that's where Fixx's people would likely have gone. She took something with her."

"Her phone," Amber told him. "And her shoes. It's too cold to be barefoot outside."

"There you go." Gage shrugged a shoulder. "It still might have worked if she hadn't put up a fight when Bear showed up to get her out."

"He was a stranger. He grabbed her. What would you have done in her place?"

"Probably the same thing—until he told me he was with you and there to help me."

Feeling frustrated, angry, and a hundred other things she didn't want to examine right then, Amber poured more whiskey. She allowed Gage a stingy quarter inch in his cup and thrust it at him. "I'm still not happy with you. I might be able to drink my mad away, but it doesn't always work. I'm not much of a drinker overall and..." She trailed off. "Who's Lydia?" The shock and trailing suspicion in his expression had amusement breaking through her annoyance. "You didn't like that question, did you?" She drank more. "Why not? Did she dump you?"

The look he gave her was nanodegrees short of lethal. "What Lydia did or didn't do is none of your business." A scowl invaded his features and made her want to take a bite of him. "How do you even know about her?"

She glanced into her cup, swirled the whiskey. "You talk in your sleep. My name came up. Well, my code name, anyway. Then you said Lydia. I think you threw a punch, but it was too dark for me to be sure. Did you hit her?"

His eyes narrowed dangerously. "No."

"Did she hit you?"

"Are you drunk?"

"Working on it. I told you, I'm not much of a drinker. Can't overindulge and effectively climb the career ladder. That's where Rachel and I differed. A lot. I wanted to make money. She preferred to marry it." Frowning slightly, Amber thought back. "She said something to me when we talked. It didn't make sense."

"Something about Fixx?"

"I don't think so. Like that, but no. Are you going to answer my question from before?"

"Change the subject, Amber."

Her lips curved into a teasing smile. "What was your rank in the LAPD? I'm guessing Lieutenant."

"Good guess."

"Plain clothes? Homicide?"

"You have moments of serious spookiness, Snowbird."

"I'm good at reading people." She checked the bottle,

poured more. "Your cop facade's not all that deeply buried. Except I think you're more reckless now that you're not one. Abel definitely is."

"And now we're back to him, are we? This is one wide-ranging conversation. Do you think Abel turned you in?"

"I don't know. I'm worth a fortune, apparently. Bear followed us. Maybe he turned me in."

"Bear followed us because he owed me more than one favor from our Army days."

"You recognized his truck's engine, didn't you? I thought it sounded familiar, but I never made the connection between the engine we kept hearing and Bear's Ram-erado." She studied Gage from the side. He really was so damn gorgeous. And hot. "Were you engaged?"

"Nope. We just served together in the Army."

Amber calmly finished her second cup of whiskey. "You're being ridiculously perverse."

He took the bottle from her before she could pour another drink. "You've had enough for one night. You're not watching for headlights."

"Yes, I am. I'm an excellent multitasker. I'm also stubborn, sometimes contrary, and I have a tendency to let things I don't like fester and grow. That comes from my Irish side. Grudges are sacrosanct and temper's a given. Like elephants, we never forget what we don't like."

"Does that mean I should worry about you shooting me in my sleep?"

"I don't know." She took the bottle back. "I haven't gotten to the festering stage yet. That's why I'm drinking. I'm hoping to bypass it. Tomorrow's another day, right?" When Gage veered off the lumpy road and pointed the truck down a treacherous incline, Amber felt her stomach bounce briefly into her throat. "Uh, do you have any idea what's at the bottom of this roller coaster dip?"

"Hopefully a dry creek bed. Or it could be a rushing river. You might want to cross your fingers."

"I did that with Rachel. Didn't work. She's so dumb, Gage." Amber rescued the bottle before it spilled. "But that's no reason for you not to tell me about your guy-plan with Bear. Guy-plans gone wrong are fodder for a good fester and subsequent Irish grudge. If you'd told me about it at the time, then asked me not to tell Rachel, I wouldn't have."

"And I'm supposed to know that?"

She stabbed the air between them. "Lydia let you down, didn't she? Betrayed and/or disappointed you in some unforgiveable way."

Grabbing the whiskey, he tipped it up and drank a mouthful. "Let it go, Amber, before *my* Irish roots start showing."

He wasn't going to talk, wasn't prepared to tell her anything about his past. It shouldn't bother her, that reticent James Dean attitude of his. He'd been sent to protect her. The rescuing Rachel part had been her idea. Not the best one she'd ever had, but Rachel was her sister. How could she be expected to leave her?

"You know what we should do." Curling a leg up under her, Amber faced Gage. "We should attack rather than run. Set a trap of our own. If we're feeling really bold, we could do it in Las Vegas. Or New Mexico. But Las Vegas would probably be the best place. Owen likes really lavish parties." She grinned. "On the flip side, he also spends time in scrungy bars where everyone smokes and drinks and has sex in bathroom stalls."

Gage stopped the whiskey bottle halfway to his mouth. "Where the hell did that come from? The scrungy bar and sex in the bathroom part?"

She bit her lip, thought back. "I'm not sure. It was just there in my head. Obviously, more information snuck in than

I realized. I know his nephew Luka liked sex in back alleys, but Owen's always so proper and clean. So polished." She struggled to think past the haze in her head. "Could that be helpful?"

"Depends." Gage used the thankfully dry riverbed as a roadway. The truck pitched and rocked, forcing Amber to uncurl and hang on. "Can you name one of his slimy hangouts?"

"Not offhand. And I'm not sure he'd be in Las Vegas at this point. Wouldn't Mockerie want him where Rachel is? Not with her necessarily, but in the vicinity?"

"If not now, he will eventually. Whoever's holding your sister will be someone Fixx trusts."

"Money can buy trust, Gage. Fixx has very loyal people on his payroll."

Gage shook his head. "This is Fixx's life on the line. You don't trust your life to a worker. A brother or a nephew or a son maybe, but not a worker."

Amber's mind drifted back to Las Vegas. "I think—I'm not positive, but I think Rachel's personal assistant Lauren might be Owen's second cousin. That would make her family, wouldn't it?"

"What about her trainer?"

"Helmut?" Amber tapped her temples with her index fingers. "Nothing here about him. He's Swedish, though, and for some reason, I'm thinking Owen's mother is Swedish. There could be a connection." Her brow knit. "I've lost the thread of this conversation. Are we planning to do something, or just trying to establish who might be holding Rachel?"

"Possibly both."

Suspicion she didn't want to feel formed slippery knots in her stomach. She hoped it was the whiskey making her uneasy and not her instincts, because to doubt Gage at that point could mean death, for her and for Rachel.

"Tom warned me Rachel would be a problem." Amber watched through the treetops as tendrils of cloud drifted across the moon. "I knew he was right, but what could I do? We had to go into the WPP. Maybe she had a point, and I should have said no to the FBI. I wouldn't have married Gareth, but who says Owen would have killed her like I'm sure he did his other wives? It's possible Rachel was his one true love." Her lips curved. "And maybe I'm a bit drunk at that. The Fixxes of the world don't love people. They love power and money and probably themselves. Gareth never believed Owen loved him. I figure that's what made him become so obsessive."

"Who's obsessive?"

She turned her head on the worn rest. "Gareth. He's OCD, or close to it. He keeps his guitars in neat little rows the same way Owen lines up his files and his books and the suits in his closet. Underwear, too, according to Rachel. I imagine Luka and Owen's brother Tony are the same. Is Mockerie?"

"Is he what?"

"OCD." Irritation rose. "Are you even listening to me?"

"I'm listening. I'm also thinking. Fixx isn't going to hold your sister in this manner indefinitely. Taking her back to Las Vegas would be the smart thing. Every time he's thwarted, his strategy should change to some extent. It only makes sense. He tried a trap here. It failed. Time to make another attempt somewhere else. That somewhere could be Las Vegas."

"Does that mean we have to wait and see what happens next? Drive in circles until Owen or one of his people contacts us?"

"Or until whoever's been assigned to follow us catches up."

Amber pulled the band from her ponytail and ran her fingers through her hair. "You've checked out everything I own: my clothes, my boots, my phone, my jewelry, even my shampoo, makeup, and moisturizer. What's left?"

He set the whiskey bottle on the seat between his legs, capped what remained. "Something I'm missing. On a more positive note, the terrain we've covered is virtually undriveable. We need sleep, they'll need sleep. I'll see if I can set up a band of interference between us and them. If it works, it'll buy us some down time."

"How do you set up…? Never mind." She waved the question aside. "If you can do it, do it. I want a hot bath and a bed with a mattress that doesn't sag. Are either of those things in the realm of possibility at whatever o'clock it currently is in the morning?"

"We'll make a quick stop. I'll see what I can do interference-wise, then we'll head south, grab some sleep. Don't get your hopes up, though, Snowbird. I'm good with tech, but I'm not a techno geek."

His "quick stop" lasted more than an hour. He used the stolen truck's radio. Apparently, it had power and range. It screwed up any cell phone reception they might have needed, but Amber was fine with the sacrifice. She really wanted that bath.

She wanted Gage, too, she reflected while he worked on rewiring the exposed connections. Unfortunately, any involvement, even a one-night stand, would only lead to complications she didn't need.

He slapped the panel back into place. "You don't ask, I won't ask. I'm done. We should be good for a while. They'll break through it eventually, but we'll get some sleep in the meantime."

"Great. Where?"

"I'm thinking Peachland."

She retied her hair. "Please tell me we're not in Georgia."

"Nope. Mississippi. Not far from Jackson"

"So we won't be striking out for Las Vegas anytime soon."

"That'll depend on the strategy we devise and what happens with Rachel."

Amber held out a hand for the whiskey. "My head's spinning, but not entirely from the alcohol. I want my buzz back."

He glanced at her. "I don't think so, Snowbird."

"Lydia," she said simply.

A muscle in his jaw twitched. He didn't swear or say anything at all. He just dropped his phone in the dock and let Elvis take over.

Of course, it was music from the King's Las Vegas years. Rather than fight the memories, Amber took a slow drink of whiskey and went back to another time, another place. Another world.

...

Even when he felt sure she was asleep, Gage resisted the urge to make a phone call. Better to let Elvis keep his thoughts centered and his mind on the immediate goal.

She still didn't trust him, not all the way. He didn't blame her. In her position, he wouldn't trust him, either. With reason in this case.

The sign for Peachland came into view and, with it, the first light of dawn. The timing couldn't have been better. The truck needed gas and the tank had a lock on it. It was a minor problem, but one he didn't intend to solve in full view of a station attendant.

The Starlight Motel sign he spotted appealed on a number of levels. One, it was here, two, it looked like something from the fifties, and three, there was a café rather than a bar attached to it. Four minivans sat in the lot. That meant families. He'd park the truck on the side of the building and hope to hell the interference band he'd rigged would hold for a few more hours.

"Wake up, Amber." Leaning across her, he unstrapped her seat belt. "Time for that hot bath and a real bed."

"Back off, Gareth." She pushed on his hand. "I'm not..." Her eyes opened. "Where am I? Why does my head feel like it wants to explode?"

"We're at the Starlight Motel, and you're hungover because you're a lightweight when it comes to holding your whiskey."

"I am," she agreed.

Because he was already leaning that way, he took advantage of their close proximity and kissed her. Not deeply, not at first, and certainly not for a long period of time. Even so, the instant burst of heat surprised him. Something tightened in his stomach as the taste of her tempted him to slide in farther and savor.

He dragged his mouth away and saw her lips quirk. "Your idea, your consequences. I know better than to do that."

So should've he, dammit. He'd only meant it as a wakeup call. And maybe a bit of enjoyment.

"Get your stuff," he told her and picked up his guns. "Memorize this. We're heading north for your brother's wedding in Raleigh. Wedding's tomorrow. We got held up in Baton Rouge, at my grandmother's. Now we're in a race against the clock. A few hours of rest and we'll be good to go."

"Got it." She climbed out to stretch. "Ask if the rooms have bathtubs."

And cold showers, he thought, heading for the lobby.

It was still dark enough for the main room to be lit. He smelled coffee and told himself not to beg. Caffeine could wait.

The man at the desk barely bothered to look up from his tablet as Gage signed the register and paid.

"Twenty-three's empty," he said in an absent tone. "Café opens at six a.m. Ham and eggs are decent. Y'all enjoy your stay."

So much for the backstory. Gage stepped out and gave Amber the key to room twenty-three. "I'll park the truck. Don't go inside until I'm with you. Keep your gun ready."

"Is it weird that that last remark is starting to sound normal to me?"

"Not weird, just unfortunate." He wanted to kiss her again, but it was better to keep a clear head. Returning to the truck instead, he pulled out his phone and drove around to the far side of the motel.

"'Bout damn time," Bear snarled at him. "When and where?"

"Two hours, give or take, depending on where you are. We're at the Starlight Motel, on the outskirts of Peachland. I need this to work, old friend."

"Uh-huh. By the way, word is the reward'll be up to three million by noon today. If this goes on, friends are going to be harder and harder to keep. Two hours, Gage. Unless something happens in the meantime."

Ominous statements, Gage reflected, issued from the depths of an increasingly murky situation. Amber didn't trust him all the way, and he didn't trust anyone more than halfway.

Not even himself.

Chapter Fifteen

A hot bath in a mediocre tub in a crappy motel raised Amber's spirits more than she'd expected. Gage left her alone, which evoked mixed feelings on her part. In the end, it was just as well. Confusion had become a state of mind where he was concerned. Did she want him? Yes. Would having sex with him solve any of her problems? Probably not, but still…

Calling Tom was an option, though maybe not the best idea on the off chance her phone really was bugged. Instead, she rested her head on the back of the tub and let the heat of the water lull her into a drowsy state.

Why couldn't Rachel have followed instructions?

Because when had Rachel ever followed instructions. She'd been a jealous, spiteful child with a temper, an attitude, and petulance to spare. Tom called it the youngest sibling syndrome. Having had four or five kids of his own, he'd recognized it right off.

"She wants what you've got and a whole lot more, Amber." Tom had winked at her across his office desk mere hours before she and Rachel had been whisked off to the Smoky Mountains. "One thing she'll never have is your compelling face. So what happens when a man like Owen Fixx comes along and showers her with compliments and pretty jewels? Suddenly, she's the center of attention and hoo-eee, she's loving that. The son likes you, but he's small potatoes compared to Daddy. This time, the prize is hers, and ain't no way in hell she intends to give it up."

Amber had propped her chin in her hands. "I should have gone to Los Angeles instead of Las Vegas. I wasn't in love with Gareth. He was just a guy I met on a plane. But then I saw the glitter and all the happy people, and I thought, 'this could be fun,' to say nothing of financially rewarding. I should have looked deeper before I jumped into the job at Owen's hotel. But who does that? I heard whispers about him, gossip, rumors, that kind of thing. And God knows, I had access to enough files that I could have turned up the sort of red flags that might have warned me to get out before I got in. Of course, digging that deep would have meant using Gareth..."

"Which you wound up doing anyway," Tom reminded her. "Don't beat yourself up for things you do that are necessary to the survival of you or a loved one. Sometimes life takes funny turns, Snowbird. Roads fork. You chose the one you needed to take. It's who you are. Someday, your sister will understand that."

Comforting words, Amber thought now, but she wasn't convinced Rachel would ever forgive her. The sad part was, at that moment, she didn't much care. She wanted Rachel back safe and unharmed. Beyond that, her feelings were numb.

At least they were until Gage's face drifted in. Then everything inside her warmed. Her blood, her skin, her mind.

Without warning, his image vanished and the world went dark. Lightning split the turbulent blackness. Thunder rumbled. Another face formed. The features were less distinct and partly hidden by the brim of a hat. She saw long hair, a portion of a scar, and teeth, not bared in a smile so much as an evil grin.

Half a middle finger beckoned her forward. Creatures flew around his head. Monkeys? No, couldn't be that. Could it? One of them looked very much like Owen. The others… she couldn't tell.

The finger continued to crook. "Come to me, Amber," the man to whom it belonged said. "You can't trust him. You never could. He'll betray you. It's what people like him do. Kill or be killed. Except you can't kill me. Can't touch me. The only thing you can do is come to me, before it's too late. Come to me, my pretty, or when I do catch up, I'll torture you. And your little sister, too."

...

Gage watched an ultimate fighting match on bad cable while Amber soaked and probably slept in the tub. It wasn't what he wanted to do, but it was safe, and he wouldn't be tempted to touch her, to have sex with her, or, God help him, to talk to her. Be seduced into telling her things he didn't want to think about, let alone share.

Fuck Lydia, and not in the good way. Why the hell couldn't he have kept his mouth shut in his sleep?

Time crawled. He'd kept Amber out of the bathtub for close to ninety minutes of the two hours he needed for Bear to find the motel. It hadn't been a difficult task. He'd asked her about her life growing up, more about her job in Las Vegas, and a little about her relationship with Gareth Fixx. The last topic had both intrigued and pissed him off at the same time. In the end, they'd opted for safe ground. Tom Vigor and her transition from Alexa Chase to Amber Kelly.

She said Tom had made the change as seamless as

possible. But then, old Tom had been in that line of work for a number of years. He had a list of commendations as long as Gage's arm. On the flipside, Tom's counterpart, Sidney, wasn't quite as decorated. Gage intended to explore that avenue when and if the opportunity presented itself.

If the opportunity presented itself. There was no wifi there. There was barely cell phone reception... And the thought of Amber wet and naked in the next room was making him crazy.

He checked the time. Close enough. Careful not to make any noise, he turned up the TV and slipped out the door.

The day couldn't have been more forbidding. Thunder rolled through the sky over the distant woods. Between peals, he spotted several jagged forks of lightning. The only thing missing was rain, and that would come at some point.

Bear sent directions in a garbled text message. Keeping with the *Wizard of Oz* theme, Gage had to admit, he hadn't seen woods like those since the last time he'd watched the trek to the Wicked Witch's castle. It wasn't a promising sign.

Damp ground fog curled around his ankles. He half expected it to develop fingers, grab hold, and drag him down into the earth.

Instead, a large hand clamped onto his shoulder from behind. Instinct had him dropping, rolling, and coming up armed.

A wicked grin split Bear's face. "Got stuff on your mind there, Gage? Maybe a dark-haired beauty with a big, fat bounty on her head?"

"You bastard." Gage climbed to his feet. "How long have you been here?"

"Five minutes, give or take. Long enough to watch you stroll toward me with your mind a million miles away. And speaking of millions, you best be keeping your lady well under the radar. Word's out. Anyone looking to get rich quick's gonna be searching for her."

"Tell me something I don't know." Gage tucked his weapon away. "And talk to me about last night."

"About the she-devil?" Bear slapped his bandage-wrapped arm. "Caused me to take on another scar—like I need one. She did what you figured she would. I lost my grip like you wanted me to. They took her back, I hightailed it, and here I am." Reaching into his shirt pocket, he produced a miniature transponder. "This baby's got range and it's working. I put her location somewhere in northern Louisiana. It's not the newest device in the world, but it's the best I had on hand. It'll do you if you really want her back. Do you?"

Gage lifted a shoulder. "Not particularly. Amber does. She's got a thing for baby sis. I'm not sure I understand why, but then, I'm an only child."

Bear chuckled. "Hell, I got two of each myself, and I wouldn't go after any of 'em, except to recoup the money they owe me. What'll you tell her if they kill the she-devil?"

"Depends how much I tell her in the first place. I'm not sure she trusts me to keep *her* safe, forget the sister."

"Love to forget her, but…" Bear glanced at his wounded bicep. "Gonna be a while before I can. You want new wheels, I got a buddy near the Louisiana border. Has a body shop and a collection of trucks. He minds his own, won't ask a lot of questions. Give him double what he wants, he'll forget he ever saw you. We closer to square now, Gage?"

Gage grinned. "Getting there." The first spatters of rain began to fall. "If I need more, I'll think about calling in a favor from someone else."

"Like old Abel?"

Bear's grim tone had Gage frowning as he flipped up his jacket collar. "You know Abel?"

"Heard about him."

"From who?"

"You. Couple years back when we did that Army reunion thing and we got so pie-eyed, we couldn't take two steps without falling down. We were climbing up off our butts for the fifth time, and you started talking about how old Abel and his wife split and he was pissed because the bitch took him for everything he had."

"Yeah, like that's never happened to anyone else. Almost happened to you once, didn't it?"

Bear shrugged. "Might have, might not have. It's no skin off my nose one way or the other. You've got bigger problems anyway. Like how you're gonna explain to Amber what really went down at Bitterroot Lake."

"I'll think of something," Gage told him. "Or lie."

The clouds let loose then, but he didn't rush back to the motel. He checked the tracking device, watched it flash a location in Louisiana. And wondered if he could trust either the light or Rachel.

. . .

Amber paced the motel room like a caged tiger. Fury bubbled inside her, hot and explosive. The moment Gage came into the room, she swung around, strode over, and slapped him.

Thunder crashed overhead as she stood there with her palm throbbing and her eyes snapping in anger.

Gage didn't react. At least not physically. He kept his hands shoved in his jacket pockets and his expression level. "So," he said, "I take it you finished your bath early."

"Lucky thing." She held his stare. "There's a high window in the bathroom. I climbed up to push it open and I saw you going into the woods."

"You dress quickly."

"I can do lots of things quickly when I want to. I followed you."

"I gathered that when you slapped me. It was the only way, Amber. Rachel wasn't going to cooperate, so Bear attached a transmitter to one of her earrings while she was struggling. If she'd gone with him, he wouldn't have had to do it. But she didn't."

"You knew she wouldn't go."

"I put the odds at twenty to one against."

Because she was tempted to slap him again, Amber spun away, fists clenched, teeth grinding. "That wasn't fair." She swung back. "Why didn't you tell me?"

"Right." The ghost of a smile quirked his lips. "You'd have gone for that all the way, no questions asked, no arguments offered. I wanted you to understand what your sister really is—a spoiled little girl who rebels when things don't go her way. She doesn't think, she reacts."

Which was true, but hearing it didn't improve Amber's mood. "Damn you, Gage, yes, she's a spoiled little girl, but she's also scared and totally out of her element."

"So are you."

"We're not the same person."

"Exactly my point. I recognize Rachel because she's a female version of Knute."

She marched back over to him. "Well, I'm not a female version of you."

"Damn right."

They stood like that for several seconds while lightning crackled and thunder crashed overhead. Rain pelted the motel roof.

The conflicting elements fueled Amber's anger. It made no sense to feel the way she did, but there it was, raw and sharp, pulsing inside her like an overexcited heart.

Gage glanced at her fists. "Hit me again, Snowbird, and I promise you, there will be consequences."

Shaking the hair from her face, she waited for the

lightning to illuminate his features before firing back an icy, "Did Lydia suffer consequences?"

His eyes turned to stone. Thunder underscored an effect that had a shiver snaking through her body.

"In a way, she did," he said with absolutely no expression. "I killed her."

Chapter Sixteen

James Mockerie sat alone in Owen's office, toying with his fourth glass of bourbon and staring at his iPad. He'd locked his gaze on a picture of Owen's wife thirty minutes ago, and he hadn't been able to wrest it away. He wanted her to beg for death. He always wanted that. Craved it. He'd let his own wife…no, not going there. Not right then. He was going to focus on Amber Kelly and her insipid, bitch sister. If torture was an option, he'd go for it. If not, he'd shoot them in turn, once in the head and a second time in the heart, as was his habit.

He'd shoot Gage Morgan, as well, but primarily for the hell of it in Morgan's case. Men were never as gratifying to torture or kill as women.

McCabe would be the exception to that rule. At some point, they were going to clash, because he knew, he fucking knew, that McCabe was behind all of this. Sequestered in the shadows, but there, pulling strings and making his life a living hell.

Meanwhile, Owen might be fun to off. He'd have to think about that if the time came to eliminate him.

James's eyes refocused on the iPad photo in front of him. "You fucked with me, Rowena. I loved you and you screwed me over. You died for that." Leaning in, he ground out a hoarse, "Why do I think you're still screwing me from the grave?"

...

Shock coursed through Amber's body. "You killed Lydia?" She couldn't possibly have heard that right. "Why? When? How?"

"In reverse order: with a gun, three years ago, because she sold me and half the department out."

"Okay." Half afraid to move, Amber kept her eyes on his shadowed face. "Is there more, or am I just supposed to go with that and maybe take it as a warning to scale back my anger?"

"Take it any way you want. It doesn't change what I did. Or what Lydia did."

She ran a suddenly damp palm along the side of her jeans. "Were you lovers?"

"Yeah. She was good, and I was stupid. I almost died for that stupidity. I almost got a lot of other people killed."

"Who did she...?"

"Work for? It wasn't Mockerie, or we wouldn't be running. The guy was a drug lord, a cocaine importer from Colombia. He had meth labs on the side and was in the process of getting fentanyl onto the streets. She was persuaded to join his team when a coworker in Vice was promoted ahead of her. It was nepotism and unfair, but hell, nine tenths of life isn't fair. Most of us suck it up and deal, right?"

"Most of us," Amber echoed. "But not all. Obviously not her."

"I was after the same drug lord for murder. I had leads and evidence. She had a growing bank balance. It's an old story, happens more than you think, more than it should. We got into a situation one night. My partner discovered the truth, dragged me out for a confrontation. We saw them, they saw us. She shot my partner, the drug lord shot me. My partner shot him, I shot her. Lydia and my partner died. The drug lord lived. Briefly." Not by a flicker did the expression in his eyes change. "Anything else you'd like to know?"

Still feeling shocked, Amber went with the first thing that came to mind. "Yes. Why did you agree to help me?"

A faint smile appeared. "Meet McCabe sometime. You'll understand. I went off the rails for a while, left the force. Left Los Angeles. I got colder and meaner. I stopped caring about myself or anyone else. Then, one day, McCabe asked me if I'd like to become a US Marshal. I thought what the hell. It was still law enforcement. So I went through the training deal. Let me tell you, it was hell and then some. But it was worth it just for my first assignment. A woman who reminded me of Krista had a son who wanted her dead. She wanted him in a psych ward. Locked down until his medical and mental issues could be properly addressed. The son was clever and quick, couldn't be caught in the usual way. So McCabe took an unusual route. It's what he does."

"And what you do now, as well." The tension in her body faded to a tingle of residual fear. Turning away, she rubbed her temples. "I feel like I'm living in the Twilight Zone," she murmured.

"You think?" Gage's smile upped the tingle in her belly to a hum. Like the lightning outside and the thunder that rattled the walls and floors. Rattled her. "So what now, Snowbird? Are you afraid of me?"

She regarded the whole of him. "I should be, shouldn't I? Would be if I were Rachel or Lydia. But I'm not either of those women." And dammit, desire spiked through her when his dark eyes locked on hers.

"You really don't want to go there with me." The shadows around him shifted slightly, made his eyes more visible in a face she could barely see. "I won't hurt you, but I'm not a nice guy."

She laughed, couldn't help it. "That's bullshit and you know it." Her hands fell. "That thing you and Bear did with Rachel pissed me off, still pisses me off, but nothing about what you've said scares me at all."

"You're worth three million dollars."

She stared at him for several long seconds, head up and challenging. "Fine. If you're so bad and I'm so vulnerable, turn me in." She walked toward him, slowly, while something much more exciting than fear swam in her veins. "From what you've told me, alive would be better than dead, but I'm sure you could manage it, a fit, fully trained ex-cop like you." She shook her hair back in a deliberately provocative gesture, let her hips swing just enough to draw his gaze. "Go on, do it. I won't resist, at least not in any way you can't overcome. Take the money and complete the slide to the dark side."

He didn't look away as lightning shot through the sky beyond the window. "Nothing about this situation is safe. You know that, don't you?"

"That and much, much more." She stopped walking less than a foot in front of him, gripped the sides of his jacket. "I don't mind being pissed off. It stimulates my senses, like the lightning outside. There's something to be said for living dangerously. Not recklessly like Rachel, but on the edge. You're an edge, Gage. I'm on it, and I intend to keep right on going."

"You're crazy, Snowbird. That interference band I rigged is eroding as we speak." His hands followed the line of her waist, then moved higher to span her rib cage. He lowered his mouth to hers. "We'll probably both be killed," he murmured.

Then, covering her lips, he took her all the way over the edge.

Chapter Seventeen

He didn't want this. Did not want to get tangled up with any woman, let alone a woman like Amber. She appealed to him on every level. She challenged him on an equal number. She was smart and beautiful, with an instinct for survival he couldn't help but admire. She also loved her sister. No idea why, but she did.

There was something quite remarkable there, given Rachel's nature. He intended to think all those things through when his brain returned to a functioning state and was no longer being controlled by his hormones.

She gave him a shove when he lifted her off her feet. The smile she sent him brought fire to her amazing eyes. Hooking her arms around his neck, she settled herself against his hips. Her legs enfolded him and bumped the need inside him to a burn.

He kissed her and damn near lost his bearings. Cupping his face, she kept his mouth on hers when he might have pulled back, for breath and a brief moment of clarity.

"Don't think," she told him. "Just feel. Enjoy. I want to

soar, Gage. Let myself go, fly, and not worry about where I land. Where *we* land. I think you're bigger on regrets than I am."

Okay, gauntlet thrown, picked up, shredded, and tossed aside. He grinned against her mouth when she began to hum.

"'My Way'?"

"Frank sang it first, but I'm thinking Elvis for obvious reasons here."

She tugged on his jacket as he laid her on the bed and followed her down. She reacted by rubbing her hips against him and making him see fiery red.

She continued to hum while she pushed aside the leather of his jacket, smiled when he rolled her on top of him and went to work on her jeans. Straddling his hips, she pulled off her T-shirt with its deep V and clingy red fabric. He saw a bra that was mostly black lace, displaying cleavage that made him want to beg.

She had an amazing body. Silky soft and glowing in the barely there light. Then lightning flickered and illuminated her for a single glorious moment.

Black lace, pale gold flesh, amazing features, and a teasing gleam in her eyes. He might have regrets later, Gage reflected, but at that moment, they were few and far between.

He had no idea how he got her out of the rest of her clothes. He only knew things flew into the shadows. Laying her back on the bed, he kissed her long and deep. Then he worked his way down her body, from throat to breast to navel, until he reached the hot, wet center of her. He took his time there, tasting, exploring, savoring.

Desire clawed at him. Fortunately, while he felt like a horny adolescent, he wasn't one. They had condoms. Despite the heat and the persistent throbbing between his legs, he put his own need on hold and focused on hers.

Her fingers curled in his hair. Her body rocked. When he

looked up, he saw her head arch on the pillow, felt her hips rise.

He heard her gasp as her fingers went limp.

"Jesus, Gage. That was…"

Cutting her off, he took possession of her mouth even as he slipped inside her.

Her cry of response was coupled with a quick intake of breath and a hard upward push as she immediately matched his rhythm.

He used his lips and tongue when he kissed her. He knew he let too much of himself flow into her, too many feelings, some old, some new. They twisted and coiled into a ball of confusion in his head.

"I taste conflict and mystery and a little bit of need." Grabbing hold of his arms, she bowed her body upward. "Lose the conflict and give in to the need."

"Happy to." As he kissed the corners of her mouth, he kept his eyes on hers and upped the tempo to match the pulsing in his brain and lower body.

Thunder crashed, and lightning spread from black cloud to rain-soaked ground. And for a moment that felt oddly suspended in time, the world beyond the motel window simply melted away.

• • •

Good-bye Yellow Brick Road. Amber's lips curved. The words ran through her head like the Elton John song. Good-bye Elvis, as well, at least for the moment. And hello Gage Morgan.

She couldn't move—a dangerous state to be in considering who was out there searching for her.

Three million dollars. Could Rachel resist that kind of money? Was she worried the answer might be no?

Because her own answer to that was no, she set the question aside and listened to his heart as it beat a little too fast under her ear. "I'm hungry," she said. "Are you hungry?"

She heard the lazy drawl in his voice when he replied, "Not enough to do anything about it."

Amber raised her head slightly. "Storm's moving west. Is that good or bad?"

"Good if you like storms, bad if you don't." Reaching over to the nightstand, he picked up the tracking device, which strongly resembled a cell phone. "The blip hasn't moved. Assuming Rachel's still wearing her earrings, neither has she."

"If they were her diamond drops…"

"Bear said they were."

"Then she's still wearing them. Unless the people holding her are savvier than I think and they've figured out she's bugged. Like I apparently am."

"Then there's that. I wouldn't worry too much about it. The whole bugging thing, especially where you're concerned, feels off to me. I can't explain how or why, but it does."

Folding her arms on his chest, Amber looked into his eyes. "I don't regret slapping you. I still think you should have told me about your plan. Is Bear going to continue tailing us?"

"He would if I asked him to, but I won't."

Stretching upward, she kissed him. "Are you sure he isn't in need of three million dollars?"

He kissed her back, ruffled her hair. "I'm not sure of anything when it comes to Bear."

"Or Abel or Wanda or Mandy?"

"Let's say I'm as sure of the people on my side as you are of the ones on yours. Does that help?"

"No." Rolling onto him, she sat up with her knees on either side of his hips. "But I'm really hoping this will."

And bending down, she kissed him until her mind went hot and blissfully blank.

...

Try as she might, Rachel couldn't unfold her arms. Fury radiated from her. It was Amber's fault that she was back in captivity. Why hadn't she said the guy she was with looked like King Kong? Why had he wrapped his forearm around her throat when she'd tried to get away? She'd thought for a horrible moment he was going to try and kiss her or, way worse, rape her. It wasn't until he'd snarled at her to shut the hell up because he was her sister's friend that she'd understood.

Too late, always too late. And now she was truly starting to believe Owen didn't love her. Maybe he never had. Three former wives dead. Would she have been the fourth?

Damn. She couldn't even delude herself anymore that her life just might return to normal. It was over. The spending sprees were done. So was the shower of jewelry. And she could kiss off her sweet little Porsche with the hot pink leather seats forever. She was down to the dumbass Jess Murkles of the world. And wasn't that just about as bad as life could get?

She'd heard talk since they'd brought her there. Because men, when they weren't being watched over by an eagle-eyed scumbag who'd posed as a friend, tended to flap their gums in all kinds of disgusting male ways.

Her sister was worth a small fortune. Her sister who'd gotten her into this mess—sort of. Who'd stuck her for good with bumpkins like Jess Murkle. Except Jess had turned her in, so that made him a traitorous bumpkin.

She should never have let herself get drunk and start talking. She'd told him too much, she knew that. But who'd have thought he'd be smart enough to figure out what to do with the information she'd given him? Damn country bumpkins to hell.

It appeared her choices were very limited. Creeps or bumpkins. She needed to go one way or the other. Unless...

Fingering a sparkling drop earring, she cocked her head and then shook it so the diamonds glittered in the mirror across the room.

Pleased with her reflection, and a burgeoning idea, she stood to admire herself. She'd bitched and complained until someone had brought her makeup and a bottle of body lotion. She could make that work for her, couldn't she? She hadn't lost her sex appeal, she was sure of it. And men were men whether they were bumpkins, millionaires, or somewhere in between.

Oh yeah. She let her lips curve into a sly smile. It was time to dude up the girls and see if they could help her swing a sweet, rich deal.

. . .

Amber tumbled into a soft, untroubled sleep. Satisfaction ruled and her body felt weightless. Until the noise began.

Slot machines whirring, people laughing, chatting, occasionally shrieking. Gareth came up behind her, squeezed her shoulders, and whispered, "You belong here, Alexa. It's your niche."

It wasn't, and she'd understood that by then. But gathering evidence took time, trickery, and a strong measure of deceit, unfortunately.

She'd let him think she cared even as she'd swiped the keys to his father's office. She'd seduced information from him, including the fact that his father's computer passwords were written down, secure in a black notebook buried deep inside a well-concealed wall safe. The safe's combination?

Easily deduced when she'd discovered that Owen was every bit as anal—and as oddly predictable—as Gareth.

He'd had three common passwords. In each case, he'd used the first name of one of his late wives coupled with the order in which he'd married her, followed by the year she'd died. Or been killed. All things neat, tidy, and as simple as they could be in Owen Fixx's world.

"We'll get married, have ten kids," Gareth had promised. He'd kissed the top of her head. "Ten beautiful musicians. We'll be our own band, and we'll have you to manage us."

God, she'd felt guilty. But death was final, and Rachel was next in line.

She twitched the dream away, went back to the delicious place where Gage had taken her. Much better. And there he was, half hidden within the darkness, secretive and mysterious—with a smoking gun in his hand and a woman lying dead at his feet.

Even with blurred edges, the image jolted her.

"Wake up, Amber."

Gage spoke while she was gasping and already partly upright.

Her hair fell in her eyes, over her face. Her breath came hard and fast. "I was... I saw... Why am I sitting up?"

"No idea." He pulled her back down. "Bad dreams maybe. They get me most nights."

"I bet." She exhaled on a shudder. "What time is it?"

"Almost four p.m." He reached for the tracking device, squinted at it in the shadow-filled room. "Shit!" He sat up. "She's moving."

Amber pushed her hair back. "Moving at this moment, or has her location just changed?"

"Location's changed. She might still be moving. We need to stay in range. I'll see what the motel owner has to offer, vehicle-wise. He might be open to cash."

Already digging through her pack for clean clothes, Amber glanced up. "You seem to have an endless supply of money. How is that possible?"

"McCabe believes in covering all contingencies. Most of those have dollar signs attached to them. He loaded me up before I left Memphis. Get everything ready, wait here, and keep an eye on the tracker." He was gone before she could answer.

So much for the blissful afterglow, Amber reflected as she buckled her pack and pulled on her boots. Dragging her hair into a tail, she slipped on a jacket and reminded herself the nightmare would end. All things did, good or bad.

The door opened. Amber whipped up her gun, spotted Gage, and breathed a sigh of relief. "We need some kind of signal. If I were trigger happy, I'd have blown your head off."

He grabbed his pack and hers, swept the room. "If you'd done that, you'd have been forced to drive a contentious vehicle and rescue Rachel on your own. The owner took five hundred for what he called his funky heap."

"That doesn't sound overly promising. Does it run, or will we be doing a Fred Flintstone with it?"

"He said it was a faithful heap, he's just got his eye on a slightly newer Jeep Cherokee. It's cherry red."

"As opposed to a camo-colored whatever this Jeep is." Amber circled the back end. "I can see where a cherry-red Cherokee would look really good."

Passing her, Gage gave her a quick kiss. "Beggars and choosers, Amber. It runs, it'll do. Where's Rachel?"

"Heading for New Orleans would be my guess. Definitely in Louisiana, moving south."

"We need to play catch up fast, before she's out of range."

"Which is?"

"I don't know. We're probably close to the limit by now. We'll stop for food and coffee after we bridge some portion of the gap."

Once they were on their way, Amber watched the mirrors, as well as the road ahead. They were driving back into the storm, which was unnerving. But the darkness required all drivers to use headlights, so if someone was, in fact, tailing them, she'd see them coming.

Gage took the interstate for a while. To make up some time and distance, she imagined. He played Reba for her and Charlie Daniels for both of them.

The Jeep did its job on and off the main roads. They picked up subs and soft drinks in a town called Primrose and, after narrowly avoiding an in-depth chat with the talkative sheriff, left via a rain-slick side road.

Tom called while they were making a fuel and restroom stop. The map Amber had Googled said they were still within the limits of the town.

"I'm glad to hear you're on the move, Snowbird. And no, don't tell me where you are. I'm calling because it occurred to me you had the right idea using Myra Pinkerton's phone way back when. On the off chance Fixx's people are somehow homing in on you through your cell, you need to ditch it in the nearest swamp. Use Gage's instead."

Pacing, Amber rolled her head to ease the tension in her neck. "I got the phone from the WPP, Tom. Don't tell me now it isn't clean."

"It was clean as a whistle when you received it. But we didn't put the bits and pieces of it together, and word's getting louder that Mockerie has more than one person on his payroll. You have to figure he has an insider at the FBI, but it's a good bet he has more in other departments. Bastard money-grubbers. I'm not saying you're bugged, but in case you are, I think you should lose the obvious potential source."

"We dealt with that source early on," Gage said. "Or so we thought. It's possible the network I hooked into has been compromised. I don't know how good Mockerie's tech is." He handed Amber a candy bar. "Any word on Fixx or Mockerie's current location?"

"Both were in Vegas as of yesterday. They've dropped off the radar since then. You got a whopping bounty on your head, little Snowbird."

"So I've heard. How's Sidney, by the way?"

Tom's chuckle contained no humor. "Funny you should ask that question. Young Sidney took an emergency leave 'round about the same time you hightailed it out of Black Creek. He didn't specify the 'emergency', he just up and left. How's that for a coincidence?"

"Convenient."

"Seems to me, he might have mentioned having a grandmother in New York once upon a time, though. We'll see. Anyway, you watch your back, or have Gage do it for you. McCabe's a good man. He uses good people. You take care and stay safe."

She ended the call, glanced over. "Do you think Tom's right about my phone?"

"Not necessarily," Gage told her. He capped the gas tank. "But there's no point taking any chances. We're tracking Rachel, so hopefully we'll get her back and there won't be any more need for phone calls."

"Where is Rachel? Can you tell?"

"The blip's been holding steady for the past ninety minutes. Unless it's broken, she's stopped moving."

"Okay, well I guess that's good." She stared at her phone. "Why did Tom's call unnerve me so much? It isn't as if you didn't think the same thing, reconfigure my cell and the rest of my possessions before this."

"Because straight-laced Sidney's taken off?""What if Rachel does try to contact me?"

Gage shrugged. "Pick your poison, Amber. We know

where she is."

"We know where her earrings are."

"Poison," he repeated.

They were standing on opposite sides of the Jeep's hood. Although the rain had stopped for the moment, thunder continued to rumble in the background. Amber released a heartfelt breath. "Fine, smash it. You and Tom really have a way of…"

A blast of rifle fire cut her off. Gage vaulted over the hood, undoubtedly intending to get her on the ground, but Amber was way ahead of him. She'd already dropped to her knees.

"There's no one here except you, me, and the station attendant." She twisted her head around. "Where did that shot come from?"

Before Gage could answer, another blast shattered the misty silence.

Gage scanned the trees to her right. "Got him," he said and gave her one of his guns. "Stay low and fire every two seconds. Aim for the cypress tree in the middle. That's where he's hiding. Or trying to. Big men with beer bellies don't conceal easily or well. An officer of the law should know that."

"Officer of… What are you talking about?"

Gage got in front of her as the next bullet whizzed by. "He's a crappy shot, even with a scope. Think back, Amber. How many people have we met today?"

It hit her and she tightened her grip on the gun. "Primrose. Sub stop. He was going back to his car. He leaned in your window, all friendly and official."

"Yeah." Gage got ready to launch from his crouch. "The friendly, official, money-grubbing sheriff of Primrose."

. . .

This whole fucking nightmare with Amber and Fixx was more than he'd been told and a lot more than he'd bargained for. Gage promised himself that, at some point in his life, he and McCabe were going to have it out. A down and dirty, fists flying, bones cracking, winner walks away free and clear fight. They knew each other too damn well, and that gave McCabe an advantage Gage wanted gone.

He wanted other things gone, as well, the biggest one being his feelings for Amber. She mattered, dammit, far more than she should. More than he'd intended or could handle. She muddled his mind and made everything cloudy and unfocused, any or all of which could get both of them killed.

Fortunately, his feelings for her right then were peripheral. His focus was straight ahead on Sheriff Asshole, who obviously kept an eye out for illegal opportunities on the dark web.

Intent on his quarry, the big sheriff continued to fire at Amber. She shot back and caused him to keep jerking sideways into the shelter of the cypress tree.

"Come on, you little beauty," the sheriff muttered. "Come to Papa and make him rich as old Midas."

Not today, pal, Gage thought. He'd crept up behind the man while Amber kept him busy. One more rifle blast and there'd be a gun barrel pressed to the base of the sheriff's neck. "You're gonna want to set that rifle down real easy there, Sheriff. What was your name again? Stroub?"

"That's what they call me." The rifle fell into a bed of moss and leaves. "Emmet Stroub." Turning, the man bared his teeth in a pleasant smile. "And right behind you is my deputy, Arnie Skinner."

"Hey, y'all."

The tip of a rifle jabbed hard into Gage's spine. Swearing softly, Gage tossed his Glock onto the spongy ground.

The sheriff kept smiling. "Arnie and me, we reckon three million bucks oughta take us and ours a good long way in this world."

Gage watched the deputy's indistinct shadow on the tree trunk ahead of him. "You won't be long for this world, either of you, if you try to collect that reward. I know who you're dealing with, you don't."

"Big talk," the deputy drawled.

He was a lanky man, Gage judged, probably stronger than he appeared in shadow. Sheriff Stroub, on the other hand, was wheezing at the mere thought of so much money.

His piggy eyes crinkled at the corners. "She's a looker, no doubt about it. Kind of woman that'll catch a man's eye every time. Caught mine eighty feet away and I was just glancing over at what I figured was a couple of tourists passing through our little hamlet."

"Ad said she's wanted alive," the deputy remarked. "Didn't make no mention of what condition she should be in. I'm liking that." He screwed his rifle into Gage's back. "Didn't mention you at all. I'm liking that even more."

"Now, you understand, we're not murderers, not generally." The sheriff waved a hand. "But when the occasion presents itself, well, what's a man to do? Nothing personal's what I'm saying here, friend. Simple fact is, you got something we want, and we're gonna take it."

"So which one of you is planning to kill me?" Gage asked.

"Oh, me probably." The deputy snickered. "Old chicken liver there can't so much as skin a rabbit without turning fifty shades of green."

Gage noted movement in his peripheral and swung around to face the would-be shooter. In the same instant, he had his elbow planted in Sheriff Stroub's belly and a second weapon drawn.

The startled deputy whipped his rifle up, then

immediately yelped and dropped it as his shoulder began to stream with blood. "What the hell?" He staggered in a half circle and went down on his knees. "You shot me, bitch! You tore up my shoulder."

"Making you a lucky man." Amber held her gun on him while he glowered at her. "I was aiming for your head."

The sheriff panted with exertion as he endeavored to right himself. Gage's elbow had knocked him into the cypress tree. From there, he'd toppled to the ground.

"Reach for that rifle and I'll put a bullet right through your badge."

"Your word against mine as to what happened here." Bracing his hands on his thighs, the sheriff wheezed in a breath. "Best for all concerned we forget this entire incident."

"Best for you," Gage agreed. "Not for us. There's rope in the back of the Jeep, Snowbird. Bring all of it. We'll deal with these two and then I'll contact McCabe."

"What are you gonna do?" the deputy demanded. "You can't truss us up and leave us here. Snakes live in these swampy woods. Big, poisonous ones."

"In that case, you won't want to move around too much. Stay calm and quiet, and maybe they won't notice you."

Amber returned with the rope. "Be grateful you're not actually in the swamp," she said. "Then you'd have to worry about alligators, as well."

"Y'all are enjoying this, aren't you?" the sheriff remarked in a testy tone. "That ain't very charitable of you."

Amber stopped tying the deputy's ankles. "Seriously? You're worried about Christian charity after what you planned to do?"

"Aw, well now, honey, that was just temptation getting in the way of my sense of decency. I'm feeling a mite less mercenary now."

"First step's always the hardest." Gage caught the rope

Amber tossed him. "Check the thing," he said and knew she understood when she stood and pulled the tracker from her pocket.

"We should go," she told him. "The rain's starting again, and Corpus Christi's a long way off."

Nodding, Gage cinched the rope a little tighter than necessary around the sheriff's wrists. He sent Amber back to the Jeep for duct tape while he texted McCabe.

Someone might or might not come before Stroub and his lackey worked themselves free, but however it went down, the two men would be out of a job, and that was all Gage really cared about right then.

After gagging them, he retrieved all the weapons and carried them back to their soon-to-be-history vehicle.

He kissed Amber before throwing everything in the backseat. "Timely shot, Snowbird. Semi-accurate and silenced, too."

"It was in your pack." She shrugged. "I didn't want to make a lot of noise. The station attendant's still cowering behind the counter from the first round of fire. I opened the door a bit to see if he was all right and I heard his voice under the cash register. He kept saying, 'I didn't see anything. Why would anyone hurt me when I didn't see anything.'"

"I'll let McCabe know about him." Reaching into the back, he located a hammer, tossed her phone on the ground, and smashed it. He climbed in and started the engine. "Where's Rachel?"

She checked the screen, frowned, and shook the device.

"Is the battery dead?" Gage asked.

"No." She shook it again. "The battery's at eighty-six percent. That's not the problem." Turning the screen toward him, she said softly, "The blip's disappeared."

Chapter Eighteen

"Rachel's moved out of range." He pointed the Jeep south. "We have the last location and her trajectory. We'll find her again. Worse comes to worst, you can call her."

"I can if her phone's being charged. Knowing Rachel, it will be. Her cell's a major lifeline, and she knows how to whine until she gets her way."

"Can't say I envy her captors," Gage remarked.

"Envy no. Appreciate her whining, yes."

Four hours and a great deal of boggy terrain later, Amber decided to risk that call. To her surprise, Rachel answered on the second ring.

"Where are you?" Amber demanded.

"In Hooterville, I think." Rachel sounded simultaneously peeved and hyper. "Bobby Lee's got a weird sense of humor. He's older than me, so he's probably just teasing, but whatever this place is, it's hick and hokey. Where are you?"

"It doesn't matter. Why are they letting you talk to me?"

"*They* aren't doing anything. Bobby Lee and I escaped. He was supposed to be watching me while the others went off to play poker and drink. I told him about my stash of jewels back in Las Vegas."

"You have a stash of jewels in Las Vegas?

"Of course I do, silly." Rachel's reply was overly bright, a sure sign she was lying.

When Gage arched a brow, Amber shook her head. "Okay, good, the jewels. Did you tell him about the gold, too?"

"All twenty-four karats."

"Rachel, I need to know where you are."

"We're heading for New Orleans. That's all I can say. Bobby Lee's nervous, so we're using a lot of back roads. You'll have to get my jewelry to me in New Orleans, Amber. Promise you will."

"I will," Amber promised. "Have you stopped for the night?"

"Yes. We're at a little hotel…"

"Called Shady Rest," Gage put in. "Never mind." He shook off the question in Amber's eyes. "I grew up on sixties reruns. Ask her for the name of the last town sign she can remember."

Amber relayed the question and received a grunt from her sister. "Oh, I don't know. It was a really dumb name. Astor, Aspirin, something like that."

"Got her." Gage showed Amber the tracker. "She's thirty miles south of Astrid."

Relieved, Amber exhaled. "Rachel, stay where you are if you can. And keep your phone charged."

"I will." Her tone changed. "Oooh, that looks really nice, Bobby Lee. You got the tub all full of bubbles? Food's on the table over here, and I've got the other goodies waiting. Night, Amber. Don't you forget about those jewels now."

Amber ended the call. "Well? What do you think? Is she running with Bobby or was that a setup?"

"My guess? She's running. Question is, is she running away from Owen's people? Or inadvertently pulling us into a trap."

...

They changed vehicles again in Genoa. Bear's friend helped them out as promised. He sold them a Range Rover SUV and even threw in a spare tire for good measure. Gage took Bear's advice, doubled the asking price, and gave the guy an extra two hundred dollars due to the lateness of the hour.

"I feel like a vampire." Amber sat cross-legged in their newly acquired vehicle. They'd taken on several mosquitoes as passengers, and she'd made it her mission to swat them all. It was either that or sleep, and she was too jacked up even to close her eyes.

Another two hours of bumping and bouncing, however, and her eyes seemed to have changed their mind.

They'd have to stop eventually. Gage looked even more tired than she felt, and that was saying something.

"Anywhere you choose is fine." She fought off a yawn. "I don't care if we sleep in the Range Rover at this point. I can't think straight, and you must be ready to plant us in a ditch."

His lips twitched. "I've driven into a ditch or two before. You don't want to know how it turned out."

Half an hour later, he surprised her by pulling into a hotel parking lot on the river. Some kind of convention appeared to be winding down.

"You're in luck," the harried desk clerk told them. "We had two early checkouts. Room 711's ready if sleep's what you're after."

At one a.m., Amber would have expected most people to be in their beds. But that wasn't the case at such a lively convention. She heard dance music playing in the lounge, slot machines dinging in the casino, and bawdy laughter rolling out of the bar.

"Flashback to my former life." She had a Saints ball cap pulled down over her forehead and she'd made a point of staying behind Gage since they'd entered through the double lobby doors.

"Wanna try your luck?" Drawing her forward, he draped an arm over her shoulders. "Don't worry. I've been watching the crowd. Most of them are too wasted to know who they are, let alone who you might be. Clerk didn't so much as glance at you."

"That's because she was busy looking at you. Blackjack's my game, if we're playing. I might have thirty minutes left in me. I'll be your muse."

Gage shook his head. "Other way around, Snowbird. You deal with the cards, I'll deal with the crowd. Poker's my game anyway."

She could believe that.

They walked casually through the casino, saw people dressed in everything from slinky dresses and suits to rough denim and flip-flops.

"Unless you wanna play three blind mice, you poison the little suckers," a man behind them slurred. "Traps are for cowards."

Amber bumped Gage's hip. "We're at an exterminator's convention."

"Keeps life interesting."

"If you're into pain and death."

"I prefer quick and painless." He drew her closer, turning her head away from a man who looked like a rat and almost teetered into her.

"Warfarin." The man's Adam's apple bobbed convulsively. "S'rat poison, you know. My doctor prescribed it for me last week. Frigging rat poison in my veins."

"Life's all about overcoming challenges, pal." Gage held the man off with a firm hand when he would have toppled into Amber's arm.

She resisted an urge to chuckle and kept her head averted. No point testing her luck unnecessarily.

She spied a baccarat table through the crowd and, behind it, an open exit door. Three men stood on the threshold inside. One of them had a long, dark ponytail and a flashy stud earring.

"Shit!" Amber stiffened, placed an open palm on Gage's torso. "We need to leave. Now."

"What do you see?" He dismissed the drunk to follow her gaze. "The guys by the door?"

"The one with the ponytail. I think it's Luka." The man turned slightly, affording her a clearer view of his features. "God, Gage, it is. He's looking around."

"Yeah, I see that." He pressed her face into his shoulder, blocked Luka's view with his body. "Don't sweat it. We're going to go out the same way we came in and take the side door to the parking lot."

Amber didn't argue. Head down, she walked with him and, at the same time, attempted to sift through the dozens of thoughts darting wildly through her head.

Had Luka and his people been that close behind them all along, or was their being there part of the setup Gage had suggested when he'd heard about Rachel's escape?

Someone had been on their tail from the start, she knew that much. Which meant at least one of her possessions was bugged. But her phone was gone and Gage had examined pretty much everything else.

So how was Luka's being there possible?

"Rachel's so-called escape has to have been a setup on both sides," she concluded. "It makes sense and— Where did he go?"

"Stay calm." Gage reached back and under his jacket. "He's not in front of us."

"Yes, he is." She stopped dead. "He's right there, Gage, next to that black marble column. I don't think he's seen us. He's holding a device that looks a lot like the one we've been using to track Rachel."

"Okay, that's it. Keep your head down and get ready to run."

She saw him whip out his gun and take aim at the chandelier overhead. "What, wait," she objected. "Are you insane?"

He fired six shots in rapid succession. Crystal shattered, lightbulbs exploded, people screamed and immediately began to run.

Gage fired again, four more times, then grabbed her hand. "Fire door," he shouted above the instant pandemonium.

Amber stole a quick look at Luka, but she couldn't see anything except his ponytail. Then even that vanished as he was shoved through the main doors by a group of panicky gamblers.

A man with a beetle brow materialized in front of them. "Hello, Alexa. Long time no see. I gotta say, you're looking real good…"

Straight-arming his gun, Gage shot him in the throat. Still smiling lewdly, the man dropped to the floor where he stood.

Shock swept through Amber's body. "You killed him."

"Yep. Keep moving."

She had to step over the dead man's outstretched hand. Gage plucked the gun he held free and pushed her through the door.

Her teeth were chattering by the time they reached the Range Rover. She fumbled the door open and scrambled inside.

Then, instead of endless questions racing through her head, her mind went numb. She couldn't think at all. But she had to.

Beetle brow, beetle brow. He'd looked so familiar. Did she know him from the hotel in Las Vegas? Yes, she did. He'd been part of Owen's personal staff. Security guard. Former mercenary. She'd never seen him smile.

She watched for Luka behind them as Gage peeled out of the lot. "Damn. Should I strip? Lose everything I'm wearing?"

"I'm good with that." Gage flicked a glance at the rearview mirror. "But you don't have to go there quite yet. I checked all your clothes and jewelry, remember?"

"Maybe it's the pull on my zipper or the strap on my backpack." She felt the sides of her boots. Her fingers passed over two small chains. "Jesus, Gage, it could be anywhere on anything."

"Or Luka and his boys could simply have known where we were headed and gotten lucky."

"I don't believe that, and neither do you."

"What I believe is that we got out of there undamaged. Luka's down a man and we're closing in on your sister."

"Right, yes, good." She forced herself to breathe, find her center, her balance. Quiet her mind. "It could be in my other boots. I bought them at the hotel… I see headlights."

"So do I. We're on a highway."

"At two in the morning? Wait, they're gone." Her mind spun in super-fast mode. "His name was Quint. He claimed to have killed twenty-five men in one hour in one skirmish in the Middle East."

"He'd have killed me in a heartbeat and handed you over to Mockerie even faster. He died quickly. You won't if Mockerie gets ahold of you."

"Consider me comforted. God, what now?" That's when

Gage's phone rang.

He put it on speaker. "Hey, Bear. What's up?"

"Not the ponytail or his crony, not anymore."

Amber's eyes widened in disbelief. "You killed Luka?"

"I didn't kill anyone, just broke a few bones, put holes in a few interesting places. They won't be bothering you for six, maybe eight weeks. Are we square now, Gage?"

"Getting closer." Gage slowed their speed a little. "Thanks, Bear. Go on home. I've got it from here."

Bear snorted. "Pretty sure you said that self-same thing five minutes before we got our ride blown out from under us in Afghanistan. Later, bro."

"Bro?" Amber wondered if the surprises would ever end. "Now you're his brother?"

"Depends on his mood."

"Well, mine's all about not being a blip on someone else's device. If I get rid of everything I'm wearing and carrying and, I don't know, wear your clothes, they can't possibly follow us, right?"

"It's a sound theory," he agreed. "Try and sleep, Amber. I'm ninety-nine percent sure they already know where we're going, with or without a tracking device."

Letting her head fall back, Amber regarded the sky outside. One hazy star twinkled through a break in the clouds. "I'd make a wish if I could narrow the number of possibilities down to a reasonable number."

Gage cut off at the next exit. "I can narrow that number down for you right now."

Unsure, she glanced at the road behind them. "I don't see anything."

"That's because you're looking the wrong way."

She switched her gaze back. And felt her heart sink into her stomach when he pointed to a flashing red light on the dash.

• • •

Owen cradled a bottle of his beloved aged whiskey. He hadn't taken so much as a sip of it when his home phone rang.

If Luka was contacting him on a landline, it must have been important. Probably catastrophic the way his luck had been running lately.

"What is it, Luka?"

"She got away."

Completely unruffled, because given his nephew's track record, that was hardly shocking news, Owen nodded. "Of course she did. Are you still following her?"

"Hard to fucking do that with both my kneecaps shot out."

Finally, Owen heard the strain in Luka's voice. He'd have sympathized if the stakes hadn't been quite so high. "Morgan?" he asked.

"No, some big ape with a crazy gleam in his eyes. Who the hell cares? Quint's dead. Morgan did him."

"Merciful end." Owen stroked the whiskey bottle as if it were a cherished pet. "Where are you?"

"They're going to airlift me to a hospital in Baton Rouge. Stuart, too, if you care. Both his arms are busted, and he has two bullets near his groin."

"Ouch." The third member of the unfortunate trio sounded worse off than his nephew. Owen thought quickly. The backup team was gone, and the lead team hadn't checked in for several hours. All wasn't lost yet, but it would be if things didn't start clicking into place.

With regret, he set the whiskey bottle on his desk. "Call me from Baton Rouge," he said to his nephew. "You might want to ask for a no visitors order from the doctor in charge."

"Why?"

"If you can smuggle one in, keep your gun handy.

Mockerie doesn't take failure well."

Luka was still swearing when Owen disconnected. With a mournful last gaze at the bottle, he picked up his cell phone and contacted his on-call pilot.

"Get the plane ready," he ordered the man. "Maximum fuel load. We're flying to Louisiana. I'll let you know exactly where before we take off."

Ending the call, he speed-dialed the lead team. When he got no answer, he left a terse message. "I'm en route. I need to know where you are. Exactly where you are."

He'd call his contact from the plane, make sure he was still on board. Mockerie had done the deal with him. Although he was newly acquired, James believed he'd finish the job he was being paid to do. Then, if he was smart, he'd disappear for good. Burrow deep and enjoy whatever time Mockerie gave him.

Just like the rest of them.

• • •

They had no time to stop for repairs, and Gage didn't have the patience right then to deal with the engine warning light. He punched the "Vehicle Needs Service" reset button, cursed Bear's friend, and concentrated on the road both ahead and behind.

Amber watched the tracker's screen. "The blip's still not moving." She tapped the device with a fingertip. "That isn't good, is it?"

"It says trap to me, but my head's been there since we found out Rachel had escaped."

"I can't think." Amber dropped her hand and the tracker in her lap, rolled her head from side to side. "My brain's too exhausted to move in logical lines. How do you do it?"

"Adrenaline. It kicks in when all else fails. Whether

you know it or not, it's kept you going since we left the hotel casino."

"That and sheer terror." She let out a long breath, regarded him sideways. "We were all we had, Rachel, me, and our brother Elijah. Our parents fought, day and night. I don't recall them ever having a quiet conversation. Remember I told you that Rachel and I both liked our new names better?"

"I remember."

"That's because our mother wanted all sons. Alex and George. Those were going to be our names. I don't know what our father wanted. I'm not sure he cared. Having kids was just something you did. Something you were supposed to do. Like getting married, which I'm not sure he wanted to do, either. He took care of us after our mother left, but only because that was expected of him, too. He gave us stuff to keep us happy and out of his hair."

"Sounds like Rachel's kind of dad."

"She wasn't always spoiled, Gage. Or, well, maybe a little. She was born more demanding. Just not quite as obnoxious as she became later."

"Or as jealous? You're more beautiful than her by a long shot."

Amber's smile was faint and slightly wistful. "But that's in the eye of the beholder, isn't it? You behold one way, Owen beheld another."

"How did Luka behold you?"

"Luka was never in the mix. He likes men."

"And Gareth?"

"He liked Alexa. I'm not her anymore. I don't want to be her again."

"I'm thinking you never really were. Sometimes, people figure out who they are by playing games, taking on different roles, testing the water. You tried glamorous and probably liked it at the time."

"I did."

"Then things changed, and you became a spy. Also quite a glamorous role, or so Hollywood would have us believe."

"It was a bit Hollywood-like, living on the edge of danger. Maybe death. But in the end? Not so glamorous. Black Creek was…a revelation. Rachel was horrible the whole time we were there. She kept wanting to contact Owen, see if she could make him understand that she'd had no part in what I'd done. She's been pissed off at me for the past month. As you can see, she still is."

"Pissed off and relying on your sense of guilt to help rescue her."

"She's not wrong to blame me for the situation she landed in, Gage. A thousand years could pass, and she'd never believe Owen would hurt her, forget killing her."

"So now she's with a guy called Bobby Lee, heading for New Orleans. I'd venture a guess that her belief's starting to develop cracks. Maybe, on a smaller scale, those cracks were there before you left Las Vegas."

"Maybe," Amber agreed. "Rachel's extremely good at deluding herself, and denial's been her constant companion since childhood." She waited a moment before asking, "If we're heading into a trap and we know it, what are we going to do once we're in? I'm assuming you have a plan to get us out."

"You'd think so, wouldn't you?"

"Gage…"

He cast her an unreadable look. "It's less about a plan and more about timing and execution. I have no idea how many people will be waiting for us, how they'll come at us, or where Rachel will factor into it."

"You still don't trust her, do you?"

"Actually, I do, in as much as I trust anyone. But I also think she's scared, and frightened people tend to be unpredictable."

Amber considered the situation from her sister's perspective. "Actually, Rachel's fairly predictable when she's frightened."

"She fights back."

"And shouts and flails."

"Can you calm her down if you want to, get her moving?"

"Probably." She ran her hands over the chains on her boots again. "Is she my sole responsibility once we're there?"

"That and shooting anyone who moves and isn't me or her."

"This is so not promising. Tell me, what happened between you and Bear that he's willing to do as much as he has in return?"

"I pried him out of a vehicle that had been hit by a car bomber in Afghanistan. His legs were caught and he was only half conscious. He kept saying to shoot him. Finally did—in the shoulder. I knocked him out, dragged him out, and a minute later, watched five twisted-up Jeeps go up in a fireball."

"Uh, okay. Wow."

"Couple months later, I took out a female soldier who was playing possum during an air strike. I saw her fingers move, Bear didn't. She tripped him, he went down, lost his weapon. I killed her. There's more, but you get the idea. It's what you do when a fellow solider is compromised. We didn't like each other when we met. Being in the Army changed that."

"You have a history."

"Yep. The odd thing is, what he seems to appreciate most is the time we went out drinking and I puked on his pants. He was every bit as hammered as I was, but he was bigger, stronger, and meaner. He dragged me outside, probably intending to punch the shit out of me. Bomb hit the bar less than two minutes after we got through the door."

"Well, yay you."

He pointed to a road sign. "Astrid's two hundred miles from here. Thirty more on top of it, and we'll be wherever Rachel is. If she doesn't move."

If their vehicle didn't die, Amber added silently. If her sister wasn't already dead. If Owen's men didn't blindside them. The list went on.

A hundred miles farther on, they were forced to stop. The Range Rover was overheating. Out of sight on a rutted road with swamps all around. Gage raised the hood, added water to the radiator. He hopped back in and drew Amber across the seat.

"What are we doing now?" she demanded.

"Taking a break." He eased her head onto his shoulder. "I need to think, sleep for five minutes if I can. We don't want to rush into another barrage of enemy fire. If we can help it."

Would it matter in the end if they rushed in or crept in? Owen's people would have things under control, and God knew how many of them would be waiting to ambush them.

On the upside, though, Luka was gone. And Quint. And whoever the third man had been.

She felt Gage's heart beating under the hand she'd set on his chest. The sensation steadied her and allowed her to slide into a sleep deep enough that the sounds of the swamp no longer intruded. Not the insects, or the frogs, or the owls.

Not even the twig that snapped close behind them.

Chapter Nineteen

Amber woke up dazed and disoriented. Far from refreshed, but not quite as muzzy headed as she had been.

Rain poured from a lead-gray sky, and every bone, every muscle, every joint in her body felt stiff and unusable.

She discovered she was alone in the Range Rover. But the hood was down, and she was still in one piece. All good things, she supposed.

The door opened and Gage climbed in, soaked to the skin and carrying a bag that smelled like heaven.

"Man with a shack and a mother who's blind saw us parked here and tapped on the window last night," he revealed. "The guy said we'd sink into Ella Mae's grave if we didn't move quickly."

"We moved?" Amber paused in her perusal of the bag. "How did I not notice that? How did neither of us notice we were parked in a bog?"

"Mud's mud to an out-of-stater." He grinned at her. "The guy's name is Gerry. You're welcome to use his outhouse before we leave."

"Outhouse," she repeated. "Well, it's better than a pond, I guess?" She relinquished the bag. "Please don't eat everything Gerry and his mother gave us."

"Take your pack. There's room inside to change if you want to."

She did want to, very badly. Not into anything she owned, but what choice did she have?

The outhouse surprised her. Pleasantly. It had running water, a warm trickle shower, and a toilet with a box of tissue paper on the back. She used all the facilities, then she brushed her teeth, changed her clothes, and even switched to her other boots, because why not? One way or another, they were heading into a hornet's nest of trouble.

Pulling her hair back, she packed up her gear and ran for the SUV.

"Better?" Gage asked.

"Definitely." She reached for the bag. "What's in here besides more of that coffee you're drinking?"

"Biscuits, blackberry jam, hard-boiled eggs, peach compote, grits, blueberry syrup, and a poppy seed cake."

"It looks fantastic."

"For a last meal?"

She dipped her finger into the compote, licked it off. "I didn't say that. No sign of anyone after us?"

"Nope, and I'm not thinking there will be." Gage started the Range Rover. "Careful pouring the coffee, Snowbird. We're rolling."

The food helped enormously. Amber freed her hair and let it dry. Her stomach would jump a lot more the closer they got to Astrid, but for the moment, she simply let her mind drift back in time. How in God's name had she gotten to such a messed up place in her life? Such a moment?

Instead of lightening up, the day grew darker and more ominous. Gage used the interstate as much as he could, then he took the appropriate exit for Astrid and switched to the back roads. Presumably, Rachel and Bobby Lee had done the same thing.

Another twenty-five miles passed before a small water tower came into view. It was set behind a sprawling three-story house with a broken sign out front that read: Cypress Inn. Honey Bee Pollen and Black-eyed Peas For Sale."

Amber arched a shrewd brow. "Your Shady Rest Hotel?"

"More than likely." Gage regarded the tracking device. "Blip's not here. We need to go west a few miles."

"By SUV or on foot?"

"There's a road." He motioned forward. "What time is it?"

"Almost five." She did a double take. "Really? Already?" A frown knit her brow. "Why?"

"I want the night."

"Do I want the details?"

"Never give the enemy an unnecessary advantage. Let them come after us. Wait half an hour, then call your sister."

"And say what?"

"Tell her if she wants to be rescued, she and Bobby Lee need to come meet us at Belmar. It's a plantation house fifty miles south of our current location. It's in ruins and unoccupied. She comes or we leave."

With a determined false smile, Amber replied, "I hate this, you know that, right? What if she doesn't show?"

He said nothing, merely regarded her patiently.

"Right." She expelled a breath. "I'm the prize, not Rachel. Considering the reams of information I can't access even if it is tucked away in some dark corner of my brain, Owen's going way over the top to capture me."

"Mockerie's going over the top. Remember who you're dealing with at the heart of it, Amber. The torture factor's paramount to him. You can't do what you did and walk away.

He's been biding his time ever since you disappeared."

"So the information I gathered isn't important?"

"His FBI contact will have returned that to Owen over a month ago. You fucked with a member of Mockerie's team. He always intended to make you pay for that at some point. Rachel handed him his golden opportunity when she left Black Creek."

"She must have said something to Jess Murkle," Amber mused. "Or his brother. Or a friend."

"Who told a friend, who put it together and made a call to Fixx. Then bam, the game was on."

Amber regarded his cell. "Twenty minutes to phone call." She sent him a fervent glance. "I hope you know what we're doing."

"So do I," he said and started the SUV.

Or tried to.

...

It took several attempts and over fifteen minutes of him fiddling under the hood before the reluctant engine turned over. The delay gave Gage time to think and rejig his virtually nonexistent plan.

Position would be key, and he was counting on Rachel to panic. True, that might get her killed, but frankly, her safety was farther down on his priority list than Amber might've been happy to realize.

It couldn't be helped. The two of them could've been facing five people or fifty. He leaned toward the lower number for the sake of efficiency, not making a big noise, and because he didn't want to think of how badly things might go if the number were high. Numbers hadn't worked for Fixx at Bitterroot Lake. Lesson learned, he hoped. He imagined Fixx would go with sharpshooters and making anyone helping

Amber disappear quickly.

Wiping his hands, Gage returned to the cab of the Range Rover and nudged Amber out of the driver's seat. The engine she'd managed to start ran rough when she took her foot off the gas pedal.

"It's almost dark," she noted. "Those black clouds to the south are helping." She raised her brows at him. "Call Rachel?"

"Keep it short and sweet. If Fixx's people are with her, they'll come; if they're following her, they'll still come."

Amber dialed. There was no answer, only her sister's voicemail.

"Leave a message," Gage instructed her.

"Rachel, listen to me. I need you to meet me at Belmar. It's a plantation house, a ruin, fifty miles south of the Cypress Inn. Leave as soon as you get this message."

Gage drew his fingers across his throat, indicating she should end the call. She looked at him and broke the connection.

"I think..." she began, but got no further. The twilight, such as it was, suddenly exploded with gunfire around them.

Gage yanked her down and away from the windshield. "It's possible we'll be finishing it here," he muttered.

But he didn't like here. The location was too open. If only barely, at least the engine was running.

"Hold on, Snowbird. We're moving."

He knew two of his tires had been hit. He could feel the difference when he turned the wheel.

The Range Rover responded as he alternated swerving the front and back ends.

His phone rang. Amber answered it from the floor and immediately put it on speaker.

Rachel's tearful voice wobbled across the line. "He'll kill me, Amber, if you don't turn yourself in. He's already killed

Bobby Lee. He swears to God, he won't kill you."

"No, he'll leave that to his boss. Owen's not the boss," she added before Rachel could reply. "You…"

The phone zinged out of her hand when a bullet blasted through the side window. "Shit," she swore. "That was close."

Gage fishtailed the back end, saw Amber hunting through the many weapons littering the floor. "Shoot behind us," he told her. "Don't bother taking aim, just pepper our wake."

They hadn't expected him to rabbit, he realized. All the shots were coming from the back end.

"Where are we going?" Amber shouted above the continued spray of bullets.

He maneuvered through a stand of sycamore and hickory trees, felt the ground growing increasingly squishy beneath the tires. "As far into the swamp as we can make it on two working wheels. Get ready to bail. Grab what you can for weapons."

He did the same even as he wound an erratic path over knolls, past humped tree roots, and through patches of murky water.

Spanish moss slapped the broken windshield. He counted three vehicles behind him, all powerful and relatively intact. No telling how many occupants might be inside them.

Amber inched upright to peer out the back window. "I see gray hair in the passenger seat of the first one. It could be Tony."

"The brother?"

"I didn't think he'd be this protective of Owen."

"Brotherly love, Snowbird."

"He also knows who pays the bills so he can veg out on St. Croix for four months of the year." She ducked as another round of shots assailed them. "The driver looks like Quint's cousin."

"Apparently, nepotism's rampant in Fixx's branch of the

organization. Hold on."

Leaping one knoll, then two, Gage landed hard but intact.

"Dirt bike riders have nothing on you." Amber grunted as he jumped another knoll. "Okay, my stomach's officially in my throat... I think they're falling back."

"As old ladies tend to do in rough terrain."

Double handing her weapon, Amber fired. "Don't let my grandmother hear you say that. She rode her Harley across the U.S., coast to coast, when she was in her seventies. She and two other women she's known since college."

Gage's mild amusement got lost in a wild spray of bullets. "Save your ammo, Amber." He eyed a trio of small hillocks. "Three more jumps and we'll lose the bastards."

She regarded him for a moment. "In case one or both of us dies here, Gage, thank you for doing this."

"Any time, Amber."

The knolls rose up, one, two, three. On the final landing, he reached across the seat, shoved her door open, and rolled them both into the swamp.

...

Rachel screamed until Owen's eardrums vibrated. He was in Land Rover Two with a pair of his most trusted men, Mort and Bronson. His brother Tony had taken point with Quint's thoroughly pissed-off cousin and three of his best marksmen. Jake, Luka's current friend and lover, was piloting Three with a navigator and two more shooters.

"We should have tied her up and gagged her," Mort muttered from the driver's seat. "Bronson can hardly hold her."

"Can't hold her," Bronson shouted forward. "She's kicked me twice in the balls."

"Simmer down, Rachel," Owen ordered. "Bear in mind

how expendable you are."

"You're such a bastard," she shrieked and clawed Bronson's face. She began to cry. "I thought you loved me."

"I do. I did." What the hell was he saying? "You suited my purpose when we met. You don't now."

She screamed again, and that time, Bronson howled with her. "Bitch punched me in the eye. I'm fucking bleeding."

Owen looked behind him. Bronson's left eye appeared to have exploded.

"You'd better stop," he said testily. "We'll have to tie her up."

Mort slowed on an uphill grade, popped the locks on the doors.

He should have realized how desperate Rachel was. And how determined she could be when she wanted something.

Jerking away from Bronson, she kicked the door open and tumbled out into the swamp. Owen was still undoing his seat belt when she disappeared in the gathering darkness.

Could it get worse? Hell yes, it could. He could lose James Mockerie's ultimate prize.

Rather than take up the chase himself, he contacted Land Rover Three. "Rachel's flown. Solo and hysterical. Reel her back in."

"Not a problem," was the response. Owen watched the passenger door behind them open and close, and motioned his own driver forward. "Keep going." He raised his radio link. "Tony, stop being such a pussy. Why can't you keep firing?"

"No point shooting at an empty car," his brother growled back. "They're on foot. We lost them in a tangled-up mess of trees and moss and prickle bushes."

Owen controlled his frustration and his rising temper. "Understood." Snatching a tracking device off the dash, he regarded the screen. And saw the red blip that was Amber heading into the heart of the swamp.

...

Amber's lungs threatened to burst. It couldn't have been air she was breathing. The swamp must've been giving off some kind of noxious gas.

She dragged Gage to a halt in a pool of green sludge. Spanish moss dipped around them. "I can't..." Unable to speak in sentences, she waved a hand between them. "Thirty seconds."

The band was slipping from her hair. For the umpteenth time, she dragged it off. She found herself holding a piece of elastic rope. "It broke. How could the stupid thing break? It cost me thirty-five dollars."

"What cost you thirty-five dollars?" With his hands braced on his thighs, Gage looked up.

She showed him the band. "It came apart at the metal join. Maybe I can tie it... What?"

"The metal join." Having grabbed it from her, he snapped off the metal end piece. "Where did you get this?"

"At a fitness store."

"A chain store?"

"Yes, a high-end one. I told you it cost... Oh, crap. That's it, isn't it?"

Rather than reply, he gave the band, minus the metal end, back to her. "Tie it, use it, and let's go."

When he pocketed the piece, she drew her brows together. "Why are you keeping it?"

"It could come in handy. You ready?"

"No, but..."

"Let's go." Grabbing her hand, he pulled her out of the water and deeper into the trees.

It was a fairy-tale forest of the bleakest kind. Flying

monkeys. Amber visualized the creatures. They were bound to appear any minute.

A snake dropped from of a tree directly ahead of her. She almost stepped on it. A scream rose, but she swallowed it before it escaped.

The guns weighed her down. Thankfully, Gage was carrying the heavier rifles. He also had the transponder she'd been wearing since…when?

Since a week or two, maybe more, before she'd been whisked out of Las Vegas. She remembered buying it, and two others. One black, one blue, one purple. She used one or the other of them all the time. She didn't like her hair falling in her eyes, but she didn't like it short, either. Problem solved with a simple band, or so she'd thought.

They ran on, dipping and weaving, never traveling in a straight line. Once again, her lungs wanted to blow apart. But fear and a strong desire to live spurred her on. How could a band used to hold hair in a ponytail have been bugged?

Rachel had been with her when she'd bought them… But no, she wouldn't go there.

"Gage, I can't…" She panted.

"Yes, you can." He held tight to her hand.

And only paused when a scream cut through the nighttime cacophony of the swamp. One long, piercing shriek that Amber recognized instantly as Rachel's.

• • •

"Go ahead and scream." The hand that had grabbed her by the hair yanked her to a halt. "Scream your head off. Give her a location."

Rachel twisted in his grasp and screamed again when he gave his wrist a vicious snap.

Tears streamed down her cheeks. "You can have my

Porsche if you let me go. Sell it."

"I don't want your Porsche. I want your sister. My life's worth a helluva lot more than a Porsche to me."

Her voice reverberated. "Bobby Lee wanted to make her come to New Orleans looking for me. I said yes, but I didn't mean it. I just wanted to get away."

"Gee, that's nice." Another mean twist, another scream. "Any particular reason you're sharing this with me?"

Was there? "I didn't love Owen just for his money," she blurted out. "I wanted to be his business partner. But now... Bobby Lee said the scuttlebutt is that Owen's falling out of favor with his boss. Someone will have to take his place eventually. Maybe it could be us."

"So you're willing to turn your sister in."

"Maybe I am. I mean, why not?"

The hand holding her hair released her. Rachel sagged with relief. Poorly controlled hysteria washed through her in giant waves. She had no idea what she was saying or why. And a moment later, she had nothing but stars in her head.

He slapped her so hard, she lost her footing and fell.

"You are some bitch." He sneered. "But it doesn't matter. Babble away all day. I'm not Bobby Lee or Owen Fixx." He showed her his teeth. "What I am is hungry for a great big slice of cunt pie. And baby, you're going to help me get it."

...

They wouldn't make it to Belmar. Gage understood that even as they ran. The swamp itself would have to do. Fortunately, there were no shacks or houses, so it was unlikely any bystanders would be dragged into the looming nightmare. There was only Rachel, a group of determined gunmen, and Amber's instinctive response to the sound of her sister's scream.

"Where did it come from?" she demanded. She didn't stop running, but he knew she wanted to.

He gave her a firm tug. "They won't kill her as long as she keeps screaming. They're probably encouraging her, hoping to lure you in."

They stopped for breath on a weed-filled embankment alongside a slow-moving waterway.

"We need a boat," Gage remarked. "Do you see anything?"

"No." She shook her head. "But the waterway expands to the right. Maybe we'll find something that way."

Rachel screamed again, and Gage felt Amber shudder.

"They're using her," he reminded her. "Try to bear that in mind. I want to find a place where I can see them coming. We can pick some of them off if we have the right kind of shelter. Barring that, we need to lose them. Another vehicle would be helpful."

"Or that boat you mentioned."

"In the swamp, a boat's a vehicle. You ready?"

"Do I have a choice?"

Standing, Gage turned right, but he didn't move as quickly as before. Something felt wrong to him. The crickets weren't chirping, at least not the ones in the immediate vicinity.

"What is it?" Amber bumped into his arm when he broke stride and slowed to a jog.

"Quiet."

She glanced behind them, past him, into the bushes and trees. "I don't see anything."

You never did, Gage reflected, when the person after you was a pro. And more so when those pros thought the way you did.

"Fuck." He said it softly and shrugged a pair of the rifles from his shoulder.

Rachel screamed again, far in the distance. Amber

looked toward the sound, Gage didn't. He heard the bushes ahead rustle, saw a man step out. The man had his assault rifle raised and pointed right at Amber.

Following the direction of his steady gaze, Amber finally spotted the man, as well.

"You?" While she seemed surprised, Gage really wasn't.

"Yeah, me."

Was there a hint of apology in his features? If there was, it came and went in a blink. The clouds had broken up enough for the moon to beam down over the swamp. Over the man in front of them. A man Gage thought he knew. A man he trusted.

Abel Bodine.

Chapter Twenty

"Why?" Gage's one-word question said it all. But the answer was obvious to Amber. Money. Far too much of it to resist. Abel had an ex with expensive taste. Hadn't that been mentioned several times while they'd been at his lodge? He wanted her back, and that would require cash.

Maybe it would work. There was little chance that Owen would pay up, but the mere idea of so much cash had blinded people before. Which was undoubtedly why Owen had made the reward such an outrageous amount.

Abel's mouth crooked into a wry smile. "I can see the wheels turning there, Amber Kelly. Except you're not Amber, are you? You're Alexa Chase, would-be toppler of illegal empires. I knew your mama, remember? Secrets are just so damn hard to keep in today's world. *C'est la vie*, as they say in these parts. You, uh, might wanna drop those rifles, old friend, before my trigger finger gets twitchy."

With his gaze fixed on Abel's, Gage let the weapons he'd unshouldered drop onto a bed of wet moss. "So now what?" he asked. "You turn us over to Fixx, and presto, three million plus bucks magically appears in your bank account?"

Abel snorted. "Do I look like a moron? I take the girl." He jerked his head. "Got a truck half a mile away, out of the swamp but deep in the hollow. When the money's in my hands, free and clear, I'll tell him where I've got her hidden."

A faint smile tugged on Gage's lips as Abel's rifle barrel fell an inch. "You really think that'll work for Mockerie?"

"No." Abel shrugged. "But it'll work fine for Fixx. I'm guessing he's pretty desperate at this point. Amber keeps eluding him. Word of advice, Gage, you might think about getting gone yourself."

"What, you're not going to kill me?"

"I'm hoping not. However"—he shrugged again—"three point five million is three point five million. Still, I'll try to keep it down to a debilitating wound for you."

"You're all heart, old friend."

As Abel smiled, the rifle dropped even lower. "Hell, you'd do the same for me if the situation was reversed."

Gage didn't bat an eyelash, didn't alter his expression in any way. He simply murmured a calm, "Don't count on it." When Amber moved and Abel glanced at her, he grabbed the gun from the back of his waistband and planted a bullet in the middle of his old friend's chest.

"What the—"

Amber stared. Abel looked down, then up, then over at her. "Bastard shot...me."

The rifle in his hand jerked. Amber felt herself falling sideways. Before she landed, she heard a second shot.

Abel gurgled out a final astonished protest and pitched forward into the weeds.

For a moment, probably no more than a split second, Amber regarded the dead man.

Unable to think of a single thing to say, she climbed stiffly to her feet and stood mutely while Gage tugged the assault rifle out from underneath his mentor.

"Come on," he said without inflection. "We need to leave. Abel had a truck. We have to find it."

"I—yes." Words continued to elude her. "Yes."

Taking a final look at Gage's trainer lying facedown in the weeds, she dragged her numb gaze away and prayed to God she'd never see Gage—or her sister—in that same state.

...

She didn't ask a single question, likely wouldn't, Gage thought as once again they ran through the slime and mud and water not quite deep enough to hold any full-size alligators.

Rachel was no longer screaming, but he imagined that was due to the gunshots everyone in the vicinity must have heard. Small but deadly, he'd had the gun he'd used on Abel up his sleeve since they'd abandoned their last vehicle. He'd hoped like hell his hunch about Abel's wants and needs had been an erroneous one. But life, mistakes, and greed had taken their toll, and now the man who trained him lay face down, waiting for the scavengers to move in and cover him.

He didn't expect to locate Abel's truck easily, or without encountering at least one obstacle. Bullets flew from inside a small, wooden structure on the edge of the waterway.

Amber stumbled slightly and went to her knees as Gage hid behind a curtain of Spanish moss. "What is that?" She panted the question out. "Not a house."

"Still." Gage searched the darkness, regarded the misty moon. "Come on, clear up, give me a view."

Amber pointed. "There's someone crouched down on the side of the building."

He held his fire as more shots came at them from the direction they'd been running.

"How many do you count?" Amber asked.

"Three, maybe more. They know we're here. We'll keep to the shadows and run. That way." He motioned behind them. "Up the incline. If we can, we'll circle back to the road."

A muffled scream reached them. Gage ignored it. Near or far, Rachel would have to wait.

Bullets whizzed past. Left with no choice, he shouldered the assault rifle and fired back. The man hunkered down next to the still eased up a few inches and took aim. Two well-placed shots and he staggered backward through a collection of old metal parts. Gage heard the crash as the guy fell to the ground among them.

He couldn't make out the source of the rifle fire to his left, but he fired at it regardless.

The swamp had been transformed into a war zone. Bullets flew in all directions. There were shouts and cries and the sound of splashing water.

"We need to move." When Amber didn't answer, he glanced at where she'd been.

And saw nothing except an empty patch of black.

...

Amber fought and kicked and would have screamed like a banshee if the arm around her windpipe hadn't cut off her air supply to the point where her vision went spotty.

A gun jabbed into her side. "You draw Morgan back here and this whole swamp's gonna rain blood, sugar. Your damn sister scratched the crap out of Bronson, and the dumbass took it. Yours truly doesn't intend to have an eye clawed out or his innards exposed by an ex-cop turned renegade sharpshooter."

Despite the man's warning, Amber kicked him in the shins. He responded by shaking her as if she were a rag doll.

He dragged her through the swamp, kept her covered

with a scratchy, wool blanket. Her head spun from both the pressure of his forearm and a residual chemical smell in the wool. Chloroform maybe. Not enough to knock her out, but enough to make her woozy.

It felt like an eternity passed before he threw her to the ground and snatched the blanket away. She heard Rachel's wet sob and, at the same time, spied her sister's tear-streaked face.

"You're here." Rachel threw her arms around Amber, smothering her. "Thank God, you're here. I'm sorry. I tried not to scream so loud, but he kept hurting me. I think I punched him in the nose before he shoved me to the ground. Where are we?"

From what Amber could ascertain with Rachel's hair in her face and the moon half visible through a layer of filmy cloud, they were in a circle of three SUVs. The lone man walking back and forth in front of them with his rifle resting on his shoulder like an ax was big, with bushy hair and a wad of gum in his mouth.

"Name's Mort," he said in a conversational tone. "That guy behind you's Jake. D'you remember Jake, Alexa, from Las Vegas? Don't matter, he remembers you. We both do, even if you never paid either of us any mind. I been trying to call the others back, but no one can hear me over the racket down waterside. You got yourself one hell of an annoying bodyguard there. He's even got the boss man shooting at him."

Amber pushed Rachel's hair aside. "Owen's here?"

"In the flesh."

The man called Jake nudged her between the shoulder blades with his rifle. "Your man's friend's responsible for Luka getting his kneecaps blown out. That friend's not gonna live too long when Luka's back walking again. Same goes for your bodyguard hero."

"Jake's Luka's lover," Rachel hissed in Amber's ear. "He's got a real mean streak."

Amber nodded, fought back a portion of her terror.

"Come on, come on," Mort muttered into his comm link. "Someone answer. I'm still hearing gunfire. You can't all be dead."

"They're not," Jake said. He used his gun to indicate the nearby trees.

Amber couldn't see what or who he was pointing at, not with Rachel still hanging onto her. But she felt a man's hand on her neck and instantly recognized his voice when he bent close to speak in her ear.

"Hey there, Alexa. I see you've found another asshole to dupe. Are you planning to dispose of him the same way you did me? Or maybe you'll be merciful and put a bullet in his head."

Knocking Rachel aside, he jerked Amber around to confront his quietly murderous face. "I've missed you, sweetheart. I really have. But it's a little too crowded here for us to have the kind of reunion I'd like. What say we take a walk in the moonlight and talk over old times?"

Amber twisted free of his grasp. "What say we skip the walk and wait for Owen?"

"I don't think so." His lips peeled back into a savage grin. "If we wait for him, he might stop me from doing what we both know you deserve."

And yanking her to her feet, Gareth Fixx crushed his mouth to hers in a vicious, vengeful kiss.

...

He'd picked them off, every last one of them, the bastard. Not that Owen was overly surprised. Morgan was fucking good.

Bronson with his bandaged eye had gone down first. A

lucky shot had gotten one of his other men. They'd fallen like ducks on a conveyor belt after that.

His brother, Tony, had been the last to get hit. Only in the shoulder, but his helpfulness had come to an end. It was down to four of them, and Owen was plenty worried about what he'd always considered the weak link in his recovery chain.

But no, it would be fine. Gareth would follow the plan as ordered. He'd wanted to be part of things from the start, and so far he'd performed admirably. It would be fine. It was in Gareth's blood to rise up and shine in the mini kingdom his father had built. There was no reason at all to doubt him.

So why did he feel a sudden urge to run?

...

Gage was pissed. They'd hemmed him in, dammit, made it impossible for him to go after Amber. He'd been forced to hold position and shoot for far too long. God knew where she'd been taken.

The only thing he could do was let one of his opponents get out unscathed. He'd opted for the weakest shooter, Owen Fixx. Strong beams of moonlight had afforded him a clear enough view of the area that he'd been able to distinguish body types, if no actual features. Owen's polished moves and lean frame had been easy to spot.

He watched his lone remaining opponent from the shelter of a black walnut tree. After turning to someone, likely his fallen brother, Owen ran, bent low toward a natural mud bridge that spanned the waterway.

A thump on his shoulder had Gage swinging sharply around. The tip of his gun lodged in Bear's whiskered throat. A grin split the man's face. "I'm fixing to wipe the slate here, Gage."

With a steady look, Gage lowered his weapon. "You count

awfully heavily on me not having a shoot first philosophy. You should have told me you weren't finished following us."

"Shoulda, coulda, woulda."

"Do you know where they took her?"

"Damn right, I know. I spotted the ring of Land Rovers. You gotta figure Fixx here'll be heading in that direction. Chances are he'll take the easy route. We go the hard way, we'll beat him by five minutes. And then…"

"Yeah, and then." Gage holstered his Glock, gestured with his rifle. "If anything's happened to Amber, first we shoot him in the nuts, then we kill him.

...

Gareth shoved Amber into the swamp, down toward the water. But not to the same place where she'd been abducted.

He cuffed her wrists with a strong hand, tightening his grip whenever she attempted to wrench free.

She made a point of doing that every few steps. As she did, she dug her boot heels into the soft ground. In the absence of a breadcrumb trail, heel marks were all she had.

"Make a peep, Alexa, and I will blow you away," he warned in a snarl. "My father might want you alive, but from the start, I promised myself I'd see you dead. Not killed by James Mockerie, but by me."

Amber's jaw ached from locking her teeth together, to prevent them from chattering. "You kill me, and Mockerie will kill you."

"No, he won't. My father'll be plenty pissed, but he'll cover for me. A meaner, smarter man than him would never have allowed me to be part of this hunt. He knows I don't want anything to do with his bullshit business. What he did want was for his kid to come through in the end. So he believed me when I told him I'd had a change of heart." Halting suddenly,

Gareth spun her around, gripped her by the throat. "You used me to bring down my own flesh and blood. I wanted you, and you wanted incriminating evidence."

He squeezed her throat so hard she thought his fingers might dig right into her flesh. She tried not to choke. "If I said I was sorry, would you believe me?"

She hissed in a tight breath as he jabbed his gun under her chin. "No."

His eyes glittered in the hazy moonlight. "I'm going to kill you and enjoy doing it. But first I'm going to pin you down and take you right here in the Louisiana mud. I'm going to make you cry, and when I've committed that moment to memory, I'm going to put a bullet in your lying throat. What do you think of that?"

Amber opened her mouth to reply, but she was cut short by Owen, who burst out of the darkness, winded and seemingly as startled to see them as they were to see him. "Gareth, no!" he rasped. "Have you gone mad? You can't kill her. Rape her yes, but not kill her."

Gareth responded by swinging Amber back against him, using her as a shield. "Shut up," he barked. "You wanted a Mini-Me, well you got one. You and her both. You taught me to be self-centered. She taught me to crave revenge. And here I thought I was a nice guy deep down. I guess the Thing was inside me after all, waiting to break out."

Owen had no visible weapon, but there'd be one somewhere, Amber was sure of it.

She made a strangled sound as Gareth's hand tightened around her neck. He had his gun pressed to her jugular.

"You need to leave," Gareth warned his father. "Now. Go back to Mort and Jake and your bitch of an ex-wife. Leave Alexa to me." He pulled the gun from Amber's neck and pointed it at his father. "This is how it's going to be. Either go back, or I'll shoot you and carry out my plan anyway."

Amber thought she spied movement. Neither Owen nor Gareth appeared to notice anything except each other.

Reaching slowly into his jacket pocket, Owen produced a gun of his own. He took aim at his son. "Don't do it, Gareth."

Gareth laughed. "You'll never use that on me. Besides, to kill me, you'll need to go through her. But it was a decent bluff."

Amber wrapped her fingers around Gareth's wrist. She struggled to breathe evenly, and not let her muscles tremble. Until...

The movement came again, a quick flash of motion that Gareth did see that time.

"What the hell's that?" he blustered.

Amber yanked his hand from her throat and, at the same time, pulled away just far enough to kick him in the groin.

To her surprise, Gareth's eyes went wide and began to blink rapidly. "Dad?" he whispered. Then, clutching his chest, he tipped sideways into a pool of thick water.

Owen stared at the weapon in his hand for a full two seconds before the truth struck him. When it did, he swung in a semicircle and began firing.

Amber heard the thwack of a bullet striking the shoulder of his shooting arm. The gun flew backward. He stumbled around to face her. To face his dead son.

Falling to his knees, he began to laugh.

Everything ran together in a blur of color and sound and motion. It happened in an instant. Amber scrambled to her feet and ran to Gage. For the first time since she'd started helping the FBI, she felt safe. Suddenly, no one and nothing could touch her.

Of course, that feeling wouldn't last. She knew it even

before Owen started muttering James Mockerie's name. First, he laughed it out, then the laughter became an agonized moan. The tears, she suspected, were primarily for his dead son.

Gage had two grazes, one on his shoulder and a second on his upper left arm. Neither were serious, or so he insisted.

Bear was waiting with the others back at the circle of Land Rovers. Owen walked ahead of Gage, head down, shoulders slumped, a broken and terrified man by all outward appearances.

"The she-devil and me, we've been keeping our distance from each other," Bear informed them when they arrived. "I got her to tie up these two assholes, didn't trust her with a gun."

When Rachel saw Amber, she jumped up and ran over to her. "I'm so sorry. About everything. I told Jess about us. I didn't mean to. Or maybe I did, but I didn't mean any harm. I was drunk, and he wanted out of Black Creek, too. I guess he figured he could get money for turning me in. But it never happened." Tears ran down her cheeks. "They killed him when we stopped for gas. I don't know what they did with his body." She choked back a sob. "I think he might have said something to his brother."

"Whatever happened," Amber said, "word got back to Fixx. Two men showed up at the bar just as I was being told that you'd been taken."

"Jess was a bastard. So is anyone he talked to about us. Honest to God, Amber, men can be such assholes. You know what I mean, right?"

Only men could be assholes? Amber controlled the anger that wanted to rise for everything Rachel had done. "Yes, I do know," she said. "I think we all know at this point."

"It isn't over," Gage told her. "For either of you. Fixx might be a broken man, but Mockerie isn't."

"We'll always have to hide, won't we?" Rachel appealed to her sister. "That's what he's saying, isn't it?"

Amber nodded. "We just have to do a better job of it this time."

Rachel subsided next to Bear, who was keeping a watchful eye on Owen and nudging Mort's hip to irritate him.

Turning to face Gage, Amber fingered the blood on his jacket. "Any chance you know where we can do that better job of hiding, former Lieutenant Morgan?"

"Off the top of my head, no. But something'll come to me. It always does."

Smiling, she hooked her arms around his neck. "So. Is this our last farewell?"

With a half smile playing on his lips, he searched her face with his eyes. "What do you think, Snowbird?" Lowering his mouth to hers, he took her far away from Owen Fixx and the horror of her life for the past several months.

Now, only James Mockerie remained.

Chapter Twenty-One

It didn't end there. It couldn't. Amber knew James Mockerie wouldn't let the nightmare fade.

Owen Fixx was another matter. He was being held on too many charges to count. Although the evidence Amber had gathered was nowhere to be found, people were dead, and all fingers pointed directly at Fixx and his family.

Owen himself was under heavy guard in New Orleans. Prison would come at some point, but for the moment, strict surveillance in the county jail had to do.

Amber suspected Owen was more relieved than upset by the guards outside his cell. If he couldn't leave, at least he'd have the comfort of knowing none of Mockerie's people could get in. Not in theory, at any rate. They'd gotten into Luka's hospital room long enough to kill him.

Upon further investigation, Gage had determined that the fasteners on all three of the bands Amber had used to secure her hair in a ponytail contained tracking devices. Amber still had no idea who'd done it, how, or when. It didn't seem possible that Fixx could have been involved in that.

And yet, if not him, then who?

Time crawled once they were placed in a New Orleans safe house. Amber hated to think what was happening outside. She only knew that being inside was making her crazy.

Finally, late Saturday afternoon, five days after the nightmare in the swamp, Gage appeared on the doorstep.

"Pack your bags and Amber's," he instructed Rachel. "You've got an hour. We'll meet you at the airstrip. One of the agents will drive you."

"We're leaving New Orleans?" Rachel asked. Her disappointment was evident, but surprisingly, she didn't complain about the decision. "Where are we going now?"

"I'll let you know when we get there. You, too," he said to Amber. "One hour, Rachel. Come with me, Snowbird."

If Gareth and Owen hadn't killed her, Amber figured curiosity wasn't likely to send her to her grave, either. But it might eat her up if Gage didn't tell her something, anything, soon.

"I'm not a fan of secrets, former Lieutenant Morgan." She poked him in the back as he checked the grounds around the safe house. "I never was, and after six plus months of them, I can honestly say, secrets suck."

"Yeah, they do." He opened the passenger door of a super-cool Lincoln SUV and helped her in. "More than you know right now. We're going to take a little ride."

"Where?"

"I'll explain later. We're going to see a man about a thing."

Well now he was being doubly secretive, which made her doubly curious.

Fortunately, the ride was short. He drove them to a small hotel in the vibrant French Quarter. Once inside, they took a service elevator to the third floor.

"Come on, Gage." She shook her head as the doors slid open. "Tell me who we're meeting here. Is it the famous McCabe?"

"No." She noticed he checked his gun, but to her relief, he didn't actually draw it. "We're here to see a much more infamous man—one who currently works in the Witness Protection Program."

Her eyes snapped up. "Sidney?"

"Not quite." He held her gaze as the elevator door clanked open. "He's a former FBI agent and, more currently, your WPP contact."

"What?" Amber felt as though she'd been hit in the midsection with a sledge hammer. "Tom? My Tom? Why is he infamous?"

"You'll see," was all Gage said.

Tom was sitting by the window, overlooking the crowd on Bourbon Street. He didn't turn as they entered through the unlocked door.

"Hey there, Snowbird," he greeted her. "Gage."

Slippery tendrils of fear slithered like snakes in Amber's stomach. "Hello, Tom. Why are you in New Orleans?"

"Gage asked me to come. I wanted to come. It doesn't matter. I'm a dead man anywhere I go. It's only a matter of time. You fail, you die. I only hope my death is quick and painless."

Gage's gaze circled the room. "How much did Mockerie pay you to switch sides, old man?"

"I'm ashamed to say." At last, he pivoted to face them. Amber saw the anguish in his expression. "I need you to understand I turned him down flat at first. Even when I finally caved in—I had bills and heavy debts to pay, Snowbird—I still didn't tell him where you were. I lied. I told Fixx the devices I'd planted in your hairbands were malfunctioning. They weren't, and in time, he figured that out. I'm truly sorry, Amber. I had to track you, but I didn't have to tell him everything I knew. Of course, when his people couldn't quite catch you, he started to threaten me. It's what people like him and Mockerie do. Even though I was in the WPP, I still had access to FBI files. Illegal access, but it got the job done. I'd already gotten the information you'd collected back and given it to Fixx. I handed it right to him, but that wasn't enough. It never is in their world."

Amber sighed. "Mockerie wanted me back. So he could torture me?"

"So he could torture you and your sister. Mockerie likes to do things in twos, and you were the perfect pair."

"Mockerie threatened you," Amber assumed. "With your life or your family's?" Disappointment rained down on her.

"Oh, both." His hound dog eyes drooped even farther. "It was no less than I expected by then. Best I could do when it started was keep them a couple of steps behind you. Then he took my youngest boy, and I had no choice but to become more specific as to your whereabouts."

"That's when Luka caught up with us," Gage told Amber.

"I'm sorry, I truly am." Tom looked away. "I want you to have this." He produced a thick packet in the form of a heavy manila envelope from the window seat. "You take it where it needs to go, or have Gage do it. It's a copy of every scrap of information you collected on Fixx and his operation. You take it and leave, now, before someone shows up and stops you."

Stunned, Amber accepted the envelope he shoved into her hands. "So you're just going to sit here and wait for Mockerie's people to come for you?"

Tom's smile bordered on tragic. "Something like that. Now go, both of you, before…" He ended on a shrug of defeat.

With one last look around, Gage drew Amber from the

room. "Come on. There's nothing we can do."

"But..." She gestured to the door he closed behind them. "Why doesn't he take his family and run? Or does Mockerie still have his son?"

"Probably. It's too late for Tom, and he knows it. We need to do as he said and get out of here."

Although the hotel walls and doors provided a certain amount of soundproofing, Amber still heard the gun go off. A single, telling shot fired from inside Tom's room.

Closing her eyes, she murmured a soft, "Oh, God." Once they were in the elevator, she forced herself to ask, "What about his family?"

"McCabe will deal with them, if he hasn't already. They'll be as safe as they can be under the circumstances."

Amber struggled to regulate her breathing. "And Owen?"

"Good as dead." Lowering his mouth to hers, Gage gave her a bolstering kiss. "It's up to you, me, and Rachel to make sure he doesn't have a chance to do the same to us."

"Us?" Uncertain, Amber regarded him. The barest trace of a smile appeared. "You're coming with us?"

Tipping her chin up, Gage looked into her eyes. "You love someone, you face the same demons she does. And I don't mean Rachel."

In spite of everything, Amber's smile blossomed. "I guess that puts me in my place. I love you, too, Gage, and God knows I'm willing to face your demons, as well. Somehow I doubt they'll be as monstrous as mine."

"Yeah, well, I'll tell you a story or two once we're on our private plane bound for the land of wherever. Trust me, my demons have never even heard of the Yellow Brick Road."

Resting her forehead on his shoulder, Amber managed a quiet, "Neither has James Mockerie."

Epilogue

Owen Fixx listened to the sound of a prisoner across the corridor snoring his way through a bad dream. Jail was the safest place to be, though experience told him nowhere would really be safe where James Mockerie was concerned.

Officers stood guard down the hall. He couldn't see them from his cot, but he knew they were there.

He stared blankly at the untouched food on his plate and tried not to think. His son was dead. His nephew was dead. His brother was injured. And he himself had hurtled halfway down the rocky road to hell.

He didn't hear the cell key turn so much as sense it. There was no squeak of hinges, only a subtle movement of shadow as the big door swung outward.

Standing, he glimpsed the figures of two officers. They were lying on the floor far down the corridor. His stomach pitched into his bowels when Mockerie strolled in.

"Silencers." James nudged the brim of his hat upward with the tip of his gun. "One of the best inventions ever. Not very many guards watching over you, Owen. I guess McCabe doesn't consider you worthy of his full attention." His teeth appeared shark-like and sharp in the muted light. "So, how are you holding up? Have you made any arrangements for Gareth's funeral? Or Luka's? Or your own?"

Owen swallowed, remembered he had water and downed all of it. "I don't care for funerals."

"That's a shame." Still smirking coldly, Mockerie raised the gun. "It could have been a triple burial. Good-bye, Owen."

He squeezed the trigger; Owen saw him do it. Squeezed it once, then a second time as was his habit.

And then he saw nothing at all.

...

It was done, McCabe reflected. In as much as he could protect any of the people involved, he'd crossed the last *T*. Owen Fixx was dead. Fixx, his son, and his nephew. He hadn't brought Mockerie down, but that end would come. Someday, somehow, some way.

McCabe drove his truck to a vantage point overlooking the Las Vegas strip. From there, he watched the lights glitter and dance and shine like a beacon to the heavens. Picking up the cell phone beside him, he held it up to the night sky. Maybe the owner of the device would see him, maybe she wouldn't. He didn't know what he believed in that area. But he knew more would happen before Mockerie fell.

And he knew some of that more was secreted inside her phone.

About the Author

Jenna began creating stories before she could read. Over the years, she has worked in several different industries, including modeling, interior design, and travel, however, writing has always been her passion. She earned a degree in Creative Writing from the University of Victoria in British Columbia and currently lives in a semi-rural setting fifteen minutes from that city. She loves reader feedback. You can visit Jenna Ryan any time at http://www.jennaryanauthor.com or leave a comment on her Facebook page https://www.facebook.com/jenna.ryan.5201.

Also by Jenna Ryan…

BLACK ROSE

BLOOD ORCHID

SCARLET BELLS

DARK LILY

Discover more Amara titles...

CODE OF HONOR
a *HORNET* novel by Tonya Burrows

Jesse Warrick used to consider himself a kickass medic, but a teammate's brush with death has him questioning everything. But when HORNET's hotel is taken hostage with half of the team inside, Jesse and the sexy new female recruit are their only hope of escaping alive...

THE CHARMER
a novel by Avery Flynn

Hudson Carlyle just met the one woman in Harbor City who's immune to his legendary charm. Nerdy ant researcher Felicia Hartigan is the unsexiest dresser ever. And she's in love with totally the wrong man. Hudson can't stop thinking about her. He's going to need a new plan, starting with helping her win over the man she *thinks* she wants. And if in the process she ends up falling for Hudson instead? Even better. Step one, charm her panties off. Step two, repeat step one as frequently as possible.

THE WHITE LILY
a *Vampire Blood* novel by Juliette Cross

While Friedrich Volya, the Duke of Winter Hill, seeks to discover who a mysterious faction is, a local schoolteacher, the raven-haired Brennalyn, is on her own mission—to spy on the duke and discover what she can for the Black Lily resistance. But when Brennalyn's secret puts her life and the life of her children in danger, Friedrich steps in as her protector, she finds out there's more to the duke than she thought.

Printed in Great Britain
by Amazon